PUZZLES, PURRS & MURDER

A Dickens & Christie Mystery

Book X

Kathy Manos Penn

Paperback ISBN: 979-8-9887177-2-0

eBook ISBN: 979-8-9855140-9-4

Large Print: 979-8-9887177-3-7

Dedication

To Stephie, Kathy, and Kelly, the lifelong girlfriends whom I first met in my Leadership Development days oh so long ago

Acknowledgement

Thank you to Rick Bradley, whom I worked with for many years in corporate America.

Rick gave generously of his time and expertise in helping me to recall team-building activities we facilitated back in the day. His suggestions were invaluable, and any adjustments made to the activities described in this book are mine alone.

When you live in different cities and take different paths in your careers, some relationships fall by the wayside. That wasn't the case with Rick, and I hope we're still emailing and connecting on Facebook for many years to come.

He willingly agreed to let me use his name as a character without knowing how his fictional counterpart would be portrayed. Typical of Rick, he took it all in good fun. Trust me, he is neither smarmy nor a player. He's a loving husband to his wife Peggy and a genuinely good person whose friendship I treasure.

Contents

CHAPTER ONE   1

CHAPTER TWO   11

CHAPTER THREE   21

CHAPTER FOUR   29

CHAPTER FIVE   39

CHAPTER SIX   53

CHAPTER SEVEN   61

CHAPTER EIGHT   69

CHAPTER NINE   81

CHAPTER TEN   89

CHAPTER ELEVEN   99

CHAPTER TWELVE   107

CHAPTER THIRTEEN   119

CHAPTER FOURTEEN   131

CHAPTER FIFTEEN   143

CHAPTER SIXTEEN   151

CHAPTER SEVENTEEN   163

CHAPTER EIGHTEEN   171

CHAPTER NINETEEN   185

CHAPTER TWENTY   195

CHAPTER TWENTY-ONE   205

CHAPTER TWENTY-TWO   217

CHAPTER TWENTY-THREE   229

CHAPTER TWENTY-FOUR   243

CHAPTER ONE

Early Friday morning in Manhattan

As we stood outside the Waldorf waiting for the taxi to JFK, Dave shook his head. "How one small woman can need two large bags and a carry-on for a ten-day stay is beyond me."

He was referring to our visit with his mother in Connecticut, and he knew full well I'd arrived with only one large bag. The second one resulted from a bit of retail therapy in New York City.

I smiled up at him and kissed his cheek. "Admit it, you wouldn't have it any other way. I needed outfits for warm days, cool nights, a family reunion, and your high school reunion. Options were a necessity."

That response elicited an eye roll. "Uh-huh, and visits to Saks and Bloomingdale's before heading home? That was a necessity, too?"

"Well, yes! And what a successful shopping trip. The perfect pair of jeans for the Billy Joel concert and a new dress for Ellie's Christmas party. Do you have any idea how hard it is to find a red dress, much less in the perfect shade of red?"

He chuckled as the doorman flagged down a taxi. "I'll miss you *and* your fashion sense, sweetheart. After all, I got a new button-down out of the deal. Now, text me when you land and when you get to the train station in Moreton-on-the Marsh. With any luck, I should be able to get Mom packed and ready and be home by next weekend."

Having to arrive at the airport three hours prior to my international flight meant I had plenty of time to catch up on the mysteries I'd loaded on my Kindle. With an additional seven hours in the air, I'd probably finish at least two books.

I opened *A Body in the Village Hall*, a mystery set in Cornwall. It was just my kind of book—a murder, an intrepid amateur sleuth, and a setting in one of my favorite spots. Try as I might, though, I couldn't get more than a few pages in without my thoughts drifting to our stay in Connecticut.

We'd had a jam-packed visit with family and friends but also squeezed in a few delightful days on our own. Typical of Dave, he surprised me with a scenic two-day stay in Vermont at the romantic Stowe Meadows B & B. Spending our last weekend in Manhattan was always part of the plan, but our Thursday night tickets to a Billy Joel concert were a spur-of-the-moment treat.

I wondered whether the concert was Dave's way of making up for extending his stay for an extra week. Despite his mom's words to the contrary, it was clear she needed help. Perhaps because Dave now lived an ocean away, she'd kept him in the dark about her decision to sell the family home and move to a nearby retirement community. The annual family reunion in her backyard had been a tearful last hurrah.

With her daughter Michelle's help, his mom had begun to sort, donate, and pack her belongings, but she was nowhere near ready for the move that was a few short weeks away. Dave and I discussed the situation, and together we convinced his mom that she could use his help and he was happy to stay.

I in no way begrudged him the extra week, but he couldn't stop apologizing for leaving me to deal with the installation of his new he-shed in our garden. Truth be told, it would go more smoothly without him.

Hiring Cynthia White to design the shed instead of purchasing one pre-made was my idea. She'd been invaluable in updating the color scheme for my cottage when I'd retired to Astonbury. The floor-to-ceiling bookshelves in my office and the sitting room were her idea, and I adored them.

Though she'd moved to London after she and Toby divorced, she still had clients in the Cotswolds, and she jumped at the opportunity to work with me again. It helped that she and Toby, the owner of our local teashop, had developed an amicable post-divorce relationship.

When I described Dave's clutter driving me crazy, her response was perfect. "Leta, how clever—not a *she-shed* but a *he-shed*. This will be a first for me. Not only would I love to design it, I can also suggest some simple additions to your cottage that will camouflage the mess. After all, you don't think Dave having a space of his own will put an end to every bit of clutter, do you?" I could only laugh. She was spot-on.

After living in a small NYC apartment for years, Dave had no idea what he wanted. It was difficult to nail him down, but Cynthia excelled at balancing his all over the board ideas with my taste. So far, we were both happy with her suggestions.

Her design firm had a big September event in the Cotswolds, so we scheduled the finishing touches to the shed interior for the same week. Over the last month, she'd sent me numerous texts with photos of the shelving and a change to a slimmer, more efficient wood-burning stove. I couldn't wait to see it all come to life.

It was no surprise that Dickens and Christie greeted me in different ways when I arrived home the following day. One was chipper, the other snippy.

Dickens literally leaped for joy, scampering back and forth in search of a ball, and nearly knocked me over. "Leta, Leta, did you bring me a treat? Wait, where's Dave? Is he coming?"

I dropped my bags in the boot room and plopped down to rub his soft white fur. "Yes, I have a treat for you, but I've got to unpack first, silly boy. How 'bout a belly rub? Will that do for now?"

"Oh yes," he barked as he rolled over. "But where's Dave?"

As I explained Dave's absence, Christie strolled into the room with both her nose and her tail in the air. "Pfft. Where have you been? Lucy took Dickens on walks with Buttercup, but she only took me in the backpack twice. What's up with that?"

She sat and stretched out a hind leg to clean. "And Timmy still isn't any good at fluffing my food. He never pushes it to the center of my dish, where it should be."

I chuckled at her grumbling. "Oh my, have you been reading *Hamlet*? You sound awfully put-upon."

Dickens gave me a quizzical look as Christie hissed, "What's that supposed to mean?"

"Only that I can see you now with your paw lifted to your chest, protesting that you've suffered 'the slings and arrows of outrageous fortune.' You are such a little drama queen."

Turning her back, she strode from the room and tossed a parting command over her shoulder. "Puhleeze, enough with the babbling. Feed me."

Ah yes, it was good to be home. And it was the first time in a while that I could talk freely to the animals. Since Dave had moved into my cottage in January, I'd been vigilant about not letting on that I could understand them. I'd had this strange Dr. Dolittle ability since I was a child, but I'd never revealed it to anyone, not even my husband Henry. I couldn't put my finger on why I was so worried about slipping up in front of Dave, but I was.

I fed the princess and texted Dave that I was home, before following Dickens to the garden. The stone foundation of the new shed still took my breath away. Cynthia had painstakingly searched for the perfect hue of Cotswolds stone to match my cottage, and her local contact came by with sample after sample until she finally approved of one.

I knew there was no way I would have managed the match on my own. The walls were up and painted, and the windows, complete with window boxes beneath them, were exactly how I'd envisioned them.

"Time to unpack, Dickens." I could never relax after a trip until I sorted my clothes. With the new outfits stowed away, and the dirty clothes stashed in the laundry room, I breathed a sigh of relief. Only then did I kick off my shoes and stretch out on the couch.

Dickens had a different idea. "Leta, did you see the people next door? They're back."

"Silly boy, Timmy and his parents are always there. What do mean, they're back?"

"No. The people on the other side. They were in and out the whole time you and Dave were gone, and they're back now."

That was odd. I hadn't seen anyone at that cottage in over a year, and before that, not very often. I remembered Deborah, Timmy's mum, telling me that an elderly woman had owned it, but she died before I moved in. As far as anyone knew, the property had never gone on the market. When I saw the occasional car or truck in the driveway for a few hours, I always assumed it was a repairman.

"Did you see anyone or only hear them, Dickens? Did they stay overnight?"

He sat and tilted his head. "No. I didn't see anyone. I heard lots of hammering and talking. Not at night and no lights. I wonder if they have a dog or a cat. I could have a new friend."

Christie strolled in and put in her two cents. "We have plenty of friends. Watson visits most nights, and Lucy brings Buttercup to visit." Christie wasn't as social as Dickens. She liked Watson, Ellie's tabby cat, and had befriended Snowball at the yoga studio, but those were the exceptions.

Dickens wouldn't let it go. "Let's see if they're here now. We can visit Martha and Dylan, too."

So much for resting. "Well, I guess we'll have to take a look. Should we take Christie?"

Christie leaped into my lap. "What kind of question is that? Let's go."

"Am I back in your good graces now? Or do you just miss the donkeys?" My questions didn't get a response, but she followed me to the boot room to climb into her backpack. Her sleek black head peeked from the top when I loaded the pack on my shoulders.

I slowed as we approached the gravel driveway next door. A man in jeans was pulling boxes from a grey Jaguar in front of the open garage. "Look, Dickens, you may be right about us getting new neighbors."

At the sound of my voice and Dickens's hello bark, the man turned. He was of medium height with blond hair and a runner's build.

"Hi, I'm Leta Parker, and I live next door. Are you moving in?"

"Ah, you must be the owner of the Schoolhouse Cottage. My grandmother always loved that place with its old school bell. I'm Lyle Holmes. I'm not moving in, but I *am* getting the place ready to rent."

He explained that his gran had left the cottage to him several years ago. "Because I spent so many summers here, she knew I'd enjoy it more than my parents. Unfortunately, I've been too busy to tend to it properly, but now I'm making the time."

The puzzle pieces fell into place. "Holmes—oh, you must be Cynthia's partner, and you're here for the Village Hall Competition. Are you staying here all week?"

"You know Cynthia? Oh, wait, you're Leta Parker. She's completing your he-shed this week. I must admit I got a kick out of it not being a she-shed."

He pointed toward his cottage. "I'll be in a larger rental cottage with a few of our designers, but an old friend is staying here this week. I told him his job was to tell me what basics were missing. Do I need to add more dishes, more linens, that kind of thing? I'm struggling to furnish a new townhome in Mayfair, and keeping straight what to put where is getting confusing. He'll give it a fresh look."

I laughed. "And here I thought that would be easy for the owner of a design firm."

"It might be if I could get Cynthia to take charge of it. Her forte is interior design, and I lean more toward the exterior architectural elements."

When Christie signaled her impatience with a plaintive meow, I introduced her and Dickens. Lyle giving Dickens a belly rub was the last straw. "That's enough of him. Martha and Dylan are waiting." She made her disdain clear by burrowing deep into the backpack.

Waving goodbye, I told Lyle I'd see him at the pub later. Dickens chattered as we crossed the stone bridge that would take us to the donkeys. "He likes dogs. Do you think he has one? Maybe we can help him find one."

Dickens's comments didn't require answers, so I let my thoughts drift as he pranced happily by my side. Was it Lyle who'd introduced Toby and Cynthia to Astonbury? Did they open the tearoom here because Toby fell in love with the village as Lyle had as a boy? And now, Holmes & White were here to update the village hall. What a funny turn of events.

Martha and Dylan were happy to see us. They reached their snouts down to greet Dickens, and nuzzled Christie when I turned around so they could reach her in the backpack.

"Sorry, guys. No carrots this time, but I'll bring some tomorrow after I visit the market."

On the way home, I didn't know what to think when my phone lit up and I simultaneously heard music. Other people had musical ringtones, but I didn't. When Dave's name appeared on the screen, I stuttered, "Hel-lo?"

"What do you think? Do you like it?"

"Did I just hear Billy Joel? How did that happen?"

"Remember when you went to bed at the hotel? And I stretched out on the loveseat for a bit? I downloaded a song as your new ringtone. Do you recognize it?"

"It's 'Until the Night,' isn't it? I can't believe it. My all-time favorite Billy Joel song is on my phone."

"I can see why you like it. It sounds like a Righteous Brothers tune. The ringtone doesn't do it justice, but I thought you'd like it."

"I *love* it. Thank you. Now, tell me how things are going with your mom. Are you making progress?"

He groaned. "I've figured out why Mom and Michelle didn't get very far with packing. Some things are quick. Others are a trip down memory lane and take forever. I can't believe she still has all my sports trophies from high school. The pile for keep versus the ones for donate or trash keeps growing. There's no way she can fit all this into her new two-bedroom apartment."

"I can only imagine living in the same house for sixty years and trying to make those decisions. Thank goodness, I only had twenty years of memories to sort through when I moved here. Christmas ornaments were a no-brainer, and the desk furniture that Henry made."

"Don't forget your frog prince collection. It's hard to compete with, but I'm glad you kept it."

Henry had given me a frog prince stuffed animal after a friend remarked that I'd kissed a lot of frogs before I found him. Not that I had that many boyfriends, but I waited a long time to find Henry. After that, he brought me frog prince figurines, stuffed animals, and books. My favorite was that very first velveteen frog with the small crown.

"I'd say you do a darned good job of competing. My new ringtone is pretty special. Now, tell me, have you come up with some way to speed up the packing process? Or should I plan on not seeing you until Christmas?"

"Not to worry. I've got good news. Sandy stopped by this morning, and I've hired her to handle the job. She'll still need me to encourage Mom, but she and her crew do this all the time and have a process. If they live up to their company name, my worries should be over."

I met Sandy at Dave's high school reunion. She owned a company cleverly called Done and Done for You, and they did just that. Whether it was helping a homeowner declutter or prepare for downsizing or simply to move, Done and Done for You were the people to call.

"That will make things easier. Who called her in? You or your mom?"

"Neither of us. When Michelle told her how relieved Mom was that I'd stayed on to help, Sandy took it upon herself to stop by and offer her services. Guess that's why her business is so successful. When I saw her standing at the door, I knew it was a heaven-sent solution to the problem. It sure is a weight off my shoulders."

I wasn't nearly as delighted as he was. *Be honest with yourself, Leta—you're not delighted at all.*

CHAPTER TWO

Talk about heaven-sent. That's how I saw Wendy's call inviting me to meet her at the Ploughman for dinner Sunday evening. Not only was my cupboard bare, I needed a sounding board. After spending the afternoon replaying Dave's high school reunion in my brain, I knew my best friend was just the person to talk to.

As I let Dickens out of the car at the pub, he dashed off with a bark. "It's Peter and Lucy."

Peter was Wendy's twin. They had similar coloring, but he was nearly a foot taller than his petite sister. Lucy, a photographer and portrait artist, had arrived last autumn, for what was supposed to be a temporary stay. A friend of Sara Coates, aka Lady Stow, she'd moved into one of the cottages that dotted the Astonbury Estate. She'd quickly become one of the gang, and we were all delighted when she and Peter hit it off.

"Hi, y'all. Thanks for taking care of Dickens and Christie. I always feel good about leaving them in your capable hands. Was Christie as finicky as ever?"

Lucy grinned. "Of course, but I got some great shots of her looking indignant. I may use one in this year's cat calendar."

"It was mostly Lucy who tended to them this trip because the garage has been busy. I stopped by on a few of my morning rides to throw the ball for Dickens, but that was about it."

Barb greeted me from behind the bar when I walked in with Dickens. "Welcome back, stranger. Wendy snagged a table by the fireplace. What will it be tonight, wine or a cider?"

Waving to Wendy, I opted for a glass of Sauvignon Blanc. Wendy raised her glass as I approached, and Dickens looked beneath the table before opting for the dog bed by the fireplace.

"Welcome home. I can't wait to hear all about the trip, especially the shopping and the concert. I want to hear it all, but first things first."

Given our mutual love of shopping, her request didn't surprise me. "Gee, you don't want me to start with the romantic trip to the Vermont mountains or the family reunion?"

"We can talk romance later. Rhys and I spent a heavenly weekend in London, so we can compare notes. Is the new dress for the Christmas party? We'll have to find a new one for me, too."

It was a year ago at a literary festival in Torquay that Wendy had reconnected with Rhys, a friend from her Oxford days. I wondered whether a move to London might be in the offing. How her mum, Belle, would manage was something that would have to be worked out. She'd lived on her own before Wendy moved in with her, and I knew Belle wouldn't stand in her way. Perhaps Peter could check on his mum more regularly.

I assured Wendy I was up for another shopping trip and then described the fashions in NYC and how my new jeans made the Billy Joel concert even better.

When I whipped out my phone and played the ringtone, she gasped. "I want one! A different song, but I want one."

She made me promise Dave would work on her phone. I waited until we finished our salads, our usual fare, before I broached the subject that was weighing on my mind.

"Let me tell you about Dave's high school reunion."

Setting her wineglass down, she tilted her head. "Filled with people in their fifties trying to look like they were eighteen again?"

I laughed. "Yes, there were a few of those. Some more successful at it than others."

She must have seen something in my face. "But you've got more to tell me, right? Spill."

"Let me see if I can explain without taking all night. First, it was a five-class reunion, with Dave's class in the middle. His sister's class was there, too. She was a sophomore when he graduated."

"Leta, you know you can take all night if you need to. I want to hear the good, the bad, and the ugly."

"It started when Dave was deep into a discussion about football, and I headed to the ladies' room. The first thing I heard when I opened the door was, 'Dave's just as handsome as ever. Why would he date an older woman?' Sure, I'm two years older than him, but that's not common knowledge, so I can only guess it was a reference to the grey in my hair."

An exasperated expression crossed Wendy's face. "Older? Are you serious? Did they stop talking as soon as you walked in?"

I took a deep breath. "Well, no. They couldn't see me in the entryway where the couch was, and they must not have heard the door.

"I didn't recognize the voice, but another woman responded. It was Dave's sister. 'I never pegged her as older,' she said, 'but she's perfect for him. You should hear the two of them talk about books and music. Honestly, he positively glows when he's around her.' It was good to know she really liked me."

Wendy waited. "But..."

"The other woman wouldn't let it go. 'There's more to a relationship than books and music. I know your brother, and talking certainly wasn't a priority when we were together, if you know what I mean. I can't imagine he's truly happy.' Thank goodness Michelle wasn't having any of it."

"It's always great to have family stick up for you. What did she say?"

"I missed a bit when the water ran in the sink, but I heard her say, 'Trust me, he is. He wouldn't have moved to England if he wasn't sure she was the one. She's sweet and smart with that charming Southern accent, and I'd give anything to have her skin. Hardly a wrinkle.' I wanted to run in and throw my arms around her neck. Instead, I turned the corner just as the other gal said, 'I bet she's had work done.' It made my day to see her blush bright red."

"Whoa! I wish I could've been a fly on the wall. All right, don't make me wait any longer. Who was that woman?"

"I'll get to that in a minute. I didn't know who she was when I was eavesdropping, and I still didn't when I saw her. I was quite proud of myself that I was able to stroll in and say hello without giving any sign I'd overheard them. Michelle introduced Sandy as one of her high school friends. The woman looked so uncomfortable, I almost felt sorry for her. Until she made a quick exit, and Michelle issued a warning."

"A warning? About what?"

"Honestly, it made me think of that Bruce Springsteen song, 'Glory Days.' I found out Sandy was Dave's high school sweetheart, and they broke up before he left for college. That didn't seem like such a big deal until Michelle said, 'You need to watch out for her. She's recently divorced, and she makes no bones about Dave being the one who got away. Seriously, we had coffee last week, and she couldn't stop with the questions about him. And tonight . . . let's just say, I think she has her eye on him.' See what I mean about the song?"

Wendy scrunched her mouth to the side, a sign she was thinking. "No. I remember the tune, but I've never been good about listening to the words in songs."

"It's about folks reliving their high school days, as in the glory days of their lives. You know I'm used to Dave getting admiring glances, but good grief, a high school girlfriend who could be looking to rekindle an ancient romance?"

"Why do I think it didn't stop there? No way, you'd be dwelling on a *mean-girls* conversation. If that's all there was, you'd be laughing about it."

Pushing back my chair, I told her I needed more wine for this part. I brought back two full glasses. "By the time I returned to the ballroom, the dance floor was crowded, and I couldn't immediately spot Dave. I hate to think what my face looked like when I did. He was dancing with Sandy. Wouldn't have thought a thing about it if not for her snide comments and Michelle's warning.

"When the music changed to a slow dance, Dave did an abbreviated bow and motioned her off the floor, but she wasn't having it. She pulled him back and put her arms around him. I couldn't believe my eyes when she laid her head on his chest and fondled the back of his neck. I'll give Dave credit. He looked uncomfortable when he spotted me on the sidelines."

I explained how he nodded toward me and escorted Sandy off the dance floor before the song ended. "With his hand on her elbow, he made a beeline for me, and introduced her as Sandy McGuire. He'd hardly gotten her name out of his mouth before she said, 'Thanks for letting me borrow him. It's been a long time since I've laid eyes on my high school sweetheart. After hearing he'd moved to England, I didn't expect to see him here. I hear you two live in the Cotswolds.'

"Trust me, after the bathroom incident, acting friendly towards her didn't come easily. I enthused about the Cotswolds, and Dave told her about getting his he-shed. She asked what I'd done before I retired, and we had the typical cocktail party talk from there. College and career, yada, yada. That's how I found out about the business she started with her ex, how she got it in the divorce, and how successful she's been at expanding it."

Wendy peered at me over the rim of her wineglass. "Wow, a gossip girl conversation, a warning, and a slow dance. I'm sure it got your dander up. Tell me you went out of your way to be lovey-dovey with Dave the rest of the evening."

I laughed. "Well, that's never difficult with Dave. Whenever he introduces me, he puts his arm around my shoulders or my waist, and there were plenty of introductions. Now that I think about it, I guess we're naturally lovey-dovey. We just acted the way we always do. And all those opportunities to slow dance were heavenly."

"Did you tell him what you'd overheard? Did you ask him what ended the high school relationship?"

"No, but when he suggested we take a stroll outside, he brought it up. He asked about my high school boyfriends, and I told him I'd had two steady boyfriends but was seeing a Georgia Tech guy by my senior year. I didn't have anyone to leave behind."

"And?"

"He explained that he and Sandy had different ideas about the future. She wanted to live in their hometown and get married. He wanted to be a journalist and travel the world."

Hearing Dave's voice in my head, I replayed the conversation for Wendy. "Our differences weren't a showstopper early on, but by my senior year, they were glaringly obvious. I was always honest about my plans, and not long after graduation, she beat me to the punch. She gave me my senior ring back, and that was that. Coward that I was, I was glad she took the initiative."

"Okay, so done and dusted long ago. Just some nostalgia cropping up on her part."

I grimaced. "Funny you should use that phrase—done and dusted. The name of Sandy's business is Done and Done for You, and Dave's hired her company to assist with clearing out his mom's house. She'll be by his side for the next week."

Wendy's mouth dropped open. "Oh, now I see. Perhaps a little too convenient. Oh well, it's a good thing he's smitten with you. And I know you trust him. If he could fend off the advances of that redhead in Torquay, he'll do fine with his high school flame."

My grimace quickly turned to a grin. "You're the only person I know who routinely uses the word 'smitten'—and always in reference to Dave. I love it!"

Wendy sat back. "Ooh, the high school girlfriend as an evil temptress. She could be the victim in our first cozy mystery if we ever get started writing it."

"Okay, enough about the high school reunion. Now that we've gotten that out of the way, let's hear about your London trip, and then I'll tell you about Vermont."

We'd shifted from the sights of London to the mountains of Vermont when Barb's voice caught my attention. I looked up in time to see her point my way, and exclaim, "Yes, that's her."

The woman she was speaking to waved and moved through the crowd to our table. She wore her jet-black hair in a high ponytail. "Leta Parker, I can't believe it's you." She must have picked up on my puzzled look. "It's me, Jilly Martin. From those team-building gigs in Charlotte and Atlanta."

"Oh my goodness, Jilly! Of course, I remember you. Are you back living in England or only visiting?"

"Been back a good while. How 'bout you? Still with the bank? You must be on holiday."

"I've lived here a few years now. This is my friend Wendy Davies." I explained about retiring from the bank, moving here after my husband died, and living in my adorable Schoolhouse Cottage.

Jilly offered her condolences and told me she'd moved back when her mum was ill and stayed on after she improved. "I didn't realize how much I missed home until I came back. Do you miss Atlanta?"

"You know what? I can honestly say not a bit. The traffic, the heat? This village is like paradise in comparison. So, what brings you to the Cotswolds?"

"Some kind of design competition updating village halls. The design firm working on the one in Astonbury is combining their design work with a retreat. My group is handling the outdoor team-building activities. I'm doing the same work here that I did in the States when I met you."

"You mean Holmes & White? Cynthia White's firm?"

Jilly tilted her head. "You know Lyle and Cynthia?"

"I just met Lyle today, but Cynthia used to live here, and she'll be putting the finishing touches on my he-shed this week." That led to a conversation about my schoolhouse cottage and Dave, and Cynthia's former husband, Toby.

"Wait a minute. Guess who else will be here? Rick Bradley. Remember him?"

This was turning into old home week. When I did leadership training and team building at the bank, we worked with several consultants, and Rick's company was one of the best. When my bank bought another one, they designed a full day activity around a search and rescue mission in the woods. The challenge was getting thirty high-powered take-charge executives from two firms to work together to devise a rescue plan. Observing their egos and posturing was fascinating.

I turned to Wendy and described the scenario. "Needless to say, their ill-concealed bickering resulted in a few dead bodies left behind. I wouldn't have wanted them anywhere near me in an emergency. When the day was done, my teammates and I could almost predict who wasn't going to make it long-term in the combined company.

"But Jilly, what's Rick doing in the UK with Powerhouse Performance based in Charlotte? Is his partner Tim with him?"

Jilly rolled her eyes and leaned closer. "I don't know the details, but I gather they don't see eye to eye these days. Maybe because Rick wants to expand to England, and Tim doesn't. Not sure. It's possible Rick's leading the expansion, and Tim's handling the US clients. Or they may have dissolved the partnership. As long as I get paid, it's no skin off my nose."

I always thought of Tim as the brains of the operation and Rick as the charm brigade. If you had a question about the design and intent, you went to Tim.

Rick was typically the one in the field. He led executive sessions, but mostly he trained people like me to facilitate the activities for leaders deeper in the organization. My least favorite part was dragging heavy equipment around to set up the scenarios for the day—and then storing it all away at the end. I much preferred debriefing the insights and ah-has with the participants.

"Rick Bradley. I haven't thought of him in ages. You worked with him more than Tim, right? Doing what you're doing now on your own."

"Yes, Rick oversaw our work in the field, especially for the more involved activities. He contacted me out of the blue, and here I am."

"Well, now you've piqued my curiosity. I'll have to email a few of my old teammates to see if I can get the scoop on what's up with Powerhouse Performance. "

Wendy chuckled. "Of course, you will, Miss Nosey Parker."

At the quizzical look on Jilly's face, Wendy filled her in on the sleuthing adventures of the Little Old Ladies' Detective Agency.

Funny how it all sounded so lighthearted the way she described it.

CHAPTER THREE

AFTER NEARLY TWO WEEKS without yoga, I'd suggested to Wendy that we do Rhiannon's midmorning class on Monday. Christie was still snubbing me, and my leaving her behind this morning did nothing to improve her attitude. "What? You're not taking me?"

"I checked with Rhiannon. No cat yoga today. Plus, I'm meeting Cynthia at the village hall afterwards to help her with the layout for her conference." When I mentioned my years of organizing meetings, she'd enlisted my help with decisions on breakout rooms and the lunch menu suggested by Toby. I saw the business arrangement as an example of how they'd moved on from their divorce.

Christie's response was an unintelligible screech as she stalked from the kitchen. Spying the dab of wet food left in her dish, Dickens wasted no time scarfing it up. Irritable versus happy-go-lucky—my four-legged friends were a study in contrasts.

Walking up Schoolhouse Lane to the yoga studio, I passed the entrance to Astonbury Estate and admired the colorful yellow and purple mums surrounding the stone columns. Thankfully, Dave had taken charge of our garden, and I knew we'd make a trip to the nursery once he returned. I enjoyed choosing flowers and shrubs but had never been much good at keeping them alive.

After I groaned my way through yoga class, Wendy and I made our usual beeline for Toby's Tearoom, where I had just enough time to grab a muffin and coffee to take to the village hall. I was adding sweetener and a bit of cream when someone jostled me. The coffee flew over the counter but fortunately missed me.

"Sorry, sorry, let me get you another one," said a male voice.

An American accent. Must be a tourist. I did my best to mop up the mess before looking over my shoulder.

The man continued his apologies but stopped in midstream when he saw my face. "It can't be. Leta Parker, as I live and breathe."

"Rick?" He hadn't changed much. A touch of silver in his sideburns, tanned face with crinkles around his eyes, perhaps a tad thicker around the middle, but he'd aged well. He was holding a bag from the Book Nook and dropped it to the floor to pull me into a hug.

"The grey hair threw me, but other than that, you haven't changed a bit."

This must be the season for grey hair comments. "You either, Rick. I saw Jilly last night, and she told me you'd be here. How's life treating you?"

"Grand. Did she mention we're working together again? I always got on well with that girl." He nodded to Jenny behind the counter and asked for two of what I was drinking.

As we chatted, he took my left hand. "No ring? Are you divorced now?"

"No, widowed. I moved here after my husband died."

His words of condolence were sincere, but that didn't stop him from eyeing me speculatively. Dave once told me I was strangely oblivious to the appreciative glances I got from men, but there was no mistaking the gleam in Rick's eyes. In a way, it took the sting out of the grey hair comment.

In his look, I recognized the Rick who had flirted with me when we worked together. I wasn't alone in that regard. There were several women in the leadership training department, and it was only the sixty-year-old who escaped his blandishments back then. Wedding rings had never been a deterrent to Rick.

I glimpsed Wendy with her eyebrows raised and knew I'd have to fill her in later. As I departed with my snack, I mentioned to Rick that I was writing a story about Cynthia's village hall project and would likely see him around. *Am I imagining a gleam in his eyes?*

Cynthia was pulling stacks of chairs from the storage closet in the village hall when I arrived. "Sorry to be late. I bumped into Rick Bradley at Toby's, or rather, he bumped into me."

A look of surprise crossed her face. "You know him?"

"Would you believe I worked with him and Jilly both? Ran into her last night at the pub." I explained how the three of us were connected. "And I understand you've hired him to facilitate your meeting this week."

"Well, it was Lyle who hired him. I gather Rick subbed the outdoor part to Jilly, but he's handling what I think of as the 'know thyself' piece. We have our usual cadre of interns and we've hired several new designers this year. The issue is that we're seeing some resistance among the old hands. I'm sure they don't mean to, but they can be quite dismissive of new ideas. Rick's segments include the Myers-Briggs personality assessment and some well-placed team activities. He thought all that would improve the team's effectiveness."

I nodded. "Wow! Myers-Briggs! I loved doing that with groups because they not only learned something about themselves but also had fun. Is he doing 360° feedback, too? It can be tough to swallow, but if a person can accept the feedback, it can be very helpful."

She grinned at me. "We could have hired you, Leta. No 360°. It was either that or Myers-Briggs, and we chose what we saw as slightly less scary. Do you want to observe the team activities for old time's sake? Or only the speakers we have lined up and bits of the design work?"

"I'm happy to hang around for most of it, as long as you don't need me when you're doing the interior of my shed. You mentioned shifting some of my artwork from the cottage." Now that Dave had been delayed, I was hoping to add the little extras this week, and surprise him with the finished product.

We agreed we could work that out tonight if I didn't mind her dropping by after dinner. Most of her team would arrive late afternoon, and she and Lyle would kick off the event midmorning the next day. "Why not join us at the pub for drinks? It will give you a chance to meet the team."

When I accepted the offer, she suggested I invite Wendy, too. Then we got to work. Including a few interns from University College of London, the group numbered ten, so we set up a standard U-shape arrangement in the main room. Two smaller rooms would work as ideation spaces where the teams would complete interior and exterior designs. In their London office, they'd already generated preliminary ideas and narrowed them down to three for each area. This week, they'd select one each to refine and then develop a presentation for the Astonbury Village Council and local business owners.

"Just think," Cynthia said, "by this time next year, Astonbury's village hall and the Green will have a fresh look. It will be in keeping with the architectural style of the High Street, but more functional and less shabby."

"If the transformation is anything like what you did for my cottage, it will make the village more appealing to visitors and potential homebuyers. Not to mention, we want to look our best when the Tour of Britain cycles through here."

"I'm confident they'll be pleased with the design. Once they approve it, we'll submit the plan to the Cotswolds District Council. You know there are over one hundred towns and villages in the Cotswolds, but the design competition was limited to the first twenty-five who signed up. I lobbied to be assigned Astonbury, since I once lived here."

"Do you think business opportunities in the Cotswolds will increase for Holmes and White as a result of the competition?"

"Yes. No matter which firm wins the medal, the village halls will all be more inviting, and that's advertisement enough. It may never equal the revenue we bring in from our London clients, but it's bound to grow."

For a moment, she looked wistful. "Too little too late for me and Toby. Both of us all consumed by growing our separate businesses, and me needing to be in London weeks on end was more strain than our marriage could handle." Her face brightened. "I'm so thankful we got through the early bitterness of the divorce. It's good to see him happy, and I'm glad I can throw some business his way."

I didn't know whether Toby hadn't seen the signs of her discontent or had tried to ignore them. Either way, he took it hard when she asked for a divorce. It didn't help that she'd wanted him to buy her out of the tearoom. I liked them both and was glad they seemed to have gotten past it all.

I made myself a cup of tea and carried it to my office. After listening to the plans for Cynthia's team retreat, I thought there might be enough material for several columns. The story about the competition and the ideas for the village hall were most important to Cynthia. But there was so much more. I knew my readers would enjoy hearing about the outdoor activities and the Myers-Briggs personality types, too.

That reminded me about Rick Bradley and my question about his business, and I knew just who to ask. I pulled up my contact list and fired off an email to Stephie Collins. We'd traveled together to do the leadership programs, and she was still in Human Resources at the bank.

I'd just hit send when I heard my Billy Joel ring tone. Dave was up early as usual. "Hello. Now tell me the truth. Have you been up for hours?"

"How did you know? I was doing some research. *The Strand* contacted me about a Tolkien article for their January issue. His birthday is January 3, you know."

I closed my eyes and shook my head, as though he could see me. "Of course, I didn't know. And how's the packing going?"

"Better. Sandy's really good at cajoling Mom, but it's a struggle. I feel only marginally guilty that I left them on their own to have lunch with a friend yesterday. You met him at the reunion. Martin and I ran track together."

"Such an odd coincidence. You're in the States catching up with old friends, and I've bumped into two acquaintances from my bank days in the last twenty-four hours." I told him about Jilly and Rick and how strange it felt to see them again.

"You'll be proud of me. I actually picked up on the fact that Rick went on alert when he realized I was single. Even though I'd never give him the time of day, even if I were available, it was flattering."

"You're too funny, Leta. The first thing out of Martin's mouth at lunch was what a looker you were. He said his wife told him to quit staring. So, tell me more about this Rick guy. What's wrong with him?"

"It's hard to pinpoint. The word smarmy comes to mind. I remember him being a huge flirt, but somehow too friendly. Like he always stood just a little too close for comfort."

Thinking of Rick made me look at my hand. "That reminds me, Dave. I seem to have misplaced my garnet ring. I know I took it to Connecticut, and I'm pretty sure I wore it to the concert. At least I think I did. When I took it off that night, I must have put it in my jewelry pouch, but it's not there now."

"You didn't wear it to the airport? No. Silly question. You don't wear it on plane trips because your fingers swell. Could it have slipped out of the pouch into the suitcase?"

"I looked but didn't see it. It's probably a case where you'll look in all the same places I've searched and see it right away. Would you mind checking in the guest room at your mom's, though, just to be sure I didn't leave it there?"

He assured me he would and that he'd also call the Waldorf to see if anyone had turned it in. It wasn't as special as a gift from Henry, but it was the first and only piece of nice jewelry I ever bought for myself. To me, it was a milestone that signified I was a successful career woman. I was long past that moment now, and I had more jewelry than I'd ever need. "I'll be awfully disappointed if it doesn't turn up, but I'll live. We'll just have to go on a quest for a new one."

Promising to call him after I met with Cynthia that night, I let him go.

A trip to the market and a bit of tidying took up the rest of the afternoon. Most of the time, I read in bed at night, but with nothing pressing to tend to before dinner at the pub, I stretched out on the couch with my mystery novel. *How quickly will the amateur sleuth and the handsome detective inspector identify who strangled the murder victim?* When the sound of the book hitting the floor startled me awake, I decided on a nap instead.

CHAPTER FOUR

WHEN DICKENS AND I walked into the Ploughman, the din was a surprise. For a Monday night, it was packed, and the crowd included regulars and lots of new faces. I caught Barb's eye and pointed to the tap, and a half-pint soon came my way.

Dickens was a hit as we made our way through the crowd. He got belly rubs while I got questions. "Oh, isn't he cute? Is he a Great Pyrenees? But he's so small!"

Over and over, I replied, "Yes, he's a GP, but he's a dwarf. That's why his legs are shorter than the norm and he tops out at only forty pounds." For a change, he didn't get indignant about being called small. Usually, he bristled at that word.

Along the way, I spied Cynthia and Lyle speaking with Rick near the dartboard. Loud cheers came from a group of youthful customers as they played. *Since when do twenty- and thirty-year olds strike me as youthful?*

Two people closer to my age were also part of the group. The man, who had thinning gray hair and a mustache, took his turn amid gentle ribbing. When I saw Lyle wink at Cynthia, I thought I knew what was coming. Sure enough, to the chagrin of the youthful contingent, his dart hit the bullseye. I wondered if he was one of the old hands Cynthia referenced the night before.

With his arm across his stomach, he took an abbreviated bow as Lyle cried, "Nice one, Bert."

Bert nodded toward a woman with curly auburn hair. "Wait until they see Madge throw."

Stepping to the line, she took three quick throws and Rick yelled, "Bravo, Madge! You didn't tell me you were that good."

She grinned at him. "Can't let you in on all my secrets, now can I?"

When the man named Bert spied Dickens, he came our way and knelt to pet him. "You're on the small side for a Great Pyrenees, boy." He glanced at me. "We've got a full-sized one at home, named Hermione, after you-know-who, I'm sure. My daughter named her. She feels safe with Hermione around. Bet you feel the same way about this little fella."

He stood and introduced himself, and we chatted about what great guard dogs the breed made. I explained about Dickens being a dwarf GP and told him about Basil. "There's a GP at the manor house, and he does what they're bred to do—he guards the sheep."

I turned when I heard my name called. It was Trixie from the Book Nook chatting with Jilly and Wendy. "Hello, Leta. Have you met Jilly?"

I tapped my pint glass to Jilly's. "Oh, we know each other from way back. Now, what brings you out tonight, Trixie? It's your aunt I usually see here."

"Aunt Beatrix got in a special order of books on Myers-Briggs for Cynthia's group, and she's also organizing the books for this week's book club meeting. That's usually my job, but she knew I had plans with Jenny and Jill tonight. We were going to meet here and take my car to Bourton, but this place is so lively tonight, we may decide to stay."

I was happy to hear the girls had become friends. They were of similar ages, and all three were hard workers who were well liked in the village. Jenny Walker was Toby's barista, and her sister Jill was indispensable at the Olde Mill Inn.

As Jilly entertained Trixie and Wendy with stories about her work, I indulged in one of my favorite pastimes—people-watching. When the Walker sisters came in the door, I noticed they got their share of appreciative glances from the young men playing darts. If I wasn't mistaken, they got one from Rick, too.

Lyle and Cynthia had moved to a table, and I noticed her giving handouts to Dickens, so I headed that way. The others joined the crowd at the dartboard.

"Dickens," I cried, "how many treats have you snagged? Too many, I'm sure."

He ignored me and moved between Lyle and Cynthia. I knew he was hoping I wouldn't be able to see how much he ate.

Hastily wiping her fingers on a napkin, Cynthia grinned. "I promise, I only gave him tiny bits, Leta. I know how you worry about his weight." She surveyed the room. "Isn't it grand to see the Ploughman doing a roaring business?"

"Yes. Barb's done great things with it since she took over, but this kind of crowd is a record for a Monday night."

"That's one reason I wanted our team to stay in Astonbury instead of Bourton. Lyle found a large rental cottage, too, since the inn couldn't accommodate all of us. Thankfully, Libby agreed to serve breakfast for everyone. This way, they can *experience* the village."

When Jilly and Wendy arrived with a round of pints, I looked around for Rick. He was ferrying drinks too, but it was a tray of shots for the darts players. I'd forgotten how much the man could drink and never seem worse for the wear.

We were laughing about my accent and how I preferred Jilly's when a question popped into my head. "Lyle, I'm curious. We told you how Jilly and I met each other, but how do you know Rick?"

"He did a semester abroad at the University of Westminster, and we knocked around together that summer. He even spent a weekend at Gran's with me and my roommate."

When I glanced at Wendy, she gave a half smile. "That's how I met my ex-husband. He did his semester abroad at Oxford. We moved to North Carolina when we married."

"Ah, I knew your accent was different, but I couldn't place it. Still British, but not as pronounced."

"I've been back a few years now, so it continues to change. What about you? Did you visit America?"

"No. My roommate and I had big plans to travel there after graduation. We wanted to experience the architecture on the East Coast—Boston, Washington, D.C., New York City—but we didn't make it." A sorrowful expression crossed Lyle's face. "Angus committed suicide, and it just didn't seem right to do the trip without him.

"I hadn't heard from Rick in years, but when he contacted me about his expansion plans last year, I was happy to connect him with some of our corporate clients. His business isn't something I know much about, but it was a simple thing to make a few introductions."

Jilly lifted her glass. "Here's to staying in touch with old acquaintances. You hired Rick, he looked me up, and here I am. Cheers."

When the conversation turned to ordering dinner, Jilly excused herself, saying she needed to run something by Rick. The rest of us ordered food and enjoyed a conversation that moved from business to holidays to books and back. Lyle shared his memories of idyllic summers here with his gran, and I shared my perspective about living in England versus the States.

Wendy, who had spent most of her adult life in Charlotte, declared that England was the clear winner for her. "It's the heat. I never grew accustomed to it. Had I lived in the Northwest, I might feel differently, but the Southeast is no place for a Brit."

I stifled a yawn and looked around for Dickens. He was sound asleep by the fireplace. *How does he do that?* "It's time for me and Dickens to head home. Do you still plan to come by later, Cynthia?"

"Yes, I should be there in an hour, if not sooner. Some of this crew will stay 'til closing, but not me. I've already told Barb I'll come by tomorrow to settle the bill."

As I departed, Lyle suggested another round for the table. I didn't see Jilly, but Rick was holding court at the bar, where it was standing room only. I waved goodbye to him and heard him holler something about leaving so soon. I made a slashing motion across my throat as in, "no more for me." Even in my youthful days, I couldn't drink that much.

He surprised me by following me to the door. "Leta, wait up. I'd love to have a chance to catch up. Maybe tomorrow night?"

I tried to mask my surprise. "Um, let's touch base at the end of the day, okay?" Catching up with Rick one on one wasn't high on my list, but I wasn't quick enough on my feet to come up with a graceful way to say no.

Dickens yawned and did a down doggie stretch on the way to the car. As he stood, he tilted his head. "Did you hear that, Leta? Someone's by the path to the inn." He trotted in that direction and barked, "It's two women."

I jogged that way. Sure enough, Jilly was propping up the woman I recognized as Madge. "Jilly, let me help. Did she have too much to drink?"

"That's the strange thing, Leta. Madge says she hardly drank at all. I saw her stagger to the restroom and followed her. I could barely keep her upright to get her out the back door."

Madge nodded and mumbled something unintelligible. I thought I heard the words darts and maybe pain, but I couldn't make sense of the rest of it.

Gently lifting her chin, I brushed her auburn bangs from her eyes. "Madge, how much did you drink?"

She rallied briefly. "A pint or two. So dizzy."

As I knelt beside her, I heard a voice and saw a man silhouetted in the doorway to the pub. He called, "Madge, are you out here?"

"We're over here," I replied.

It was Bert. "What's happened? Did you stumble? Are you alright?"

Jilly told her story again as Bert took over propping Madge up. "She told you the truth, Jilly. She doesn't drink much, especially compared to some of us. We were supposed to walk together back to the inn. When I missed her at the bar, I waited and then decided to check out here."

The three of us conferred. Since the inn was on my way home, I told them I'd deliver Madge, so they didn't have to cut their evening short. If we could get her into my car, Gavin or Libby would help me at the inn.

Bert draped his jacket over Madge's shoulders. "I'll ride with you. Kind of you to step in. It's Leta, right?"

Easily lifting Madge to her feet, Bert helped her to the passenger seat of my car. On the drive, he explained that Madge was a city girl and scared of the dark woods. "Doesn't help that she was mugged a few years back in the city. When the git jerked her bag from her shoulder, she fell and broke her wrist. Guess that's why I worried when she didn't return to the bar. I didn't think she'd gone off on her own."

"I'm glad you came looking for her. It makes me think that Holmes & White is a close-knit organization."

"You're right, and Madge and I are among the old-timers. Been there since the beginning."

Leaving Dickens in the car, I opened the front door and called for my friends while Bert helped Madge. A welcoming shout came from the sitting room. "In here. Is that you, Leta?"

The two were sipping wine in front of the fire. "Make yourself comfortable. Are you here to tell us about your trip?" I saw Gavin glance behind me expectantly. "Where's Dave?"

"I'll explain later, Gavin. Right now, I need your help with an intoxicated guest. At least, I think that's what her problem is. Can you tell me which room belongs to Madge? And I may need a key."

As he and Libby followed me to the foyer, I told them what I knew. Bert had settled Madge in the easy chair by the door, and she opened her eyes when we approached. "I . . . I don't know what's wrong with me. My . . . my legs are heavy."

She was a slight thing, and when Gavin pulled the key from the desk, he and Bert had no trouble helping her stand. Together, they helped her up to her room, with Libby and I climbing the stairs behind them. From there, Libby took over.

When she returned to the sitting room, she had a puzzled look on her face. "I guess alcohol affects people in different ways. Madge—is that her name? She seems more lethargic than drunk. It was like undressing the Raggedy Ann and Andy scarecrows out front. Whatever. I made her take two paracetamol tablets with a large glass of water. As a precaution, I put the wastebasket by the bed, but I don't think she'll be ill."

I couldn't help smiling at the mention of the scarecrows. In keeping with the season, Libby had dressed her two in matching orange shirts tucked into brown corduroy overalls.

"Whatever it is, I hope she's better in time for the meeting. Now, I've got to get home pronto. Cynthia is coming over to pick out artwork to move to Dave's shed. Thanks for your help. I'll give you guys a holler when I get a spare moment, and we'll catch up."

Bert walked me to the door. "Thanks for helping, Leta. I'll let Cynthia know when she gets here, so she can check on her. I think I've just connected the dots. You're writing the article about us, right? About the competition?"

"Yes, and I'll see you tomorrow and throughout the week. I hope Madge feels better by then."

At home, I shooed Dickens into the garden, and tended to Christie as she came meowing down the stairs. "I'm hungry, Leta."

She made her pronouncement as though it were a revelation. "Christie, you're always hungry right before bedtime, no matter what time that is. The only question is what you want. Treats or a dab of wet food?"

She stretched and flopped on her side, a move Henry had dubbed a flop-and-roll. "Treats. I think treats."

I had time to play a few rounds of Words with Friends before Dickens alerted me to Cynthia's arrival with his welcome bark.

She came in carrying two flat rectangular packages wrapped in brown paper and twine. "Consider this a shed-warming gift."

Christie leaped to the kitchen table and pawed at the twine. "For me, right?"

"Be patient, Christie." I knew she wanted the wrapping, not whatever was inside. Quickly untying the twine, I tossed it to the floor, where she pounced on it.

When I unwrapped the first package, I laughed in delight. "What? How?" It was the cover of the *Strand* magazine, the one with Dave's J.M. Barrie article inside. The midnight blue cover displayed his name prominently with the caption "Previously unknown J.M. Barrie children's book."

She beamed at my reaction and handed me the second package. The matching frame held the dust wrapper from Dave's book, *Barrie & Friends*. "It was your idea, Leta. You mentioned framing some of his articles, but I thought these would be more colorful and make perfect companion pieces.

"And, since you gave him the portrait of Dickens and Christie as a Christmas present, I think we should move it from your office to his shed. What do you think?"

I would have agonized over what to hang, but she made it simple. "You're a godsend, Cynthia—but then, after the magic you worked on this drab cottage, I knew you would be. It's so cheerful now with the white walls and touches of red and green. Simple but tasteful. And these pieces are perfect for the he-shed. I can't wait to see the look on Dave's face."

Her gift triggered an idea for me. "Cynthia, if I come up with a dust jacket for a Tommy and Tuppence mystery, could you have that framed, too?"

"Sure. I can even locate one myself. Is there one in particular you'd like?"

I chuckled. "If you can find *The Secret Adversary*, the first one, that would be great. Ever since Dave and I dressed as Tommy and Tuppence for my costume party, those have been our nicknames for each other. I think he'll get a kick out of having one of their books framed in his shed."

"I'll find it. Nothing pleases me more than a happy client. By the way, keep an eye out for a delivery. It's the key to keeping Dave's environment clutter-free, and I think you'll love it."

"Oh my gosh, Cynthia, you must be a mind reader."

"That's always the goal. Now, I'm off to the inn. I want to check with Lyle about his opening presentation and then climb into bed. I'll see you in the morning."

The inn. Bed. "Wait. I can't believe I didn't think to tell you this earlier." I explained the Madge situation and suggested she look in on her.

Like a mother hen, Cynthia clucked her concern. "Poor Madge. It's not bad enough that her back's been acting up, and now this. She's been with us for years, and it's not like her at all to overindulge. I hope she isn't coming down with something. I'll be sure to stop by her room, and I'd better let Lyle know, too."

As Cynthia was leaving, Dickens darted in the door and joined Christie in wrestling the wads of brown paper into submission. *Who needs toys when you have crinkly paper?*

I glimpsed headlights in the driveway next door as Cynthia drove off. *That must be Lyle's friend. I'll make it a point to drop by tomorrow to welcome him.*

CHAPTER FIVE

IT HAD BEEN A later-than-usual night for me, and I'd only just started the coffee when my phone rang. It wasn't Billy Joel singing, so I knew it wasn't Dave. "Hello?"

"Leta, it's Jilly. Cynthia suggested I call you. Would you mind terribly doing me a favor?"

I stifled a yawn. "No. What do you need?"

"It's Rick. He was supposed to meet me outside the village hall, and he's late—quite late. And the stupid sod isn't answering his phone."

How I was supposed to help was unclear to me. "Could he be driving and unable to answer the phone?"

"No. Doesn't have a car, so he'd be on foot. He's staying in a cottage on Schoolhouse Lane, and he told me the cottage next door had a school bell. It has to be yours, right? Can you run over and bang on the door, please? If he's still asleep, I'll kill him."

"Next door to me? Um . . . okay. Let me throw on some clothes, and I'll do it. I'll call you back in a few minutes."

Thoughts tumbled through my head as I ran upstairs. *Rick is the friend staying in Lyle's cottage? Guess Lyle drove him over last night. Good thing, as much as Rick was drinking.*

"Come on Dickens, we're going next door."

The sun was up, but there was still a slight chill in the damp air. "There's a light on, Dickens, so he must be awake. I wonder if his phone is dead or on silent mode."

Barking a greeting, Dickens darted across the street. "Hi, Watson. Are you here to see Christie?" Most mornings and evenings, the handsome cat from the manor house visited my door. He was one of the few felines Christie seemed to like, and I thought of him as her boyfriend.

I caught the names Martha and Dylan and assumed Watson was giving Dickens an update on the donkeys. When I heard Basil mentioned, I knew it would be a few minutes before Dickens joined me. Basil was his favorite companion.

Banging on the door of Lyle's cottage, I called, "Rick, it's Leta. Are you up?"

Since my persistent knocking wasn't getting me anywhere, I moved to the left of the door and peered through the kitchen window. The kitchen was dark, but I could see a light somewhere off to the right. *The hall, maybe, or the sitting room?*

I rapped on the kitchen window. No luck. Next, I tried the door handle. I wasn't sure how I felt when I discovered it was unlocked. The last thing I wanted was to visit Rick's bedroom to wake him up. *I guess that's better than finding him in the shower.* Imagining the jokes he'd make about either situation made me cringe.

It was cold inside, and the dim light was coming from the sitting room, where I saw a wing-backed chair and the edge of a table beyond it. I glimpsed a hand hanging over the left arm of the chair. *Did Rick drink so much that he couldn't make it to bed?*

As I approached the chair, I took in its position, angled close to the table but not directly facing it. *Oh. It's a jigsaw puzzle.*

Two things happened simultaneously. I reached to touch Rick as I softly called his name, and Dickens bounded into the room, giving his alert bark. "Leta, Leta, it's bad." Those were his exact words when we'd found the body at the cricket pavilion.

It wasn't the phone that was dead—it was Rick. I stood stock-still, not wanting to get any closer, but knowing I had to. "Dickens, stay."

Stepping closer to what I was sure was a dead body, I was careful not to disturb it. I gingerly touched Rick's neck, searching for a pulse. Nothing. But then, since I could see his half-open, lifeless eyes, I already expected that.

Pulling the phone from my pocket, I rang Gemma. When my call went to voicemail, I hung up and dialed 999. It was as though I was hearing my voice from a distance. "I need to report a death on Schoolhouse Lane." When the operator asked if I was sure the person was dead, my response was snippy. "Well, yes. He has no pulse."

I jumped when my phone rang—a sure sign I was wound tight. I heard coughing before Gemma spoke. "Leta, I just got an alert about a death at your home. I'm on my way. Are you all right? Is Dave?"

"We're fine. I mean, I'm fine, and Dave's in Connecticut. I mean, oh hell, I mean the body is next door—not the Watsons', the cottage on the other side of me. I don't know the address."

"Huh? Right, take a deep breath. I'm out running, and I'm on my way. Don't touch anything." She coughed loudly and murmured something unintelligible.

It was two miles from her small cottage next to the Olde Mill Inn. Depending on which direction she'd taken for her morning run, she could be here any minute. I shook my head and steeled myself to do what I was so good at—take in the details of the scene. When Gemma wasn't irritated or furious with me, she gave me credit for being especially observant. It was as though a strange calm came over me, or maybe it was the focused observation that calmed me down.

Breathing deeply, I forced myself to look at Rick's face. I'd already noted the partially closed eyes, but it was the purple bruises on his neck that made me shudder. His head tilted into the right corner of the chair made the marks hard to miss. He wore the burnt orange zip-collar sweater he'd had on at the Ploughman, unzipped far enough for me to see a grey tee shirt at his collarbone.

If not for the eyes and the bruises, I could fool myself into thinking he'd simply fallen asleep, one arm draped toward the floor, the other in his lap. As I looked closer, I saw that his sweater and tee shirt were stained with red wine. *Did he fall asleep drinking wine?*

I didn't see a wineglass, but a nearly empty tumbler sat near the top right corner of the table. It held dregs of amber liquid, not red wine. When I leaned in to sniff it, I caught a whiff of whiskey. *What is that white stuff?* I nearly picked up the glass for a closer look but caught myself in time. The best I could tell, some substance besides liquor was in the bottom.

My gaze returned to Rick and progressed to his feet and the few colorful puzzle pieces scattered beneath the table. *Wait. What's that?* Something drew my eyes back to the lower edge of his sweater. His belt was undone, and the loose buckle peeked out from beneath the sweater.

I wondered if his pants were unbuttoned, but I wasn't going to get close enough to check that. *Back to the table, Leta.* Loose puzzle pieces lay on the table, and someone had connected most of the edge pieces, but that was all.

Without moving further into the room, I studied the fireplace on the wall beyond the table. Rick must have lit a fire when he came in the night before, because there were a few slightly charred logs in it. It had been a warmish September day, but a stone cottage could feel chilly after the sun went down.

My eyes traveled to the mantel. Sitting beside a trio of candles was another glass, this one with amber liquid in it, too. *So, he had a guest.* I moved closer to the fireplace, but I didn't detect anything white in the glass. A pleasant aroma caught my attention, not one I readily recognized. It wasn't the smell of whiskey, nor the partially burned logs.

Turning to the left, I saw a worn plaid couch against the wall perpendicular to the fireplace. It looked comfy with its matching hassock and plump throw pillows in hunter green and blue. The green one was on the floor by the side table, which held a nearly full glass of amber liquid. It matched the other two tumblers, and beside it stood a bottle of Cotswolds Single Malt. *Two visitors? Did they bring him back and come in for a drink? Did Lyle supply the bottle of whiskey for his guest, or did someone else bring it?*

I moved closer to study the glass. Nothing white in this one either, but peachy-beige lipstick stained the rim. *At least one person was female.* That thought prompted me to check the glass on the mantel again. No lipstick marred that one.

The wall facing the fireplace had an overflowing floor-to-ceiling bookcase with an easy chair in front of it. It would be a treat to go through the collection, and I wondered whether Lyle had done anything more than dust the shelves. Glancing at Rick again, I realized the table with the jigsaw puzzle was in a bay window with its plaid curtains drawn. A small rustic chandelier provided the light. It was a cozy setting. I shook my head as I amended that thought. It was *once* a cozy setting. I doubted Lyle would ever see it that way again.

The sound of a cell phone came from the kitchen. I found it on the counter next to the fridge, but the ringing stopped before I could get to it. It was a natural reaction to reach for a ringing phone, but I knew Gemma wouldn't see it that way. Fortunately, my phone rang before I could give into temptation.

"Leta, did you find him?"

"Um, yes. But . . . Jilly, I don't know how to tell you this. Rick's dead."

I heard a sharp intake of breath. "Dead? He can't be. He was fine last night."

I waited to let her digest what I'd told her. "I'm sorry, but he is. The police are on their way. Correction—they just arrived. I'll call you later."

Gemma stood in the doorway, alternately panting and coughing. "Leta, who are you talking to?"

"The person who asked me to find Rick. That's why I'm here. Jilly—Jilly called me to come wake him up. And I found him dead, and she just called me again, and I had to tell her, and..."

Tears filled my eyes as the delayed reaction set in. For once, Gemma showed her compassionate side. "Shh. It's all right. Let's take it one step at a time. Where's the body?"

Wiping the tears from my eyes, I pointed to the sitting room. Gemma must have seen something in my posture, because she pulled a chair from the kitchen table. "Sit. I'll be back."

It wasn't like me to be meekly obedient, but I took a shuddering breath and sat. *Get a grip, Leta. You've seen dead bodies before.*

Dickens pressed his warm body against my leg and licked my hand. "I'm here, Leta. You're safe."

It wasn't long before I heard Gemma speaking. "Righto, I'm on the scene. How far out are you? Yes, she was right. He's dead, and we need the SOCOs." She blew out what sounded like an exasperated breath. "Yes, I'm sure."

She murmured to herself as she returned to the kitchen. "Could murder a cup of tea, but don't want to disturb anything." My horrified expression must have alerted her. "Sorry, poor choice of words. I know, I'll call the Tearoom."

Squinting at her phone, she cleared her throat and punched in a number. "Toby? It's Gemma. We have a situation, and I need tea, buckets of it. Can you or Jenny run some over to Schoolhouse Lane, the last house before the bridge? Yes, and could you bring some honey, too, please? I've got this awful cough."

That task accomplished, she pulled out her notepad and jotted a few notes. *Gee, does she carry that thing everywhere?*

As we waited for tea and reinforcements, Gemma went back to the sitting room. I heard her murmuring as though she were thinking aloud. When she returned, she was stuffing the notepad and pen in one pocket of her windbreaker and pulling a hanky from the other.

She's sick as a dog. What on earth is she doing running? "Gemma, you sound awful. Should you even be here?"

"Probably not." She pulled out a chair and joined me at the table. "You know I don't like to jump to conclusions . . ."

"But it's murder, isn't it? I saw the marks on his neck. He didn't do that to himself."

"You noticed those, did you?"

I flashed on the dead man Libby had found at the river two years ago. "Oh no. This is just like Max the Magician. But his killer's in prison."

Gemma scoffed. "Don't let your imagination run away with you, Leta. Yes, there are certain similarities, but this isn't a copycat. Max's killer used a scarf."

A coughing spell ensued. "Someone used their bare hands on this victim."

"Don't . . . don't you have to be strong to do that?"

"Most likely." She studied the kitchen for a moment and turned to me with a knowing look. "Leta, what story does the kitchen tell?"

I blinked and looked around. "You know, I didn't consciously take it in, but let me focus. I see a set of keys on the table with a business card. Rick probably tossed them there as he came in. Two bottles of red wine next to a tray with a crystal wine decanter—one matching glass on the tray, two in the dish drain, and a dirty one on the counter. At least three people drank wine *and* whiskey."

Pointing at me, Gemma said, "Perspicacious. I heard that word the other day, and it fits you to a tee. Something about strong intuition and insight. You don't just *see* things. You put the images together, and you ask the right questions. I've known constables who wouldn't immediately make the connection between the tumblers in the other room and the wine goblets in here." She studied the counter. "I guess they couldn't be bothered to use the decanter."

Her comment sounded strangely like a compliment. I never knew which Gemma would show up. This morning, the kind and appreciative detective inspector was here. It could just as easily have been the rude, dismissive version.

I scratched Dickens's head. "And Rick was buying shots at the Ploughman last night. I'm sure he drank plenty there."

"Right. You mentioned that name earlier. Who's Rick? Did he buy the place?"

"No. He's staying here this week." My thoughts were a jumble. "The owner's fixing it up. Rick is—" Gemma's coughing spell interrupted me.

When Dickens left my side to sniff the floor near the cabinets, Gemma's mouth twitched. "It's almost comical to watch him move from left to right and turn at the corner. He's just like you, isn't he? Searching the room the way you methodically take in a scene."

She was right. He did the same thing most mornings along the garden wall. "Funny you should say that. When he does that in the garden, I call it corner checking."

"Well then, do you feel up to doing your thing in the sitting room? Or would you prefer to wait in here?"

"Would you believe I've kind of already done that?"

When she nodded and rolled her eyes, I followed her into the other room.

Standing in nearly the same spot as before, I held up my phone. "Since you're taking notes, I'll take photos, if that would be helpful."

That earned me a Gemma look. "It would, but don't think for one minute I'm falling for your innocent act, Nancy Drew. Just because the crime scene is next door to you doesn't mean this is a case for you and your friends."

Well, she didn't say no, did she? I took that as permission and snapped photos as I laid out my observations. She didn't say anything as I clicked away, and when she took a moment to blow her nose, I snuck a shot of Rick, too. Not something I particularly wanted to have on my phone, but I did it anyway.

Leaning close to the body, Gemma used her pen to lift Rick's sweater. "I guess you saw the belt buckle. Did you see that he or someone unbuttoned his waistband?"

"Or someone? Because there's lipstick on one glass? And no, I didn't get close enough to disturb anything, so I didn't see the button."

Pursing her lips, she turned to me. "Yes. There's also a smudge of lipstick on his cheek, and if I'm not mistaken, it looks like drips of wine on his face. Odd."

Those were three details I'd missed, but Gemma also noticed the things that had caught my attention, even down to the odd white substance in Rick's glass. "Almost looks like Goody's headache powders, and that's just plain sinful. Who would ruin a glass of good whiskey with that stuff?"

It was a rhetorical question, so I kept quiet. We'd made it to the side table with the glass and the bottle of liquor on it before Dickens ran in and dropped something at my feet. "Look, Leta. It's a cork. Is it important?"

I picked it up and handed it to Gemma. "I don't know that it matters, but the two wine bottles on the counter weren't open. There must be an empty bottle around here somewhere." I slapped my palm on my forehead. "Of course there is. If they drank wine, where's the empty bottle? Maybe it's in the trash or in the fridge. I wonder whether Lyle supplied the wine or Rick brought it with him."

"And who's Lyle when he's at home?"

"Lyle Holmes, Cynthia's partner in the design firm. I met him yesterday. This is his cottage. His business card is on the fridge, and there's one here on the table."

"Okay, let's hear it. No one's been around this place in an age. Did he recently buy it?"

As I told her the story of Lyle's gran and how he was getting the cottage ready to rent, she jotted notes.

She looked up when I stuttered to a stop. "What's that look on your face, Leta? Is there more?"

I nodded. "Yes, I know the—"

There was a knock on the door, and Toby called, "Gemma, can I come in? I've got the tea."

"Coming Toby. Hold on." She pointed at me. "Stay here, Leta. I'll get it. The less said to Toby, the better."

Unfortunately, Dickens blew that plan when he ran to the kitchen door to greet Toby.

"Hello, boy. What are you doing here? Is Leta with you?"

Dickens was doing his best to answer Toby when Gemma made it into the kitchen. "Quiet, Dickens. Move." Dickens was more obedient than I'd ever be, and I could picture him sitting at attention, hoping Toby had biscuits for him.

The talking was more hushed, and I could only hear snippets of Gemma's murmurs between coughs. "Here . . . help you . . . Toby . . . lifesaver."

Toby's deep voice was easier to make out. "Why is Dickens here? Where's Leta? Is something wrong?"

More murmurs before Toby said his goodbyes. "Okay, glad she's okay. I'll check on her later. No worries."

When Toby left, Gemma called me to the kitchen and poured us tea. "Now, where were we? And more to the point, where's my team?"

As if in answer to her question, her phone rang. "DI Taylor. What? When? Well, thank goodness no one's hurt. Yes, I'll secure the scene."

She blew out her cheeks. "Bloody hell, the SOCOs were in an accident with a tractor. A car from Gloucestershire is on the way to get them. Hold on, let me call Dad."

In short order, she got Gavin on the phone and asked him to find the police tape in her cottage and deliver it. "Yes, Dad, I'm fine. I'm afraid there's been a murder, but for goodness' sake, don't tell Mom."

Gulping her tea, she looked at me. "Before this is over, half the bloody village will have been here! Now, let's get back to Lyle Holmes. I can tell you have more to tell me about him."

She was wrong. I'd told her all I knew about Lyle and his cottage. The thing I had yet to explain was that I knew Rick and Jilly.

To give Gemma credit, she listened patiently to the history. Other than a clarifying question or two, I got through my story without interruption.

She stared at me in disbelief. "Let me get this straight. You ran into not one, but two people from your past—in less than twenty-four hours? People you haven't seen in what, ten years? That's an awfully big coincidence. And they were both hired by Cynthia's design firm?"

"Yes, it's been forever since I've seen either of them. Technically, Lyle Holmes engaged Rick, and he brought in Jilly. Not that it matters."

"Maybe none of it matters, but I don't believe in coincidences."

"Excuse me! What could the three of us knowing each other have to do with Rick's death?"

"His murder, you mean. I don't know, but I can't ignore it. How likely is it that a complete stranger walked in here and killed him?"

"Well, let me assure you I didn't come over here, do him in, and then call you. And Jilly wouldn't have called me to wake him up if she knew he was dead. That kind of stuff only happens in those murder mysteries on television."

"Which you're no doubt an expert on!"

Thank goodness Gavin pulled up before we could throttle each other. "Gemma, I've got the tape." He came to an abrupt halt in the doorway. "Is this where I say, 'It's all over but the shouting?' What's going on here?"

Gemma coughed and wiped her nose. "Oh, just the usual, Dad. A dead body and our local Nosey Parker in the thick of it."

Finally, the other version of DI Taylor is here. "This sounds like a perfect time for me to leave. I promised Cynthia I'd be at the village hall all day. Goodness knows how she and Lyle will get through the next few days."

I couldn't help myself. I was already in problem-solving mode. "It's not like they can cancel the event. The village council and business leaders are expecting a presentation, and there's a competition going on."

As if to confirm my thoughts, my phone buzzed with a text message from Cynthia. "Is it true? Is Rick dead? And the police are there?"

I showed the message to Gemma. "What do I tell her?"

Before Gemma could answer me, another message popped up. "Is it Gemma? Can I talk to her?"

Gemma grabbed my phone and hit the phone icon. "Cynthia, it's Gemma. I'm in the middle of an investigation. Make it quick." She put the phone on speaker.

"An investigation? It's true, then? Rick's dead?"

"Yes."

"But what do you mean—investigation? Wasn't it a heart attack or something? Oh, I know, the police always come when someone dies, right?"

Gemma rolled her eyes, a typical Gemma reaction. "Look, Cynthia, I'm here, and what I can tell you is that I consider this a suspicious death. That's all you need to know."

"But, but . . . "

I grabbed my phone. "Hold on a minute, Cynthia."

As I put the phone on mute, Gemma sputtered, "What the hell?"

"Look, Gemma. When Cynthia gets over the initial shock, she'll go into business mode. She needs to know whether she can get on with the event and what she can say to her team. They all met Rick last night, so she's got to tell them something. Address that now, and she won't bother you again."

Now I know what the expression glared daggers *means.* I took the phone off mute and handed it back.

"Cynthia, let me be very clear. You can carry on with your event, and you can tell people that Rick is dead, but you don't have any details to share. That's it. I'll have questions for you and your partner later, and I know where to find you." She handed my phone back.

I told Cynthia I'd be there as soon as I could and asked her to tell Jilly.

Gemma looked from me to her father. "She just earned herself a new nickname, Dad. *Bossypants.* I loved that book by Tina Fey, but I don't need her doppelgänger in the middle of my murder investigation."

It was a shock when Gavin gently reprimanded his daughter. "Gemma, I realize you're in command mode and have a job to do, but there's no need to be insulting. For goodness' sake, girl, Leta found a dead body this morning. You're fortunate she had the presence of mind to help you out with Cynthia. One less thing for you to deal with."

The look on Gemma's face wasn't one I'd seen before—something akin to embarrassment mixed with shock. Walking past father and daughter with Dickens at my heels, I stifled a snarky comment, but I couldn't help whispering to Dickens when we were out the door. "Exit stage left."

CHAPTER SIX

CHRISTIE GREETED US AT the door. "What's going on over there? Watson waited ages for you to let him in, but he finally gave up."

"Dickens, will you fill your sister in, please? I've got to shake a leg. What I really want is to crawl into bed and pull the covers over my head, but Cynthia's sure to need an extra hand this morning."

Texting Cynthia and Jilly that I'd be there ASAP, I washed my face and changed clothes. Today's attire was jeans and a purple hip-length top. I grabbed Dickens's leash. "We've got a busy day, boy. Let's go."

"What about the dead man, Leta? Will he still be there when we get back?"

"For heaven's sake, Dickens. I hope not. Gemma will have it sorted by then." And maybe throwing myself into helping Cynthia would keep the symptoms of shock at bay. I knew from experience that lightheadedness or dizziness might set in, followed by lethargy. I didn't have time for that today, but I knew that when the delayed reaction finally hit, it would be like a ton of bricks.

As I left home, I rang Wendy and gave her the news. Just saying the words "dead body in the cottage next door" made me shudder. And adding the detail about Rick being strangled didn't help.

"I can't believe I just met the man last night, and he's dead. And you must feel awful. You reconnected with an old friend, and in a flash, he's gone. You don't need to be by yourself. I'm on my way."

"No, I'm headed to the village hall now. The event is still on, and my job is to write about it. Can I call you when I'm free? Hopefully sooner rather than later?"

"If you stay for lunch, I'll see you when I give my talk about Sunshine Cottage and the J.M. Barrie connection. I'll walk with you back to your cottage. You can talk. You can cry, and we'll get through this."

Knowing I could lean on Wendy was the tonic I needed. At the intersection of Schoolhouse Lane and the High Street, I spied Toby trundling two large urns toward the village hall. *I hope there are muffins on that cart, too.* "Hold up. Need some help?"

"Hi, Leta. No, I'm fine, but Cynthia's beside herself. I take it Gemma filled her in on your discovery."

"Aargh. Please don't call it *my* discovery. If that gets about, there'll be no end to people asking me questions."

"Right. Lips sealed. How are you doing? Not only did you find a man dead, but I figured out yesterday that you knew him."

At his inquisitive look, I gave him the short version of working with Rick in my banking days. I'd never known Rick all that well, and if I'd learned from a former co-worker that he had died in the States, I would have been sad—but this? Favorite person or not, he didn't deserve to be murdered.

Jogging ahead of Toby, I opened the door to the village hall. Together, we set up the coffee and tea paraphernalia. "Thank goodness, you have muffins, and they're lemon to boot."

Cynthia emerged from one of the small rooms off the hall. She looked pale and shaky, and I imagined I looked much the same. "Oh, you two are a sight for sore eyes. Leta, I don't know how I'm going to get through today. I hope Lyle is in better shape than I am."

I pulled her into a hug. "You'll do it because you must, and I'll be here as support. Is Lyle on his way?"

"No. He's having breakfast with the team. When we're all here, he'll tell them about Rick and then proceed with the program. We don't know how else to handle it. Just saying that aloud sounds so cold, but . . . the village leaders are coming to present to us, and we can't blow off the competition."

The situation reminded me of the literary festival I'd attended the previous year. When the chief organizer died, the local bobby told the participants, and the event went on. The victim would have wanted it that way. I shared that with Cynthia, and it seemed to make her feel better.

I recalled a lesson from my corporate days. "In my early leadership training days, I got some good advice. Think of it this way. If you were standing in front of a room of people and you saw snow start to come down outside, what would you do? Would you keep talking as though nothing was going on? No. You'd say, 'look, it's snowing.' You might even encourage the group to run to the windows.

"Why? Because there's no way people can focus on what you're saying until you acknowledge the situation. You can't ignore it. That's some of the best advice I ever got, and do you know who it came from? Rick Bradley."

Yet another memory came to mind. We'd employed Rick's advice when we learned a well-loved senior leader had died of a massive heart attack the night before a major meeting. My boss at the time shared the news and asked for a moment of silence. Then we carried on.

Until I heard her voice, I didn't realize Jilly had joined us. "Right on, Leta. I heard Rick say that to countless numbers of fledgling trainers and even old hands. It was one of his standard stories."

"Thanks, Jilly. Perhaps either you or I should share it with the team after Lyle tells them about Rick. Before he does his official kickoff. It would be another way to explain why we're continuing with the conference, and also a way to honor Rick."

A hint of a smile crossed Cynthia's face. "That's perfect. I'll let Lyle know."

When Toby poured Cynthia a cup of tea and suggested she walk with him to the river, Jilly pulled me aside. "Leta, please tell me what happened. I can't believe Rick's dead."

Tears came to her eyes as the words poured out. "I know he had high blood pressure, but that doesn't kill you, does it? He was fine when I left him. He was the picture of health. How can he be dead?"

When she drew a breath, I answered as best I could. "Jilly, all I can say is it looked as though it happened in an instant." *Not an out-and-out lie. It didn't look like there was a struggle. It was quick.*

"Where . . . where did you find him? Was he in bed? When it's my time, that's how I want to go. Just fall asleep and not wake up."

She seemed unable to stop babbling. *Is this morbid curiosity or nervous energy in reaction to the shock?*

I couldn't help thinking of Henry's death in Atlanta. As we were cycling uphill one morning, he rounded a curve ahead of me. I didn't see the accident, but I heard the sounds and knew he'd been struck by a car. By the time I jogged to the top, a runner was administering CPR, and I think I sensed then that he was already gone. My reaction was stunned silence as I knelt by his side, tears running down my face.

Shaking off the memory, I realized I'd tuned Jilly out. She was still talking, but in a low voice, almost to herself. When I touched her arm, her mouth dropped open. "Oh my goodness, Leta, I need to focus. What am I going to do about today?"

"If it's the outdoor activities, you know you can handle it, Jilly. You've done it any number of times."

"But what about the rest of it? I can't do what Rick does."

"What else is there?" And then it hit me. "You've done the personality types, right?"

"Nope. I only watched Rick and Tim when I worked with them. I've never stood up and explained the sixteen types, much less how to use the information. I know I'm an ENFP, and I love that phrase that describes my type as 'giving life an extra squeeze,' but I can never remember what the letters stand for."

I was certified in Myers-Briggs, but trying to remember the details from all those years ago wasn't easy. "I admit, I can't recall the taglines given to each type, but yours seems just like you. And the letters are for Extravert / Intuitive / Feeler / Thinker. I'm an ISTJ, an Introvert / Sensor / Thinker/ Judger, and my two taglines are 'doing what should be done,' and 'work before play.' They fit me to a tee, but sound much less exciting than yours."

As odd as it seemed to think about personality types at a time like this, that's where my brain went. It wasn't difficult to call to mind the description of my type. I was responsible, organized, impatient, demanding, and detail oriented.

Of course, being impatient and demanding didn't always endear me to people. Combined with the rest, however, it explained why it was almost second nature to me to throw dinner parties and organize girls' trips. And my managers appreciated my ability to plan corporate events for hundreds of people. I liked to think I was becoming slightly less impatient with age, but I suspected I was fooling myself. *I'll have to ask Dave.*

"Um, Leta, I think you just solved my problem."

"I did? How?"

"If you're a person who does what should be done, I'm betting you'll step in to take Rick's place. You will, won't you?"

She can't be serious. "Jilly, I'd like to help, but I haven't done this kind of work in years. There's no way I can step in at the drop of a hat."

"Sure you can, Leta. The personality piece isn't until tomorrow. Knowing you, you've got a book about Myers-Briggs somewhere. You can scan it to refresh your memory while the group is working on the design this afternoon. Piece of cake, right?"

No, it wasn't, but Jilly was counting on me. Maybe she knew the personality types better than she claimed, because she'd hit on what I saw as my ISTJ weakness. If someone desperately needed my help, I'd go to almost any extreme to pitch in. And that tendency sometimes landed me in hot water.

Throwing my hands in the air, I agreed to her request. "It will be more of an informal presentation, though. It's not like I have a PowerPoint deck at my fingertips."

"Not a problem, Leta. Just talk them through it. You can use me as a poster child for ENFP and maybe Cynthia for whatever she is."

I was picturing two books on the shelves in my office and hoping I had highlighted sections throughout. That would help me recall interesting details. Maybe I could also email a few of my former co-workers to see if they had easy reference material.

As I was scrolling through the contacts on my phone, Jilly cleared her throat. "Um, Leta, there's one more thing."

That doesn't sound good. "What, Jilly?"

"The outdoor activities. I planned to set it all up and provide directions, but Rick was going to do the debriefs after each activity and then tie it in with the personality stuff later. We need someone to handle all that."

"Seriously, Jilly? You're not looking at me to do that, too, are you?"

"Um, yes." She spoke the next words so rapidly, I could hardly make them out. "I bet you know it like the back of your hand. The opening questions seem always to be the same, but responding to them is the bit I can't do. I know you can. I've seen you do it. It'll come back to you. Just like Rick's snowstorm story. Say yes, please."

Spluttering was all I could come up with. "Hell's bells, Jilly. Just when am I supposed to get up to speed on that?" As soon as I uttered the words, I knew I'd made a mistake.

"That piece isn't until Thursday. We'll find Rick's notes, and you can read them over." She clapped her hand to her mouth. "Leta, we need the sealed envelopes, the ones with each person's Myers-Briggs report. They must be at the cottage. And his notes, too. It's probably all there together. Rick was old-school, and I bet they're in a folder somewhere."

There was no need to argue. Jilly would come up with an answer to any objections I had. Anyone who knew me understood full well I wouldn't leave her or Cynthia in the lurch. It might not be pitch perfect and up to my standards, but I could pull something together. *Right, if you stay up all night.*

Talk about staying busy to keep the shock from setting in. *Maybe working my tail off for the next several days isn't such a bad thing, after all.*

CHAPTER SEVEN

By the time the design team arrived and started grabbing coffee, tea, and muffins, I'd sent off a few emails and texted Dave. Hopefully, someone would come through with notes or even a PowerPoint presentation I could use. The text to Dave was a quick one to let him know I'd be on the run all day and would call tonight. We'd had a brief conversation Monday afternoon about Jilly and Rick, but only a goodnight text since then.

Jilly was in a corner whispering to Madge, who looked slightly under the weather. She was one of the few without a hot drink in her hand.

When Jilly walked away, I approached her. "Good morning, Madge. How are you today?" She looked confused until I whispered that I'd been the one to get her to the inn.

"Oh no. I'm so embarrassed. It's bad enough that the innkeeper saw me like that. I don't have any recollection of how I got from the pub to my bed, but she said she tucked me in last night. She even checked on me this morning before breakfast. Gave me some paracetamol too, though I have to be careful about combining that with my meds."

"No worries. I still shudder when I think of similar moments from my younger days, and I'm thankful there was always someone there for me. You know Bert helped, too, right?"

"Yes. He told me. Thank goodness it was Bert and not one of the other designers. They'd never let me forget it."

She sipped from her water glass. "I'm not a heavy drinker, and I try to watch my intake because I know I'm a lightweight. I don't think I drank that much last night. Maybe two pints over several hours."

Her brow furrowed. "I can't remember much beyond playing darts. Hmm . . . I wonder if I ate something before I took my last pill."

"Did you do any shots?"

"Heavens no! I never drink whiskey." Her eyes grew wide. "When the Cotswolds Single Malt was going around, one of the interns said I couldn't possibly design a Cotswolds village hall without trying it. I wasn't about to fall for that, and Rick helped me out by placing a pint in my hand." She shuddered. "I remember taking a few sips, but not much after that."

I cringed at a memory of doing shots. "You just reminded me of an episode I'd rather forget. Even now, when I see people doing tequila shots with salt and lime, I feel ill."

She chuckled and assured me she wouldn't be drinking for the rest of the week. When she wandered off, I looked around for Lyle and saw him with Jilly. Soon after, he convened the group.

His opening comments about how they'd decimated the supply of muffins after eating a huge breakfast got a few chuckles. "When's lunch?" called one slim young man.

"Aye, we're bottomless pits when the food's on you, Lyle," said Bert.

He pointed to the young man who'd mentioned lunch. "Have you seen what Freddie can put away?"

Lyle laughed and put his hand on the lectern. "We have several full days ahead, and we'll cover what that entails in a moment." He looked down and took a deep breath. "I have some sad news to share. I learned early this morning that Rick Bradley died last night."

Observing the reactions from my position on the side of the room, an unwelcome thought surfaced. It was unlikely that a stranger had strangled Rick. And that meant the killer was in this room.

In a book or on TV, a facial expression would reveal the villain. Not here, though. No one looked suspicious. They all appeared stunned. Some had their hands to their mouths. A few, like Madge and Cynthia, had tears in their eyes.

Lyle allowed a moment for the gasps to die down before proceeding. He shared the same story he'd told me at the pub—meeting Rick one summer in London and reconnecting recently. "Rick was a consummate professional. That's why I hired him to work with us this week. I can hear him now telling me that the show must go on, and so it will—difficult as it may be."

Motioning to Jilly, he asked her to share the agenda. She elaborated on Lyle's opening by sharing Rick's snow story. "That's a lesson I learned from Rick early on when I worked with him in the States, and I echo Lyle's sentiment. Rick would expect us to carry on."

She pointed to me. "You may have met her last night, but let me formally introduce Leta Parker. Believe it or not, she also knows Rick from years ago, and that means we're in luck. In her banking days, Rick trained Leta and her colleagues. Remember the questionnaires you completed? She's agreed to take on that portion of the agenda, so we won't miss a beat this week."

Cynthia chimed in from the side of the room. "Leta, thank you. And you thought you only signed up to write articles about us."

Quickly going through the plans for the day, Jilly turned things back to Lyle. He reminded them of the work that had earned them a spot in the Village Hall Competition, and spoke of his and Cynthia's expectations for the week—not only developing the best design for Astonbury, but also growing as a team. "We're known as a top-notch design firm in London, and Cynthia and I consider this our opportunity to make a name for Holmes & White in the Cotswolds. Let's make the most of it for the company, for the team, and for ourselves as individuals."

When he concluded his remarks, he called a ten-minute break. Next on the agenda was a combination bus and walking tour with George Evans, owner of Cotswolds Tours.

Pulling Lyle aside, I told him he'd done a nice job sharing the news about Rick. "It wasn't an easy message to deliver, especially since he was your friend. But you set the right tone."

Dickens jogged to my side as Lyle answered me. "Thank you, Leta. Jilly prepping me was a big help, and her follow-on remarks were well-done. And thanks for everything you're doing. I understand you found Rick this morning. Cynthia told me it wasn't the first time you've had this experience, but it still had to be awful."

Aargh. Not a reputation I want. "Trust me, it *was* awful, and I'm doing my best to block it out. Keeping busy helps. It's funny. When I saw the headlights in the driveway late last night, I figured it was your friend arriving. I didn't know Rick was the friend staying in your gran's cottage." I blinked as I realized it couldn't have been Rick driving. "Oh! Wait. I guess they were your headlights, since Rick didn't have a car."

Dickens nudged my leg. "There were two cars, Leta." I shushed him so I could hear what Lyle was saying.

A blank look appeared on Lyle's face, but before he could say anything, Jilly approached us. "Bloody hell, Leta, I forgot all about the icebreaker. It's supposed to be right after lunch, and I don't have the pieces."

"The pieces? Which icebreaker are you talking about?"

"The puzzle activity, the one where we split the team into groups. You know how Rick loved jigsaw puzzles. That's why I wasn't surprised—" She stopped midstream. "Um, that's why he so often relied on that activity to make a point about teamwork. I bet the satin bags with the puzzle pieces are in the cottage, along with his notes. I can probably fumble my way through it if we can at least find the bags."

Lyle wiped his brow. "Thank goodness you two are handling all this." He moved toward the front door. "And here's George. Looks like one thing will go according to plan."

Jilly was all but wringing her hands. "Leta, please tell me you can get into the cottage to find the puzzle bags and Rick's notes. And we need those envelopes with the Myers-Briggs results, too. It's not like the shows on the telly, is it? Where there's police tape strung all over?"

Exasperated, I blew out my breath. "Yes, Jilly, it probably is, but I'll see what I can do. And if I heard you correctly, we need it after lunch as the lead-in to the group's brainstorming session, right?"

"Righto, Leta. Thanks a million."

Before I could face calling Gemma, I needed a moment to collect myself. "Dickens, what do you think about tea at Toby's? Maybe an infusion of sugar will help me focus."

Dickens thought that was a grand idea, though I was pretty sure he'd gotten plenty of nibbles while the design team was munching the morning snack.

When I entered the Tearoom, Toby waved me to a table. "You look done in. Tea and a scone coming your way."

Dickens nudged my hand as I sat and absentmindedly ruffled his ears. "Leta, did you hear what I said about the cars?"

"Hmm. I think I missed that. What about cars?"

"I knew you weren't paying attention. Watson saw two cars last night. One when Cynthia was leaving, and one much later."

"Did he see who was in them?"

"Only heard voices. One time, it was men, and then it was a man and woman laughing."

If Lyle brought Rick to the cottage, then Watson hearing a woman later jived with the lipstick evidence. Too bad he didn't know which woman. It had to be someone on the design team or Jilly, unless it was someone from the village. I was finding it difficult to sort through the possibilities.

The shock had set in, and I'd proceeded straight to lethargy—never mind lightheadedness and dizziness. If I was going to speak with Gemma and locate Rick's materials, I needed to snap out of it.

Thankfully, Toby arrived with food just in the nick of time. "You're a lifesaver, Toby. I was fading fast."

He sat with me for a moment as I sipped my tea. "Would you like me to make up some lunch for you to take away? We're prepping the food for the design team now, and Jenny can easily fix a container of chicken salad for you. That way, you can go home and collapse."

"Thanks, but no. The good news is I'll be eating with the team. The bad news is I've gotten roped into helping with their meeting, and there's no way I'll get to rest today."

When I outlined my responsibilities, Toby looked aghast. "Leta, that is so you. You're telling me you haven't done this kind of work in years, but you're going to jump in and save the day? They couldn't find anyone else to do it?"

"I doubt that option even occurred to Jilly. It was my misfortune to be standing there when she realized she had a problem. To her credit, she could have easily told Lyle and Cynthia those parts of the agenda were off the table. Instead, she found a solution."

Walking home, I rang Gemma and explained the problem. "This project is important to the village, and I'm trying to do everything I can to help. I'm hoping the meeting notes, the props and the sealed envelopes are there somewhere. May I pop next door to look, please? You know I'll be careful."

"Yes, but only because I'm here now with the SOCOs. I'll be leaving shortly."

That was almost too easy.

CHAPTER EIGHT

Next door, I knocked tentatively and heard Gemma call, "Come in, Nancy Drew." *Gee, which Gemma am I going to get now?*

Cautioning Dickens, I pushed the door open. "Careful. Don't get in the way, and for goodness' sake, don't disturb anything."

If possible, Gemma looked worse than she had when I left her. "He's better behaved than you are, isn't he?"

"As long as it doesn't involve food, yes. Eat in front of him, and all bets are off."

"Don't even mention food. Hot tea is about all I can handle. Now, about your meeting props. They weren't in the sitting room or the kitchen, so I checked upstairs after the SOCOs did their cursory search. It looked as though the victim was in there only long enough to drop his holdall and put this on the dresser. I think it may be what you're looking for."

She handed me a pair of nitrile gloves like the ones she was wearing. "Here, put these on. I can't let you take this with you, but you can look through it."

The folder looked awfully thin. "Rick's been doing this for so long, he probably doesn't need notes, but maybe, just maybe, there's enough here to help me."

"Couldn't tell you. I will say the item on top made me gag a bit."

Sitting at the kitchen table, I opened the folder. The first thing I saw was a lined, gold-edged piece of paper. Folded in half, it had a handwritten R on the front. "Gemma, is there a guest book somewhere?"

"Yes, opened to the first page, but no one has signed it yet."

"This page may have been torn from it." When I unfolded the page, I saw a perfectly formed lipstick print in a peach color, followed by the line, "Hope it was good for you, too." Below the words was a small hand-drawn heart with a lipstick print beneath it.

Gemma smirked. "The only thing missing is the scent of perfume. My question is, did he bring this with him, or did someone slip it into the folder last night? Either way, it doesn't seem like a note written by someone bent on killing the man."

"True. I can't say I knew Rick well, but he never struck me as the sentimental type, someone to keep a love note. Unless it's a recent conquest he wants to remember."

"Well, that's certainly a telling comment. Does he have lots of those? Conquests, I mean?"

"Let's just say if he doesn't, it's not for lack of trying."

Setting the note aside, I flipped through the typed pages. I was happy to see a copy of the agenda, a page with the MBTI taglines, and some background on Holmes & White. All of that would come in handy for me. The puzzle instructions weren't there, but it occurred to me I could Google the activity and find them.

The last thing in the folder was a newspaper article with the headline, "RIBA award goes to Holmes & White." Beneath it was a picture of Lyle accepting a plaque. A brief article followed.

"Gemma, does the word RIBA mean anything to you?" I flashed the page of newsprint at her. "Maybe it's explained in the article."

She Googled it while I read the article. Almost simultaneously, we found the answer—Royal Institute of British Architects. They held an annual design competition and awarded a plaque to the winner. The award had to be a boon to Lyle and Cynthia's business. I handed it to Gemma to read.

When she finished, she returned it. "Interesting. Sounds like a big deal in the world of architecture. But you didn't mention this hand-printed note. Why would the victim write 'roommate' in the margin?"

"Oh. Lyle told me last night that he and Rick met at university. They didn't exactly room together, but he and his roommate hung out with Rick all one summer, when he was here from the States."

"Does everyone in this group know each other? You knew Rick and this Jilly person from the States. Lyle and Rick met at uni. We both know Cynthia. Are there any other connections you're aware of?"

"Not offhand, but I can nose around while I'm with everyone for the next few days. Um, let me reword that. If I hear anything, I'll let you know."

Gemma's laugh led to a coughing spell. "More like what you said first, isn't it? You won't be able to help yourself. Next, you'll be off to question Barb at the pub trying to find out what she knows. Don't even think about it. I'm headed there after I stop by home for my cough syrup. Then I plan to speak with everyone involved in this event."

"I have no intention of *interviewing* anyone. You know I've turned over a new leaf since Dave moved in. Maybe I'll pick your brain for something to put in the book I'm writing with Wendy, but that's it." Except Wendy and I barely had an outline, much less a book.

By now, Gemma was grinning. "Let's see. It was early January when Dave arrived. It was April when you and the Little Old Ladies planted yourselves smack-dab in the middle of another murder investigation. I'd say you're probably due to get in my way again."

"Not likely. Now, I understand why I can't take the folder with me, but may I take pictures of the contents? It's exactly what I need." When she nodded, I snapped shots of *everything*—including the article and the love note. I took it as a sign of how rotten she felt that she didn't notice.

"Gemma, I really need to look for the puzzle pieces. They could be in the bag you mentioned—the one upstairs. You didn't see a bunch of 8 ½ x 11 envelopes, did you? I desperately need those, too."

Gemma gave an exaggerated sigh and asked me to follow her to the bedroom, where she carefully unzipped the holdall on the bed. I was in luck. The white envelopes were tucked in a side pocket, and she almost instantly located two satin drawstring bags near the bottom. "You know, in the movies, we'd find uncut diamonds or such in these bags, so hold on."

She carefully poured the contents on the bed and found only heavy cardboard puzzle pieces. "Looks innocent enough. Okay, I'll clear it with the SOCOs. Off you go."

"Thank goodness. Now I can study everything, and maybe, just maybe, I can get through tomorrow without making a complete fool of myself."

It didn't take long to find the directions for the puzzle activity online, so I jotted those down and leaned back in my desk chair. With Christie purring in the file drawer and Dickens curled at my feet, it was tempting to pull out my Myers-Briggs books and refresh my memory. I'd always been fascinated by the topic. Hopefully, one of my former co-workers would come through with an outline I could use, though with the time difference, I wouldn't see any responses for several hours.

Scratching Christie's chin, I debated how best to fill the time until the afternoon session. "What do you think, little girl? Listen to the lunch presentations so I can get details for my article? Or take a quick shower instead?"

The response was typical Christie. "Do you need to ask? You look like something the cat drug in—not *this* cat, but maybe Watson. Go for the shower."

"Hey, I don't look that bad." I pulled a small mirror from the pencil drawer. *Maybe she has a point. I can't erase the dark circles beneath my eyes, but I could apply concealer.*

She leaped to the desk and patted my chin. "Admit it. You look bedraggled."

"Well, when you put it that way, I can't see that I have a choice." How many women, I wondered, take beauty advice from a cat?

As I climbed the stairs, my phone played its Billy Joel tune, and I smiled as I answered the call. "Do you have any idea how much I love hearing that song followed by your voice?"

I pictured Dave smiling as he answered. "Does that mean you miss me?"

"Always. And I have lots to tell you, but you go first."

"The good news is that we're making better progress with Sandy's help. She's a taskmaster and has no qualms about pushing Mom to decide what goes or stays. The donate and trash piles are growing faster than the keep pile, thank goodness."

"And the bad news?"

"The attic is full of books. You can't believe the books."

I had a vivid memory of Dave trying to select which books to bring with him when he left his NYC apartment. Packing had come to a standstill at that point. "That sounds more than bad. It sounds almost catastrophic."

"Well, Sandy knows a bookseller who specializes in used books, and he'll be here tomorrow. That may or may not help me. If he makes an astronomical offer, I'll worry that I need to go through them more carefully, that there's some priceless treasure buried in these boxes. As it is, I'm flipping through them at an alarmingly slow pace. I had no idea my dad was such an eclectic reader."

"Do you still think you'll make your Sunday flight?"

"Yup. You'll see me then. Now what's going on at home?"

Home. How I loved hearing him say that. "Let's see. I told you about running into Jilly, right? And I think I texted about Rick Bradley?"

"Uh-huh. And meeting Cynthia's partner, Lyle. How was dinner out with the team, and where are you now? I just realized you must be at the village hall."

So much for getting a shower. "I'm at home. Let me tell you about my morning, and then I'll tell you the rest."

Other than exclaiming at the mention of a dead body next door, Dave let me get all the way through my second visit to the scene of the crime. "It's not bad enough I found a dead body—someone I know, I mean knew—now I have to study so

I can pitch in tomorrow. As I keep saying, though, being busy should keep the jitters at bay."

"Do you feel uncomfortable staying at the cottage by yourself, Leta? Can Wendy stay with you?"

"I'm not exactly uncomfortable. It's not like there's a serial killer at large, but I suspect I'll have trouble sleeping tonight. Kind of the way you feel after watching a horror movie, jumping at every sound. Maybe inviting Wendy to spend the night isn't such a bad idea."

He encouraged me to do that, and I promised I would. "I want to tell you about the evening at the pub, but I've got to run. I need to hear at least a bit of the lunchtime presentations, and then I've got puzzle duty."

"Leta, call me before you go to sleep. I want to know you're tucked up safe at home, okay?"

That would be easy. I had no intention of being out late or even out. It was more likely I'd be in bed early, surrounded by books as I jotted notes for the next day.

I missed the Earl of Stow's talk about the annual tree lighting on the village green, but I was in time to hear Peter's presentation about the Tour of Britain. He'd spearheaded the successful effort to bring the Tour to Astonbury, and we were looking forward to seeing the cyclists next year. Wendy wrapped up the lunch hour with the charming tale of J.M. Barrie purchasing Sunshine Cottage for her grandmother. The discovery of a previously unknown children's book by the author had put Astonbury on the literary map.

When Lyle thanked the presenters and called for a twenty-minute break, the hall filled with chatter. The group seemed to have recovered from the morning's somber news, and kicking off the afternoon with the puzzle activity would keep them engaged. In meetings like this, it was critical to counteract the effects of a full stomach with something lively.

Surrounded by a group of designers, Wendy motioned me over. "Leta, they're interested in Dave's article about Mum's book. Do you have a copy at home? I've told them they can pick up a copy of *Barrie & Friends* at the Book Nook." She winked at me before turning back to the group. "Dave and Leta live just around the corner in Schoolhouse Cottage, the one with the school bell still attached. George pointed that out to you on your tour today."

After I promised to bring copies of Dave's article when I returned the next day, Wendy pulled me aside and whispered in my ear. "Ever since we spoke this morning, I've been replaying our evening at the pub. I bet if we do that over a glass of wine later, we'll remember something significant."

That caught me off guard, but it shouldn't have. This was exactly what got us in trouble with Gemma. I liked to think that each of us on our own wouldn't dare think about getting tangled up in a murder investigation. But together? It was inevitable.

I could tell myself all day long that there was no need for us to be involved, but I could almost hear Wendy's rationale. "For goodness' sake, Leta, you *knew* the victim, and it happened right next door! How can we *not* get involved?"

Pursing my lips, I shook my head no. "I can't think about it now, Wendy. I've been coerced into leading this next segment. We'll talk about it later."

Sure, I had jokingly dubbed us the Little Old Ladies' Detective Agency after Gemma rudely referred to Wendy, her mum, and me as little old ladies. I'd even had a handful of business cards printed up, along with a few colorful canvas bags. And, yes, we'd helped to solve a murder case or two—or three. We'd even added a dowager countess to the mix. When you put the four of us together, we were a force to be reckoned with.

Belle, Wendy's mum, and Ellie, the dowager countess, had branched out and were now specializing in the lost dog business. *I can't believe I'm using those words—branched out.* That venture kept them busy and out of harm's way *most* of the time. On one occasion Ellie had fired off a shotgun, though, so I wasn't sure.

Where is Dave when I need him? He'd been involved in a few of our escapades, but he was still the voice of reason. When he suggested that Wendy and I try our hand at *writing* murder mysteries, I knew it was an attempt to distance us from the real thing. In fact, he'd famously said, "Wendy and Leta won't have time for detective work. They'll be much too busy writing."

After giving me the go ahead, Lyle and Cynthia retired to the upper floor. I blew my wooden train whistle to get the group's attention. It was a gift from my co-worker Stephie and still had pride of place on the bookshelf in my office. *I sure hope she replies to my email soon.*

Watching the last few folks settle into their seats, I put my hands on my hips. "What Jilly didn't tell you is that I was once a high school English teacher. Be forewarned. Do *not* make me ask for your attention twice."

They didn't quite know how to take that remark until I broke into a grin. There were a few joking remarks about rulers and knuckles, and I made them laugh with the story of how I'd been paddled in high school science class for talking. "It's a Southern thing, and it's ancient history, but it's not something I'm likely to forget.

"Now, let's get to work. For this first activity, I'm going to split you into two teams. Please count off." Once they finished, I asked the even and odd numbers to assemble at the large tables at the opposite ends of the room.

"You'll see that each team has a bag of puzzle pieces. Here are your instructions:

The aim of the exercise is for each team to assemble the jigsaw puzzle as quickly as possible using the pieces provided. Both teams have the same puzzle. You will receive no additional instructions.

You may begin."

Quickly, they dumped their puzzle pieces onto their separate tables and began moving them around. No matter how many times I used this activity, it was always fascinating to observe the team dynamics. Sometimes, a team nominated a leader. Other times, a leader emerged. Some teams worked it out through collaboration without a clear leader.

The team Madge was on didn't designate a leader, but she quietly took control—in a good way. She asked questions and invited suggestions as they assembled what they had. At the other end of the room, it was a different dynamic. Several vocal people had commandeered the pieces, resulting in the others standing back disengaged. When Bert said, "There's no way we can do this on our own. We need to see what the other team has," the group ignored him.

On Madge's team, as I had come to think of it, she voiced the same idea, but in a more palatable way. "Does it look like we're missing some pieces?" When the group agreed, it was easy for her to follow with, "Then, let's see what the other team has."

There was a naysayer on each team, but once the groups merged, they quickly realized there was only one puzzle, and it came together in no time. For me, getting them to share their insights was the best part. They were an energetic group who often spoke over each other as Jilly recorded their takeaways on a flip chart. It didn't take much to get them to elaborate on what they did well as a team and what they needed to improve.

To wrap up, I reminded them that the week was not only about working effectively as a team, but also about identifying their individual strengths and areas for improvement. "The rest of today, you'll focus on the design of Astonbury's village hall. Before you do that, please take a moment to jot down one thing you learned about yourself while working on the puzzle. I won't ask you to share that, but you'll want to call it to mind when we discuss the Myers-Briggs assessment tomorrow."

Lyle stepped up to thank me and announce a break before an afternoon of brainstorming design ideas. I was officially off duty for the day—at least in my mind.

Wendy had ducked out while I was wrapping up, and I was surprised to find her waiting outside. "I know you need to prepare for tomorrow, but will it take all day and night?"

"What I really need is two days and nights, but I'll have to make do with the hours I have."

She was insistent. "Well, you can't skip dinner, so I'll bring food and a bottle of wine, and you can take a two-hour break. What time is best—six or seven?"

"You have a bee in your bonnet, don't you? It wouldn't kill me to eat cheese and crackers for dinner, you know."

"Done. I'll be at your place at six." It was easier to give in than to argue.

CHAPTER NINE

THE MORNING SUN HAD turned to misty rain, so a cup of tea was top priority when I got home. With my laptop, a notepad, and several reference books, I made myself comfortable on the couch in the sitting room. Before I dove in, I checked my email. My friend Stephie had replied to both my requests—the one for info on Rick's company and the other looking for Myers-Briggs material. I scanned the one with the attachment first. *Phew. A PowerPoint presentation, complete with speaker notes.* She also included a few pointers on the topic, so I was in luck.

The other email was much longer. She opened with how surprised she was at my running into both Jilly and Rick. After a few small-world comments, she got to my question about Rick.

There was plenty of gossip about Rick and Tim's company—Powerhouse Performance. In typical Stephie fashion, she'd listed the rumors as bullet points and typed *Truth* or a question mark next to each one. For a few, she had added a comment. The heading for the list was "Who Knows What the Whole Truth is?" It was the stuff of soap operas or an awful movie.

- Rick was a no-show for a meeting with our HR Director—Truth

- Tim filled in for Rick last minute at an all-day corporate event—Truth

- Rick had some health issues—Truth

- Rick went to rehab for drinking? I think this was the health issue.

- Rick's name is no longer on website for company—Truth

- Rick is divorced—Truth

- His wife had an affair? More likely Rick had the affair.

- Rick & Tim dissolved their partnership?

- Rick wanted to expand to England? Why on earth would he want to do that—unless he was running away from something?

- Rick had money problems?

- Same old "flirtatious" Rick—Truth

- Kickback scheme with a corporate training manager? Not at our company, but elsewhere.

Wow. The rumor mill is working overtime. Her take on all of it was that his drinking and *handsiness*—was that even a word?—had gone too far. The fact he was actually developing business in England was news to her. That made her think that the rumors about Rick and Tim dissolving their partnership were probably true.

Adding a final bullet point—Rick dies in suspicious circumstances—would make Stephie's list sound like an outline for a murder mystery.

And then it hit me. I'd sent my inquiry about Rick and Tim *before* Rick's death. And I didn't mention it when I asked for help with the meeting. I said I'd been roped into doing presentations, but not why. Stephie had innocently closed with a note to say hi to both Rick and Jilly. She had no idea.

Do I put that news in an email? My fingers gave me the answer before my brain did. I found Stephie's number on my contact list. It was likely I'd get her voicemail, but I had to try.

Her rapid-fire greeting brought a smile to my face. "Girl, seeing your name come up is a treat. How on earth did you get drafted into making presentations? I mean, you always loved doing all that, and you were great at it, but are you bored, or what? And I can't believe you ran into Jilly *and* Rick." *She hasn't changed a bit.*

I delayed the inevitable by telling her about the design competition and Cynthia designing my he-shed. And that led to explaining about the new man in my life. I might never have gotten around to the bad news if not for Stephie's busy schedule.

"I'd love to chat more, but I've got to run. Can we plan a call so I can catch up on everything?"

"Yes, but one more thing." *How do I say this?* "Steph, Rick died last night. Both Jilly and I are in shock."

"What? No! How awful." Hearing voices in the background, I knew she must be walking down the hall. "I'm at the elevator. I'll call you later—" And then I lost her.

My brain swirled with memories from my training days, Stephie's bombshell list of Rick rumors, and flashes of Rick last night at the pub. Telling myself I had to prep for the next day, I returned to the PowerPoint presentation.

After rereading the same page several times, I closed my eyes and rested my head on the back of the couch. *I'm never going to be ready at this rate.* I turned instead to my yellowed copy of *Gifts Differing*, my favorite book on Myers -Briggs and, sure enough, it drew me in. It was tempting to read the entire book, but mostly I reviewed the passages I'd highlighted years ago. Only after that detour could I focus on Stephie's slide deck. I printed it out, absorbed it, and then added my thoughts.

The presentation would last about two hours, including the back-and-forth with the design team and several activities. Practicing as I stood looking out the window took only thirty minutes, and I was happy enough with my first run-through to set it aside.

Next, I considered how to debrief the outdoor activities. It was critical to ask questions that would make the group think about their dynamics—questions that would trigger lightbulb moments for them, both personally and as a team. Equally important would be how I responded to their answers.

I was amazed at how quickly it all came back to me. *Probably because it applies to so much more than business relationships.* Without conscious thought, I routinely used the lessons in my personal life—with my husband and family, with friends, and now with Dave. What I called the art of the pregnant pause was a tried-and-true way to get people to open up.

Henry sometimes accused me of practicing my schtick on him, especially when we argued. When I used the words, "Help me understand," or "What I hear you saying is," he was bound to retort, "Don't start, Leta." If Dave had noticed the same tendency, he hadn't yet mentioned it. Perhaps it helped that he hadn't known me when that was my job day in and day out.

By five, I was satisfied I'd done enough prep work and decided I deserved a walk. Christie grumbled when I moved her from my lap, but Dickens was raring to go.

Before I donned my parka, I put a dab of wet food in Christie's dish. "It's still misting, so we won't be gone long, little girl."

She took a moment to pause from daintily licking her food to look up at me. "Will you be back in time to feed me properly? This isn't very much."

"As if you ever eat more than a dab at a time. Yes, we'll go as far as the donkeys and back. You won't even miss us." She might miss her food, but not us.

Dickens was fine with the brisk pace I set. "You know no matter how fast we walk, Dickens, I'll have to towel you off when we get home. But you like that, don't you?"

He didn't respond. Instead, he pulled toward the cottage next door—Lyle's cottage. He lifted his nose up and sniffed before moving on.

When we reached Martha and Dylan, I absentmindedly fed them the carrots they loved. Dickens was happy to put his paws on the fence as they bent their heads down to snort and nudge him. I rested my elbows on the fence and stared into the distance, random thoughts tumbling through my brain.

I pictured a cartoon image of a tiny devil floating by my head and an angel fluttering on the opposite side. Prodding me with a tiny pitchfork, the devil didn't mince his words. "You *need* to investigate, Leta. You *knew* Rick." The angel, with her gossamer wings and a tiny wand, whispered, "Now, now, Leta, you must behave. There's no need to get involved."

Why do I even have these conversations with myself? I never failed to get involved because I enjoyed the challenge of sleuthing. Sure, I could easily blame Wendy for being the instigator, because she pushed when I protested. But she didn't have to say much to convince me to proceed.

I wondered about Dave. Why didn't he ask whether I planned to get involved? Was it because it was a foregone conclusion that I would?

In the early stages of our relationship, when he was far away in NYC, he worried about my unintentionally dangerous activities. His attempt to persuade me to be more careful developed into our first argument, but it also helped me to articulate why I found the work fulfilling.

It just so happened that he got his first taste of sleuthing soon after that. Like me, he discovered he enjoyed putting the puzzle pieces together, though he still had misgivings. These days, he'd fallen into the same pattern I had. He tried to resist, but not for long. That's why he was now an ad hoc member of the Little Old Ladies' Detective Agency, and we'd dubbed him the clueless old codger.

But he couldn't play Tommy to my Tuppence if he wasn't here. Would that alter his perspective? We were building a new life *together*, and since he'd moved in, this would be the first case without his presence.

Straightening my shoulders, I turned toward home. "Enough, Dickens. We might as well get to work."

I wondered if Jilly had any insights into what led to Rick turning up in England. Had he run *away* from a scandal or *toward* a new venture? Maybe it was a combination of the two. As for what had transpired since he landed in Astonbury, once Wendy and I put our minds to it, we'd ferret out the details. Getting people to talk to us was our superpower.

I dug in my pocket when I heard the Billy Joel ring tone. "How did you know I was thinking of you, Dave?"

"Am I supposed to answer that my ears were burning?"

"Were they?"

His soft chuckle was music to my ears. "Our thoughts must have met somewhere over the Atlantic. I hate that I'm not there for you. Would you believe Mom suggested she could finish the packing without me, and I should fly home? I know she thinks you're the gal for me, but this is proof positive."

"That is so sweet of her. Are you two nearly done?"

"Are you kidding? The only way she can finish without my help is if she decides right this minute that everything not already in a box is going to the dump. Even with Sandy constantly here, we're barely going to make it."

My antenna went up. *Sandy constantly there?* "I thought Sandy had people to do the hands-on part with the clients. It's hard to imagine her doing all that with a business to run."

"You know, Michelle said the same thing. All I know is that Mom really appreciates her being here. I think she must have a special place in her heart for Mom. Maybe it's all the nights she spent here with my sister their senior year."

Uh-huh. I'm sure his sister suspects Sandy has an ulterior motive. If I hadn't overheard her remarks in the ladies' room or observed her wandering hands, maybe my thoughts wouldn't be running in that direction. Add Michelle's warning, and I was bound to be suspicious.

I bit my tongue. "Have you managed to do any writing?"

"You know me, I work best late at night. Just me and the crickets. Now, tell me how you're doing. Did you ask Wendy to spend the night?"

That made me laugh. "Ask Wendy? She invited herself and she's bringing dinner. Given that I knew Rick, I've got to think through what I might have seen or heard in the brief time I spent with him yesterday. And Wendy was at the pub last night and apparently has ideas of her own."

"Well, that answers my other question. I figured you wouldn't be able to help yourself, and you'd be making notes before long. What does Gemma have to say?"

"What do you think? I've been warned to stay away. Little does she know I've already gathered data about his background from a source in the States. If nothing else, she should be grateful for that. But how likely is it that someone followed him across the pond to do him in?"

After bringing him up to speed on the little I knew, I promised to call or text after Wendy and I documented our observations. As I pulled the keys from my pocket, I heard Christie beckoning from inside. "I'm back home, and there's a hungry cat meowing on the other side of the door, so let me run. Love you."

If a cat could put its paws on its hips, I was sure Christie would. "Where have you been? You said you'd be quick."

"Good grief, Christie. Give me a minute. I've got to towel off your brother."

As I dried Dickens and cleaned the mud from his paws, my mind once again wandered. The last thing Rick said to me was that he wanted to catch up. Was it a friendly request from an old acquaintance? Or was it something more serious? *There you go again, overthinking every little thing.*

CHAPTER TEN

WENDY SHOWED UP WITH homemade spinach quiche, cookies from Toby's, and a bottle of wine. "I hate to tell you this, but you look plumb wo' out."

I nearly choked on my tea. "You know, don't you, that whatever Southern accent you picked up while you lived in North Carolina has long since disappeared? Plumb wo' out doesn't have quite the same ring coming from a Brit."

That got a grin. "And yet, Rhys says I have a strange but charming lilt. Must depend on who's listening." She uncorked the bottle. "As for you, the more you drink, the stronger your accent gets."

Quickly slicing and serving the quiche, she gave a pinch of crust to Dickens before putting our plates on the kitchen table. "Shall we dig in before we get to work?"

"I may be tired, but I haven't lost my appetite. Why is it that quiche isn't on every restaurant menu like it once was? This hits the spot."

We carried the wine to the sitting room, where Christie promptly took over Wendy's lap while I added another log to the fire. "You know, I loved the *Outlaws* album by Willie and

Waylon, and I always think of that song 'Put Another Log on the Fire' when I do this."

Grabbing her neck, Wendy made a gagging sound. "I may have lived in Charlotte for years, but I never acquired a taste for country music. I'm rock and roll all the way."

Dickens chose the rug in front of the hearth, and I sat on the couch with my legs tucked beneath me. "I guess it goes without saying that we're working on the case, right?"

"Duh. Of course, we are."

"Okay then. Let me tell you what I learned from my co-worker, and then we can talk about our pub observations."

When I read Stephie's email, Wendy's reaction to the term *handsiness* was similar to mine. "If that isn't a word, it should be. Is that your recollection of him?"

"It wasn't that as much as it was that he stood a little too close. Remember when we taught high school—the way eighth graders didn't seem to understand personal space? I liken it to how I felt around them. It was some kind of unwelcome vibe. At least unwelcome to me."

Wendy nodded. "I get it. He seemed a bit of a flirt, and there's no doubt he was attentive. He commented on my accent and couldn't help but notice that I was a dab hand at darts. Of course, I owe that ability to Peter and his friends. The only way they'd let me hang out with them was if I could hold my own."

I jotted Wendy's observations in my notebook. "Did you feel like he was flirting with intent or merely flirting?"

"What a lovely way to put it, Leta. I didn't sense any intent with me. I'd say he gave appreciative looks to Trixie, Jenny, and Jill, but didn't flirt with them. He was . . . chummy with Jilly. They've worked together before, right?"

"Yes, in the States. She worked with him for a year or two, I think."

Wendy scrunched her mouth to one side. "If he flirted with intent, it was with one of the designers—Maggie, Mattie, or something like that."

That got my attention. "You mean Madge? The curly-haired woman in the blue-jean skirt and boots?"

"Yes, that's her. I loved her boots, didn't you? Pretty good dart player, too."

"Was he handsy with her?"

When Wendy closed her eyes, I knew she was rewinding the scene. "Now I'll never get that word out of my head. Yes, a little bit. He touched her arm when he spoke with her, but not in a possessive way. I wouldn't even remember it if that word hadn't come up. I think of it as being familiar. Not a bad thing unless it's unwelcome. But we both know it's frowned upon in a business environment."

"Was he more *familiar* with her than he was with the others? Like maybe they already knew each other?"

"Now that I think of it, maybe he was. Like I am with Toby or Gavin. Nothing beyond friendly in my case, of course. But I suppose it could have been something more for the two of them."

She tilted her head. "And after one of her dart throws, she kind of winced and went to stand with her back against the wall. I thought maybe she'd pulled a muscle. Anyway, Rick went to check on her, but that was it."

Perhaps I was reading too much into Wendy's observation. "Were you at the bar when he was holding court over there?"

"No, but he kindly sent one of the interns over with a round of shots for those of us still playing darts. Why? Where are you going with this?"

"I'm not sure. Let me tell you about Madge."

My description of Madge feeling dizzy and sick got Wendy's attention. "When I helped Libby get her up to bed, I figured she'd misjudged her drinking, even if she claimed she didn't partake of the whiskey."

"Hmmm. She didn't *think* she drank enough to feel sick." Wendy squinted in thought. "Do you think someone slipped her something?"

It's amazing how often we think alike. "Yup. That's exactly what I'm thinking, but I can't say why. Probably because I've watched so many reruns of *Law & Order: Special Victims Unit.* In a nightclub, a man's hand hovers over a drink sitting on the bar."

Closing my eyes, I pictured that happening at the Ploughman. "Could it have been Rick?"

Wendy's mouth dropped open. "From being handsy to spiking drinks? That's a big leap, isn't it?"

"I guess. Except it seems so commonplace on TV." An image of Rick listening to our conversation popped into my head. "I can imagine him now blustering about having plenty of willing partners. He'd be highly indignant at the mere suggestion that he'd need to ply a woman with alcohol or, worse, slip her a pill."

"Would it make you feel any better if you asked your friend Stephie whether there were rumors about that kind of thing?"

"Good suggestion. I'll do it right now." When I finished sending the message, Wendy and I were both quiet.

She topped off our glasses. "That kind of behavior could have caused a scandal, but I'm not sure it tells us anything about his death."

"Unless one of his victims took revenge. But then I'm back to the unbelievable scenario of someone following him to England to kill him. How likely is that?"

"About as likely as some random killer choosing him as a victim." She studied me. "I think we need cookies, especially you."

"Can't argue with that. Do you want decaf, too?" We agreed to change into our pajamas while the coffee brewed.

As I was washing my face, Wendy appeared in the bathroom doorway. "Let's set aside what we know from the pub and focus on what you saw this morning. Are you ready to return to the scene of the crime?" She must have seen my horrified look. "In your mind, Leta. Not literally."

"Well, thank goodness for that. I wouldn't put it past you to want to sneak over there."

She smirked. "Not now, but you never know."

Armed with coffee and cookies, we settled in the sitting room. Dickens sat by my knee on high alert for cookie crumbs.

Wendy set her plate and mug on the side table and offered to take notes this time. "It feels odd, doesn't it, not to have Mum and Ellie with us? I hope they're enjoying Cornwall."

"At the moment, I'd love to be with them." The senior members of the Little Old Ladies' Detective Agency were spending a few weeks at Knight's Rest, the resort we'd visited the year before. "It *does* feel strange, and you know we'll have to fill them in sooner rather than later. I wonder whether Matthew has already called his mum with the news." I chuckled. "Nope. If he had, we'd have already heard from them."

Wendy nodded. "You're right. They'd be burning up the phone lines with questions. We need to be sure they don't get it in their heads to come home early. They have a whole itinerary mapped out."

"I've just had a brainstorm. Why don't we kill two birds with one stone? We type up your notes and email them to Ellie. That way, they'll feel included. Later, we turn the notes into an outline for our first book. If we flesh it out, it can be almost like a serialized story in an old-time magazine, except the installments will be more frequent."

Wendy's face lit up. "Fabulous! They're not due home until Sunday. Surely, we'll have this solved by then."

"Us or Gemma."

Dickens piped up. "Or me and Christie."

Handing him a smidgen of cookie, I grinned. "Will Dickens have a role in our Constable James series? And speaking of our favorite constable, I wonder whether he or Gemma plans to interview me again?"

"That's a great approach for tackling what you saw today. I'll play the role of the constable. Start with Jilly's phone call, and I'll ask questions as you go along."

I was describing my initial glimpse of Rick's body when Wendy interrupted me. "The way you're telling it, I'm not seeing a struggle. Surely, he fought back?"

"You know, it didn't look like he did. In fact, it was almost as though he sat quietly and let his attacker choke the life out of him. That doesn't seem possible."

Wendy squinted. "No, it doesn't . . . unless he was passed out drunk. We know they were all drinking heavily at the Plough-man."

The white substance in Rick's glass flashed to mind. "Maybe someone drugged him. What if thinking Madge was drugged is way off base, and it was Rick instead?" I described Rick's glass and the other two. "Only his glass had powdery residue in it. I wonder how long it will take the lab to test it. And how we can find out the results."

Wendy's eyes twinkled. "We'll have to ask the star of our mystery series to keep us informed. It's the price of fame, right?" We had several titles in mind for our Constable James mystery series, but writing the books was another thing entirely.

Her comment temporarily lightened the mood before I dove back into the details of the murder scene. She took notes as I described what I'd seen—the bruises on Rick's neck, the lipstick on his cheek, and the three tumblers, one with a lipstick print.

"Wendy, I know I'm skipping around, but there was also a lipstick print upstairs on a note. If you were Gemma or Jonas, would you make me take it all in order, or let me digress?"

"You've had more experience with her than I have. Forget the playacting. Tell me about the note."

"I'll do better than that. I took a picture of it."

Pulling the photo up on my phone, I handed it to her. "Note the lipstick color and give me the phone back."

"Eww. Tacky. Who do you think wrote it?" She swiped through a few photos and stopped at the newspaper article. "What's this?"

I motioned for the phone. "We'll get back to that." I scrolled through the crime scene photos. "Look at this glass. I'd say the writer of the note is whoever drank Cotswolds single malt with him. Well, whichever woman drank it with him, that is. Oh! And I forgot, there were wineglasses too."

I got the quintessential Wendy look—her mouth scrunched to one side. "Now I know why the police on the telly say, 'Take it from the top.' Let's go back to what you saw in the sitting room before we move to the kitchen."

The rest of my observations told us only one thing—that Rick had more than a single visitor. The absence of lipstick on the other glasses didn't tell us anything about the gender or identity of his other guests.

We debated what the wineglasses told us. Wendy suggested two people could have had a cocktail before a third person joined them. I offered that the wine might have been a pre-pub libation, with the whiskey coming later that night.

"Except, Leta, that doesn't explain the note. It has to be from last night, doesn't it? So, did the third person arrive after that romantic interlude or leave before it occurred?"

Because of Dickens and Watson, I had an idea of the order of events, but I couldn't convey it to Wendy as an eyewitness account. Instead, I presented it as a possibility. "Lyle brought him home, so maybe the two of them had a drink together. Then, he left before a woman arrived—or just after. Rick and the woman started with wine and moved on to whiskey. Next was a romantic encounter of some sort." I paused. "And then it falls apart for me."

Wendy nodded. "Right, because it doesn't seem plausible that Rick's romantic partner wrote that note and then strangled him. Nor is it realistic to think a woman had the strength to strangle him. I don't think I do."

"But we agree there was a romantic interlude, right?"

Leaning her head on the back of the chair, Wendy sighed. "Maybe we're reading too much into the billet-doux. What if it wasn't from last night? If we take it out of the equation, where does that leave us?"

"Wine prior to the pub. Dinner and drinking at the pub. Lyle brings him home, they have a drink of whiskey, and he leaves. A woman arrives. When I think about it, the bed wasn't disturbed. The only signs that the two got closer than a few drinks were the lipstick stains and the belt buckle."

I yawned. "We're left with the same problem. If we don't think a woman could have strangled him, a love note and some signs of affection don't change anything. Shoot, the loose belt buckle and unbuttoned pants could be a sign of discomfort after overeating—and nothing more."

Christie chose that moment to leap into Wendy's lap. Stretching her paw toward the collar of Wendy's robe, she meowed, "What about motive?"

It was easy to lose sight of how attentive Christie could be. She was right. We hadn't touched on motive at all. "You know, when we brainstorm with your mum and Ellie, we always discuss means, motive, and opportunity. Gemma thinks manual strangulation was the means. Anyone with a car had the opportunity. What we don't have is an inkling about motive."

Wendy scratched Christie between her ears. "You're right. We're pretty much clueless on that front. Do you think if we had Ellie's laser pointer, it would suddenly be clear?"

"No, but Christie would be happy." It was hard to tell which Christie liked better, Belle's lap or the pointer Ellie brought to our brainstorming sessions.

When I glanced at my watch, Wendy got the hint, and we agreed to ponder motive the next day. I shooed her up the stairs to bed while I made the coffee for the morning.

It was as I was climbing the stairs, Dickens and Christie at my heels, that Dave called. "How's my girl? All tucked in for the night?"

"Almost. I've done as much prep as I can for tomorrow. Wendy brought dinner and wine, and I filled her in on the happenings next door. And now? We're both in our jammies and headed to bed."

"I'm glad to hear Wendy's there. Did you make much headway?"

"Some. Not enough. We realized we have lots of digging to do to identify a motive."

"So, Tuppence, what's your next step? And how will you manage without the senior little old ladies and your clueless old codger?"

I employed my faux upper crust accent. "I say, Tommy, old chap, Wendy and I will divide and conquer. I'll investigate the American angle, and Wendy will interview the locals. Where we go from there is anyone's guess."

When he chuckled, I added, "We plan to send our notes to Ellie and Belle, more to keep them from feeling left out than anything else. But you never know. They might have an idea, and I can send the notes your way, too."

"I can see it now. The killer is right under Tuppence's nose, but it takes Tommy to solve the case from afar."

"My, my, what would Dame Agatha have to say about that?" We joked about Agatha Christie's Tommy and Tuppence mysteries as I yawned.

"Okay, sweetheart, I can tell you need your beauty sleep. I'll check on you tomorrow. Love you."

CHAPTER ELEVEN

When Christie pawed my chin, I opened one eye to glance at the clock. "Go away. It's only six, and I don't have anywhere to be until ten."

She climbed on my chest and licked my nose. "You need to be in the kitchen feeding me."

"Why is it you can wait until seven or eight some mornings, but never when I can sleep in? What's special about today?"

Leaping to the floor, she stalked from the room in a huff. "Your phone's making those funny noises. You might as well be up."

Funny noises meant texts, and reading those required glasses. I retrieved my red reading glasses and my phone from the bedside table. *Aargh. Jilly wants me there at eight. Why?*

There was also a text from Gemma, telling me she had laryngitis and a fever and to expect a call from Constable James. *I hope Libby puts her to bed and makes her stay there.*

In the kitchen, I let Dickens out, pulled grits and a can of cat food from the pantry, and started the coffee. "Christie, where are you? You wake me up and you're nowhere to be seen."

She came tearing down the stairs and did zoomies into the office, the sitting room and back. "Here I am."

"About time. Did you wake up Wendy, too?" By now, she had her nose in her wet food, so there was no immediate reply. When she'd licked most of the dab of food, she looked up at me. "Wendy went home to feed Tigger, and you need to fluff my food."

That meant I needed to add another forkful of food and push it all into a small pile in the middle of the dish. "And how do you know she went to feed Tigger?"

"That's what she said when I walked on her chest. 'As long as I'm awake, I may as well go home and feed Tigger.' Didn't you see the note she left you?"

I looked around the kitchen and saw the note tucked beneath the pottery dish on the table. Wendy had outlined her list for the day. After tending to Tigger, she planned to squeeze in a yoga class, send our notes to Belle and Ellie, and then speak with Jill, Jenny, and Trixie.

As the coffee brewed, I had a brainstorm and rang her. "When you send the email, why don't you give them an assignment? Ask them to find out what they can about this RIBA award. I doubt it's important, but it would make them feel useful."

"Sounds like a good way to ensure they stay in Cornwall. If you think of anything else we can assign them, shoot me a text. Chat later?"

I updated her on my morning messages, and we agreed an innocent visit to the pub that night was in order. While I prepared breakfast, another text came through from Jilly. 'Did you see my text?'

Oh, for goodness' sake. She said eight, and it's only 6:30. My thumbs didn't exactly fly across the keypad, but I responded. 'Yes. See you then.' Immediately, my phone rang.

"Leta, since you're awake, can I come over now? I'm at Toby's. I can bring muffins."

"Do I have a choice? Hurry, I'm making grits."

The grits were thickening when Jilly arrived, and I added cheese and butter as she pulled half a dozen muffins from a bag. The word woebegone came to mind when I saw the dark circles beneath her eyes and her blotchy complexion. Her lipstick did nothing but emphasize her pallor.

"Six muffins, Jilly? Is this some kind of bribe? As in, you have another piece of the meeting you want me to help with?"

She ducked her head. "Um, yes, and no. It's a bribe, but not for what you think. And Toby said they'd freeze well."

Spooning the grits into bowls, I placed them on the table. "Food first. Then business."

Jilly looked like she wanted to protest, but she acquiesced. After all, it takes no time at all to finish a bowl of grits and start nibbling a muffin. As I removed the empty bowls and topped up the coffee mugs, I nodded in her direction.

She gulped. "It's Rick, Leta. I have to know how he died."

Without conscious thought, I employed my pregnant pause technique. Jilly squirmed and grimaced before blurting, "I was there that night."

"There? Next door?"

"Yes, we were confirming the logistics for the week."

Blinking in surprise, I pictured the tumblers in the cottage. *The lipstick?* None remained on her lips now, but a glance at her coffee mug confirmed what I should have surmised earlier. She drank with Rick at the cottage, and, if I was right about the lipstick shade, she also left the billet-doux. Given Rick's reputation, I could imagine them winding up in bed together.

In a soft voice, I prompted her to continue. "And he was fine when you left, Jilly?"

"Yes, but . . . please, I need to know. How did he die?"

Think, Leta. What happens if you tell her? "Why does the how matter?"

She wrapped both hands around the coffee mug. "I . . . I may have . . . accidentally caused his death."

Huh? You either strangle someone or you don't. "How, Jilly? What happened?"

"It's hard to explain. I was irritated with him because he kept putting me off about preparing for the meeting. He acted as though it was this huge imposition. The reality was he was having such a grand time at the pub, he couldn't tear himself away. But not long after you left with Madge, he joined me by the dartboard.

"He gave me a bear hug and said seeing you and me together made him nostalgic. We watched a game or two, and then he asked if I still wanted to go over the meeting details. Of course, I did! Hadn't I been nearly begging him to do that? That's when he suggested we catch up on old times and review the agenda over a bottle of wine at his cottage."

Then it was Jilly's car lights I saw as Cynthia was leaving. "You drove him to the cottage?"

"No. We went separately because I wanted to pop by the inn to grab my notes, so he left ahead of me. I checked in on Madge, too, before I left. By the time I made it to his place, he had a bottle of wine open on the kitchen counter.

"We carried our glasses to the sitting room, and it was like old times reminiscing about our days working for your bank and other clients. I learned a lot from Rick and Tim. Working for Powerhouse Performance gave me the knowledge and confidence I needed to start a business here."

"And the agenda? Did you get to that?"

"We would have if Rick hadn't found a stack of jigsaw puzzles and started on one while we talked. Then he wanted to switch to whiskey, and I knew I couldn't do that and still drive. It wasn't far back to the inn, but I'd already had more than I should have." She frowned. "The man was nothing if not persuasive."

"Meaning what, Jilly?"

"I agreed to have a tot of whiskey, but only if he'd walk me through the agenda in detail. Working with Holmes & White was a splendid opportunity for me, and I wanted to be sure it all went like clockwork."

This fit with my sense of Rick and the tales I'd heard about him using his charm to get his way. Both he and Jilly must have hollow legs. There was no way I could drink that much any night, much less before a big meeting.

"I washed the wineglasses and corked the wine while he grabbed the bottle of whiskey. When I saw he'd poured me a full glass, I blurted, 'Keep this up, and I'll be spending the night on your couch.' That was a mistake. I should have known better."

I saw the words from the lipstick note. 'Hope it was good for you, too.' *Was this shaping up to be a seduction scene?*

"Did you? Spend the night, I mean?"

"No!" She leaned across the table. "But when he said, 'the bed would be better,' I let him think I might. I don't do *coy* very well, but I encouraged him to build a fire and let me think about it. It was an opportunity to turn the tables on him."

"Sorry, Jilly, I'm not following you."

Anger flashed in her eyes. "I might as well admit it. I was furious with him about Madge. It was all too convenient. Madge gets sick. He suddenly invites me to his cottage. When I saw the full-to-the-brim whiskey glass, I knew what he had in mind. And I was positive he invited me over as second choice."

She took a deep breath. "While he was outside getting fire-wood, I crushed two of my sleeping tablets in his drink."

It's rare that I'm speechless, but before I could form words, Jilly continued.

"And it worked—better than I could have imagined. I handed him his drink when he came in with the wood, and he took a huge slug. He built the fire, sat in his easy chair, and drank more. I made a pretense of sipping my drink as we prepped for the next day. We weren't far into the agenda when he started slurring his words, and before I knew it, he nodded off."

"Seriously, Jilly, you spiked his drink? Because you thought you were second choice?"

"Maybe it was stupid, but it worked like a charm. When I planted a kiss on his cheek, he never stirred, and inspiration took hold. I unbuckled his belt and unbuttoned his pants, and then I thought of the note. He'd have woken up wondering whether we actually did anything. It was nowhere near as bad as giving him a roofie."

Except that he was dead. My, how the world has changed since my single days. Roofies?

"Leta, you saw the note when you found the folder, right? To me, it seemed like turnabout's fair play, nothing more."

The dots weren't connecting for me, but it didn't matter. She thought she was second choice, so she drugged him. And while the sleeping pills may not have killed him, they rendered him unconscious—and vulnerable. *If not for the pills, would he have fought back? Would he still be alive?*

My silence must have been too much for Jilly. "Leta, please tell me. Was it the sleeping pills? Did they cause a heart attack or something? Please tell me that wasn't it."

I sensed there was more to Jilly and Rick's relationship than she was letting on, but did that make drugging him any more acceptable? Not in my book. How could she be grateful for what he'd taught her yet turn around and exact some kind of revenge on him? Feeling like second choice didn't seem like a justification for what she did.

Her story is like a puzzle with missing pieces.

Still, whatever had gone on between them in the past or more recently, it didn't change the fact that Rick didn't die from an overdose. Someone strangled him to death, and Jilly didn't need to worry that she may have accidentally killed him.

I could put her mind at ease about how he died, but it would be up to Gemma and the Gloucestershire police to determine what to do next. It didn't sound like they'd spoken with her yet, and I thought that was odd. *When they do, will they believe her story or see her as the likeliest suspect?*

In as few words as possible, I explained that her sleeping pills didn't cause Rick's death, but that the police were bound to analyze his tumbler of whiskey and discover he'd been drugged. There was no way I was going to tell her he died from strangulation.

"Jilly, I hope that puts your mind at ease, but here's a word of advice. I take it the police haven't questioned you yet, and that's probably because they have no idea you were there that night."

She interrupted me. "DI Taylor asked to meet me yesterday evening, and I waited in the conservatory at the inn. It was the innkeeper, Gavin, who came to tell me she called to postpone. All night long I worried about what that meant. Did she suspect me? Did she know I'd been there? That's one reason I called you."

That explained the delay. Gemma was already too sick to see her. "I hear she's sick, Jilly, so that's probably all it is. Regardless, you need to contact the police ASAP and tell them you had drinks with Rick at the cottage and need to talk to them."

I pulled up Jonas's number on my phone and read it aloud to her. "This is for Constable James. He's the one to call while DI Taylor is out. When you meet with him, tell him everything. He'll see through any evasiveness in a heartbeat. Your 'turn-about's fair play' story is going to raise eyebrows, and you need to be prepared to explain it. Don't embroider, don't rationalize. Tell him the facts. Being upfront will work in your favor."

"Okay." She tilted her head. "You talk like you've had experience with investigations. Are you friends with the local police, or what?"

Friends? Little does she know. "Not exactly, but the DI in charge of this is your innkeeper's daughter—Gemma Taylor, and Constable James lives in Astonbury. Now, get going. I'll see you by 9:45 at the latest."

Time to shift gears. I pictured myself ducking into the red telephone kiosk near the village green to don a cape—red, of course.

CHAPTER TWELVE

WHEN I WALKED INTO the village hall with Dickens and Christie at 9:30, the group had just finished watching a short film on Cotswolds architecture. Seated in a chair up front, Lyle was leading a brainstorming session on which elements could find their way into the Astonbury designs. His team seemed very much at ease offering ideas and debating the pros and cons with the boss. Years of experience told me it was his confident, easygoing manner that fostered that atmosphere. I didn't know enough about architecture to tell how knowledgeable he was, but I sensed genuine respect in the room.

Cynthia stood in the back of the room holding a cup and approached me as I softly closed the door. "He's doing so well. Working with small groups is his forte, but I wasn't sure he'd be able to pull it off after yesterday.

"He was relatively calm after Gemma interviewed him, but her later text tipped him over the edge. It's bad enough that his friend is dead, but knowing his gran's cottage was where it happened is just plain awful. It was always his retreat, and I don't know if he'll ever be able to see it that way again."

She's lost me. "What was in the text, Cynthia?"

"A request that he make himself available for a walkthrough of the cottage."

"Oh my gosh, I hadn't thought of that possibility. But it makes sense. He's the best person to see whether anything is out of place or missing or just plain off."

"I'm sure he is, but he has so much on his plate already. This competition, his divorce. Even winning the RIBA award is a stressor. He's not big on speeches."

"I saw mention of the award. Remind me what RIBA stands for."

"Royal Institute of British Architects. It's the first time we've won such a prestigious award, and I'd wager that honor was our entrée to this competition. Lyle came up with the concept for transforming the Ambleside Anglican Cathedral into a community center, and it's been five years in the works. Madge and Bert led the teams that saw it through."

"There was a newspaper clipping about that at the cottage, but I didn't get a chance to read the details." I'd have to share this additional information with Ellie and Belle.

"Can't imagine Lyle hanging on to that. We have a copy in the office along with the plaque, but he's not one to keep articles or make a big deal out of his role."

It didn't seem important to tell her it was among Rick's papers. I was sure he intended to congratulate Lyle, and that intent spoke well of Rick. He'd done his homework, and probably planned to use the cathedral project as a case study on the team's strengths and weaknesses. What did they do well? What could they have done better or improved? Maybe I could reference it in debriefing the outdoor activities.

Since I'd been knee-deep in Myers-Briggs yesterday, personality types were top of mind for me. The more I learned about Lyle, the more convinced I was that he was an INTJ—an Introvert /

Intuitive / Thinker / Judger. If I wasn't mistaken, that type was sometimes called the Architect personality. Lyle was the poster child for it with his calm, focused demeanor.

Wrapping up the discussion, Lyle called for a break—my cue to set up my laptop and prepare for my presentation. I looked around for Jilly, but it was Cynthia who joined me up front. "Leta, I'm sure they all know who you are by now, but I want to introduce you again and emphasize that this is more than fun information. It's about understanding and appreciating differences. It's about leveraging those differences to work as a team."

I was pleased to hear how seriously she was taking this. "Heck, Cynthia, you sound like you could teach it. It's easy to intrigue them with the humorous bits about the personality types. Getting them to think about how it all plays out in their behavior and interactions with others is a different kettle of fish. Your intro will make them take it more seriously. And I'll remind them that today's insights will connect to the outdoor activities, too."

"Trust me, Lyle and I took the assessment years ago, and we know we're fortunate that we complement each other. From the early days, when it was just the two of us, he's been the visionary, and I've been the detail person. We work well together."

She'd given me an idea. "Cynthia, after I provide the overview and give them their results, why don't you share that background with the group? That's more meaningful than any example I could come up with."

When she called Lyle over to run the idea by him, he was all in. "Makes us seem brilliant, doesn't it? Go for it."

They spent a few minutes teasing each other about their partnership before he turned to me with a speculative look. "Leta, Cynthia tells me you have some experience with the police around here. Is there any chance I can pick your brain? I've a meeting with a constable this afternoon, and I'd like to know what to expect."

"Sure, Lyle. How about when we break for lunch?"

By now, the group was taking their seats, so I quickly shifted gears. Myers-Briggs was a topic I enjoyed immensely. As I described the four pairs of preferences that made up the personality types, I peppered the specifics with humorous anecdotes. They were an attentive audience who easily grasped the concepts.

"I'm an ISTJ. You might think that introverts are extremely shy, and some are. I'm an introvert who enjoys meeting new people and going to parties. Not all do. What most of us have in common, though, is that after expending energy socializing, we crave quiet time. For me, that means crawling into bed with a good book or playing Words with Friends."

I played out Sensor vs. Intuitive, Thinker vs. Feeler and Judger vs. Perceiver the same way. Holding up my yellowed copy of *Type Talk*, I pointed to the back cover. "There are plenty of books about Myers-Briggs, but I especially love this one for the taglines they give each personality type."

They got a good laugh when I shared mine—Doing what should be done. "How boring is that? I like schedules and plans, and I struggle to be spontaneous. Sure, I can invite friends over for dinner at the drop of a hat, but mostly because I can easily throw together a Greek meal I've made dozens of times. A pinch of this, a dash of that. Ask for something new, though, and I'll follow the recipe precisely. I don't make up new dishes.

"My friend Wendy, whom you met yesterday, is an ENFJ—the opposite of me in several ways. As an Extrovert / Intuitive/ Feeler / Judger, she's good for me because she's adventuresome and much more of a risk-taker than I am. That's the beauty of different personalities. We sometimes drive each other crazy, but we play well together." I nodded to Cynthia.

Laughing, she walked to the front. "I never thought about it, but you two *are* very different. You have similar interests—books, fashion, and shopping—but Wendy's like a little dynamo, all over the place."

"Cynthia, you nailed it."

She turned to the group. "Here's another real-world example, one from our company." She pointed to Lyle. "He's an INTJ. Long before I knew anything about personality types, I described him as visionary and never ceased to be amazed at the ideas he had. Once he decided on a concept, he was determined it would succeed. You know him. Success isn't enough. *Smashing* success is what he strives for." There were laughs combined with a few groans when she told them that Lyle's INTJ tagline was 'Everything has room for improvement.'

"Me? I'm an ENFJ like Wendy, though I wouldn't say I'm adventuresome. I'm creative. After all, I'm an interior designer, but for me, helping clients see the vision is the best part. I enjoy painting the picture. I guess that's why my tagline fits—'Smooth-talking persuader.' You may have seen that play out in client meetings." She asked the group to think of examples of her and Lyle in team meetings and whether the descriptions seemed to fit.

After that, it was time to give them their individual packets and a handout with more explanation of the sixteen personality types. I allowed twenty minutes for them to jot down their observations. What surprised them? What didn't? What confused them?

As typically happened, some people agreed with the results, while others balked at them. I repeated that these were not boxes that defined people from start to finish. "Think of these as innate preferences that can shift and evolve over time. Look at me. I'm an ISTJ who's a retired corporate trainer and executive coach, and more recently, I'm a columnist." *No need to mention the Little Old Ladies' Detective Agency.*

"Do you know which professions show up on the top 25 list for ISTJs?" I glanced at my notes. "Accountant, dentist, engineer, graphic designer, statistician, and police officer—to name a few. I have zero interest in any of those careers. Only one on that list fits me, and that's event planner. Believe it or not, I did event planning from time to time and enjoyed it immensely." *I guess it could be argued that police officer fits, but I'm not going there.* "So, repeat after me, but replace my personality type with yours. Not all *ISTJs* are alike."

After a humorous activity using Dickens and Christie to highlight the characteristics of Sensors and Intuitors, I unfolded a large piece of paper taped to the wall. "Here are the sixteen types. Please put your name by yours. Your lunch assignment is to pair up with someone different from you and compare notes. If you wind up with someone with the identical type, consider your similarities and differences. Why? Because, as you know, not all ISTJs are alike."

That got some chuckles. I gave them the timeline for their village hall bus tour with George and dismissed them. Several folks approached me to ask if their partners could take the assessment, and I promised to get them the link to the website that offered a free version.

Jilly had arrived shortly after Cynthia's introduction and was now busy scratching Christie's head. She looked much better than she had earlier. "Leta, the exercise with the animals was a hoot. I've seen it done with an orange, but Dickens and Christie are more entertaining."

Nudging Jilly's hand, Christie meowed her agreement. "Of course we are. I adored my group. They described me so well. I couldn't quite believe how much they appreciated my beauty."

She was right. I assigned her to the group of Sensors, and they jotted down an overwhelming amount of detail—ebony, black, silky, pink pads, soft pads, pink tongue, yellow eyes, black nose, clean ears, red elastic collar. The list went on and on.

Dickens ran up and skidded to a stop. "No! My group was the best. They told stories about me. I'm a brave mountain dog from the Pyrenees. I blend in with the snow and the sheep to protect them. They talked about shepherds and said they'd seen Basil on their tour with George. When did they meet him, Leta? They told stories about how my bark scares off predators and evil-doers."

Little did the Intuitor group know how accurate they were. Dickens was my little hero dog and had scared off several villains. And Basil, his large friend, had saved my life by pulling me from the river. I whispered in Dickens's ear. "I bet they met Basil when they toured Astonbury Estate yesterday."

"There's more, Leta. Someone said I was royal. Am I really? I think they may write a book about me. How cool is that?" He licked my hand. "One person said I was small, but another said I was small and mighty. I like that. Can they visit us?"

As I chuckled at my lovable animals, Jilly said she planned to email Tim in the States to suggest he trade the oranges for animals. "It makes the same point, doesn't it? The Sensors go into great detail about how the orange smells and feels and looks. Pretty much what this group did with Christie. With an orange, sometimes, they even peel it and count the segments so they can describe every bit of it.

"The Intuitors were more random, more big-picture. I loved hearing them describe Dickens like a character in a book. His bravery, his gentle yet strong demeanor. They didn't spend any time talking about the length of his hair or how it curled or felt."

I was only half listening to Jilly as I watched to see if the group paired off as requested. "Let me know what Tim says. I can't imagine him putting a menagerie on the payroll of Powerhouse Performance." From the corner of my eye, I glimpsed Lyle leaving the building.

Grabbing Christie's backpack and Dickens's leash, I told Jilly I had a busy afternoon ahead and hastened after Lyle.

He was standing outside with his phone pressed to his ear. "Believe me, I know how important this is. I'm terribly sorry. Can we possibly reschedule for next week?" He went on in an apologetic vein as I stood off to the side. Judging by his frown, the conversation wasn't going well.

My phone lit up with a text from Wendy. "Class over? Ready for lunch?"

I quickly typed a response. "Not sure. Meeting with Lyle. Connect after lunch?"

When Dickens tugged on his leash, I let him run to Lyle, whose scowl immediately changed to a smile. "Dickens! Hello. Did you get lunch?"

"Trust me, he doesn't need any food. Do you want to grab some, maybe at Toby's instead of here? That would give us more privacy."

"Yes. I wanted to join the team on the bus tour, but this walk-through of the cottage put an end to that idea. Can't do both. And I have clients to deal with, too."

"Toby's it is, then." Once we placed our orders and snagged a table by the window, I put Christie's backpack on the extra chair. She indicated her satisfaction with the surroundings with a soft rumbling purr. Dickens attached himself to Lyle's leg, hoping, I was sure, for a handout.

"Leta, was Cynthia serious when she said you were a detective? She alluded to Jessica Fletcher, but she was joking, right?"

"Not exactly. Since I've retired, I've unofficially played detective here and there. I guess you'd say I have a good eye. And Wendy does, too." *That and more, but no need to say anything else.*

He gave me a puzzled look. "So, it's you two who Cynthia refers to as the little old ladies. That seems a bit unkind."

I explained that the unflattering moniker originally came from Gemma and that my friends and I had adopted it in jest. "Let me tell you about the Canine Caper, as we call it." That case involved missing animals, not murder.

When I got to the part about Ellie firing her shotgun during a snowstorm, his mouth dropped open. "Crikey, point her out if she comes this way so I can duck. The Dowager Countess of Stow carrying a shotgun is quite a story."

He quizzed me about Constable James, and I told him not to let Jonas's youthful look fool him. "He's an up-and-comer with a lot on the ball. DI Taylor, his boss, thinks highly of him. My advice would be to tell him everything you know, even details you see as unimportant. I find things go much easier when I volunteer information rather than waiting to be asked." *Except when I volunteer suggestions they don't want to hear.*

"For example?"

"Well, I can't tell you what approach Jonas—I mean Constable James—will take, but he's sure to ask you to look around each room for anything amiss or missing. When I was in the sitting room, I noticed the bottle of Cotswolds Single Malt, and wondered whether you had left it for Rick, or he'd bought it. Did you leave it there for him?"

"As a matter of fact, I brought it over when I picked him up last night. He considered himself a connoisseur of whiskey, so I thought he'd appreciate having a bottle on hand."

"There you go. Tell Jonas you provided it. That detail will immediately clear up whether Rick had a visitor who brought the bottle along."

His brow furrowed. "You know I haven't set foot in the cottage since the crime scene tape went up, so you know more than I do. What else do you have questions about? Maybe I should think about how I left things when I was there last."

I pictured the mantel. "Did you leave a whiskey glass in the sitting room?"

"I think Rick and I both did. When I dropped by to take him to the pub, he poured us each a glass. He was quite appreciative. For all I know, though, I may have carried mine through to the kitchen and rinsed it. Force of habit, you know. My wife trained me well."

When Toby delivered our order, we ate in silence for a few minutes. "Lyle, I noticed the jam-packed bookcase. When this is all over, would you mind if I took a look at the collection? I bet your gran has some British novels I've never heard of."

"There's no telling. I know she has every Josephine Tey book ever written and a good many of the early Mary Stewart books. You're welcome to browse and borrow to your heart's content."

My mind drifted to books, and Lyle caught me off guard when he posed his next question. "Leta, they haven't told me what Rick died of, just that they consider his death suspicious. I know you're not a real detective, but did you see something that made you think he didn't die of natural causes?"

If Gemma hadn't told him, I certainly wasn't going to. "It was quite a shock, Lyle. He looked as though he'd fallen asleep sitting up. A jigsaw puzzle was spread out on the table in front of him. That's all I can tell you."

"Oh yes. Gran had plenty of puzzles. It'd be nice to think he died peacefully playing a game. Just put his head back in a comfy chair and went to sleep.

"Rick was a man of many hats. He liked board games and puzzles, but he was also quite active—a runner and a tennis player. He told me he had to take up walking after some nagging knee issues, though. I think he was delaying a knee replacement."

"I can relate to the knee issues. Both of mine bother me from time to time, but no one's mentioned a knee replacement yet.

"I tell you when he spoke of his work as a consultant, it was obvious he'd found his calling. He was forever reading books on teamwork, leadership, and all that. He was as likely to quote Stephen Covey as he was Malcolm Gladwell. And then, before you knew it, he'd tell you about a biography of a long-distance runner."

He studied his half-eaten sandwich. "We weren't that close, but I'm going to miss him."

CHAPTER THIRTEEN

Lyle was due to meet Jonas in thirty minutes and thought a stroll to his cottage in the cool, crisp air would help to settle him before the ordeal. Leaving his car by the village hall, he joined me and Dickens and Christie as we walked.

"Leta, you've got your hands full. What if I carry the backpack?"

Christie meowed her answer. "A nice big back for me to snuggle against? Sounds good. Almost as good as having Dave here."

Lyle probably thought I was smiling at his offer, but it was Christie's words that brought the smile to my face. Though she'd warmed to Dave, she didn't often say as much. Thankfully, I no longer had to listen to her constantly compare him to Peter, and I considered this comment another positive sign.

As she nuzzled his neck, Lyle reached behind him to scratch her head. I could think of no better way to lessen his apprehension at the imminent visit to the scene of the crime. He wasn't grinning, but the worried expression he'd worn throughout lunch was disappearing.

Jonas passed us and pulled up to Lyle's cottage as we approached my gravel drive. Emerging from the car, he waved to us. I was sure he didn't know it was Lyle Holmes walking by my side, so I hastened to make the introduction.

He didn't roll his eyes like his boss often did, but he gave me a questioning look. "Leta, are you running an escort service these days?" As soon as the words were out of his mouth, he blushed beet red. "Bloomin' Nora, I didn't mean that the way it sounded. Sorry."

I laughed and let him off the hook. "I promise not to tell Dave if you don't." *That gaffe was a good thing. At least it made Lyle smile.*

Looking from me to Lyle, he seemed to make a decision. "Since you're here, would you like to join us? Listening to Mr. Holmes as he walks through the cottage may trigger a memory, maybe a detail you overlooked that day." *Tuning into details—another of my Myers-Briggs traits.*

In the past, Jonas would have come across as tentative and wondered aloud whether Gemma would shoot him. There was no hesitation in this request. This was a more confident, self-assured Jonas James than I'd previously encountered. I was sure this change was a result of the commendation he received in the spring, combined with Gemma's increased reliance on him.

"Great idea, Constable James." I thought about bringing Dickens and Christie along until an image of two sets of paws caked in fingerprint powder dissuaded me from the idea. *What a nightmare that would be!*

They both expressed their dismay about being left behind as I closed my cottage door behind me. Well, dismay from Dickens—more like indignation from Christie.

Next door, the two men waited for me in the kitchen. This would be much easier on me than on Lyle. I would picture the body I'd found, but it wasn't the same as Lyle imagining it in his grandmother's cottage.

"Mr. Holmes, when DI Taylor interviewed you yesterday, she told you we considered this a suspicious death. I need to make you aware that we're now investigating Mr. Bradley's death as a homicide. Anything you can tell us about your recollection of the last time you were here will be helpful."

He paused, allowing time, I thought, for Lyle to absorb the news. "Let's start here in the kitchen. Please take your time looking around. You can touch anything you want to, open cabinets or whatever, because the SOCOs have finished here. Left a mess, I'm afraid, but they're done. Just point out anything that looks odd or different."

Lyle gazed around the room, and his eyes focused on the drainboard. "It looks like it did when I straightened before Rick arrived. Since Rick and I had drinks when I picked him up that night, shouldn't there be glasses in the dish drain? Or maybe we didn't wash them. I can't recall."

I waited for Jonas to imitate Jack Webb and tersely say, just the facts. *Does he even know that famous line? Goodness, that makes me feel old.*

"Good question, Mr. Holmes. The SOCOs took everything like that away, but there were two wineglasses in the drain and a dirty one on the counter. There were also two bottles of wine on the counter." Jonas flipped through his notebook. "Both were Côte de Beaune-Villages, a pinot noir, I'm told. Is that what you drank?"

"No, we drank whiskey. You probably found that bottle, too—Cotswolds Single Malt. I brought it for Rick." A line etched between his brows. "He must have brought the wine down from London."

He turned toward Jonas. "You said Côte de Beaune-Villages?"

"Yes. Does that mean something to you?"

"It's probably not important, except that it can be hard to find. I recognize the name because it's Madge's favorite pinot. Cynthia and I bought her a case of it when we won this year's RIBA awards." Almost to himself, he mumbled. "Got Bert a burl wood humidor and a selection of cigars."

This must be what it's like to work for a small, close-knit firm. I received some awards and gifts during my career, but never anything with this kind of personal touch. I thought the information spoke to what a great place Holmes & White was to work for. Jonas must have thought it interesting in some other way because he scribbled in his notebook.

"Any other observations in this room, Mr. Holmes?"

When Lyle shook his head, Jonas led us upstairs to the bedroom and once again asked him to point out any oddities. The holdall was gone, taken by the SOCOs, I assumed. The bedcovers were rumpled, but not really disturbed. That confirmed my recollection that no one had slept in the bed. At least that part of Jilly's story was true—unless the couch had come into play.

"This was Gran's room," Lyle murmured. "I packed away her patchwork quilt but didn't change much else. And this is pretty much the way I left it for Rick. Please tell me he didn't die in here."

Once Jonas told him Rick died in the sitting room not in the bedroom, we moved downstairs, where Jonas took the same approach. Lyle stood in the doorway to the sitting room for what seemed an eternity before pointing toward the fireplace. "Now that I think about it, I didn't wash my whiskey glass. I sat it on the mantel when we left for the pub. Is that where you found it?"

"Yes, and we found Mr. Bradley's glass on the game table. Well, I call it a game table because it had a jigsaw puzzle spread out on it."

Lyle closed his eyes. "Yes, he enjoyed puzzles." His face brightened. "I remember he and Gran doing one when we visited her that summer." He must have seen something in Jonas's face because he added, "I met Rick at uni."

At the bookcase, Lyle motioned to me. "Here are the Josephine Tey books I mentioned, Leta. And I'd forgotten the Ngaio Marsh books. Looks like two shelves of those."

We stood together for a few moments admiring the selection until Jonas cleared his throat. "Mr. Holmes, if I could bring you back to why we're here."

"Sorry, let me think a moment." Lyle focused on the couch and the hassock and leaned over to study the side table. "I'll have to polish this. I can hear Gran now, tsk tsking at the ring mark. It looks like red wine."

He can expect more of that if he plans to rent it out. Must be where Jilly sat her goblet. A thought was stirring in my brain, but I couldn't capture it. Something about the wine, maybe.

Lyle's question interrupted my reverie. "Constable James, you said there were two wineglasses in the dish drain and one on the counter. Do you know who was here with Rick?"

"We're pursuing several leads."

Staring into the cold fireplace, Lyle spoke softly. "I'm still trying to come to grips with his death. It was bad enough when I thought it was from natural causes. And now, you're calling it a homicide." He raised his chin. "Do you think the person who drank with him is the one . . . the one who killed him?"

When Jonas didn't immediately answer, Lyle's eyes got big. "Flamin' hell, you said three glasses. What happened here? How did he die?"

I couldn't tell whether Jonas's silence was an attempt to trigger a revealing reaction, or he was carefully choosing his words. Finally, he replied. "He was strangled." He pointed to the wing-backed chair. "In that chair."

As though he'd taken a blow, Lyle staggered and braced himself on the mantel. "Strangled? Who would do that?"

"That's what we're trying to work out." He motioned Lyle to the sofa and asked me to prepare tea, making me feel like I was a junior officer in a BBC mystery.

The kettle was on the stove, and I located tea and a teapot in the cupboard. Snippets of conversation floated in from the sitting room as I worked.

Jonas asked Lyle the questions Gemma had likely asked in the first interview. Rick had only recently moved to London. How well did Lyle know him now? Did they socialize or was it strictly a business relationship? Did he know of anyone who would want to harm Rick? Could Rick have been involved in anything illegal? Had the two of them argued?

I couldn't make out many of Lyle's responses, but that last question resulted in a loud, indignant reply. "Of course not. What are you asking? Do you think I did this?" I pictured him waving his arm toward the wing-backed chair.

As I returned to the sitting room with a tray, Lyle asked, "Is there anything else about the cottage that you want to know? If not, I'm leaving."

Jonas tucked his notebook in his jacket pocket. "No, Mr. Holmes, you've given me what I need, for now." He confirmed Lyle was lodging at the inn and requested he be prepared to make himself available for further questioning as needed.

"May I get someone in here to clean up now? I've no doubt Gran is turning over in her grave at the state of her home."

That settled, Lyle thanked me and left. I placed the heavy tea tray on the game table and sat on the hassock by the couch.

"Jonas, was that just the standard line of questioning, or do you suspect Lyle?"

Pouring two mugs of tea, Jonas handed me one. "Leta, at this stage, we suspect everyone who had any contact with the victim. The entire staff of Holmes & White, others who were at the pub that night, even you and Wendy. After all, you have a history with the victim." He winked when he said my name.

"Don't even go there. Being questioned at the police station in Torquay was one time too many."

"Ah, I'd forgotten that story. Don't fancy a repeat?"

"Perish the thought. Now tell me, Jonas, you must have narrowed the list. Have you questioned everyone?"

"I've crossed a name or two off, like the woman who was passed out in her room. Madge. Same one Mr. Holmes remarked on when he saw the bottle of wine."

"Right. I delivered her to the inn that night. It would have taken a miraculous recovery for her to be involved. It *is* odd, though. I wonder why Rick had several bottles of her favorite wine."

"And would you believe it, Leta? Another woman on the list called me this morning to say she needed to talk to me." A smile tugged at his lips. "Mentioned your name, by the way, and I'm meeting her at the village hall."

"I know you're teasing me, but it sounds like it was a good thing I urged her to contact you. I'd have thought she would be among the first people you questioned, given that Rick hired her."

"It's a wonder Gemma got to as many as she did, given how sick she is. She had no business questioning anyone with that fever, not to mention having to whisper questions."

It was hard to imagine Gemma under the weather, but it could be a good opportunity for Jonas. "It could work out well for you if she stays in bed for a week."

He laughed. "Well, I'm sorry she's so sick, but the staying in bed part may happen, if her texts are any indication. She's already grumbling about her mum keeping a close eye on her. She said Libby found her trying to talk on the phone and scolded her up one side and down the other."

It was my turn to smile as I pictured Libby plying Gemma with a variety of soups and teas. She routinely delivered a basket of muffins to her daughter every morning, and now she'd add soup for lunch and dinner. Perhaps even hot water bottles and whatever home remedies she had in her arsenal.

"Jonas, do you seriously suspect Lyle?"

"Can't strike him from the list yet. It's a bit too convenient that the victim was staying here at Mr. Holmes's cottage. You found the door unlocked and the keys on the counter, but the killer could have had another set, and Mr. Holmes certainly does. And using your bare hands to strangle someone? That's more a man's weapon."

"Did Gemma ask him about the keys?"

"Yes. He says there are two sets, his and his gran's—the one he gave the victim. So, was the door left unlocked, or did Mr. Holmes unlock it on a second visit that night?"

Because I knew about Jilly's visit, I thought it likely she left the door unlocked, but Jonas didn't have the benefit of that information. "And motive, have you any ideas on that?"

"This is where Gemma would call you a meddling Nosey Parker, isn't it? But you've yet to lead me astray, Leta. What do you think the motive could be?"

"I honestly have no idea. Rick hasn't lived in England long, so what could he possibly have done to get on someone's wrong side? If it was a crime of passion, if he'd argued with someone that night and provoked him, wouldn't you agree there'd be signs of a struggle? My immediate thought before seeing the bruises on his neck was that he'd died in his sleep."

"Exactly the questions I'm asking myself. When I get the analysis of the residue in his glass, that may help. Then there's the mystery of the love note upstairs and the lipstick on the tumbler. They point to a female visitor, who might have done it, especially if the powder turns out to be a sedative. A woman might not have had the strength to overpower and strangle a wide-awake man, but a drugged victim? That's different."

"You could be right." All of that implied premeditation. And if that was the case, the evidence pointed straight to Jilly.

I hadn't seen her since she was in her twenties, but I considered myself a decent judge of character. Yes, she'd changed her look with long hair, dyed black, but could the woman I'd known ten years ago have changed into a cold-blooded killer? More than that, if she was the killer, would she admit she'd been at the scene of the crime?

Of course, I'd been wrong before.

On the way home, I saw that I'd missed a call from Dave. His message was garbled, something about a busy day with Sandy visiting jewelry stores.

What? What do jewelry stores have to do with getting the house packed up?

When I returned his call, he answered right away. "Good morning, sweetheart, or I guess afternoon. Was your presentation a smashing success?"

"Yes, especially my improvised activity with Dickens and Christie. They were stars."

By now, I was in the kitchen where my four-legged assistants could hear me. Christie preened and meowed, and Dickens gave an excited yip.

"So, what's going on with you? It didn't all come through. You're taking time out from packing?"

"Only because Mom's got a new crazy idea. She's decided she needs to sell most of her good jewelry. Michelle's already taken what she wants, and I'll see if there's anything you might like. Most of it is way too ornate for your tastes, but I'll send you some photos."

"Wouldn't she be happier taking it with her and making those decisions when she has more time?"

"Exactly what I said, but there's no arguing with her. She says she'll never wear it again. Sandy tried, too. We've given up, so we're making the rounds of jewelry shops that buy outright. Sandy's got connections with those and a few that work on consignment."

He sounded exasperated, and I didn't blame him. He was being an attentive, helpful son, but the task was getting larger, not smaller. "At this rate, you'll still be there at Halloween. Seriously, do you think you'll make it home on Sunday?"

"I'll be there, come hell or high water. Michelle will have to get involved again if we're not done." His voice faded out briefly. "Hey, Mom's got breakfast ready, so let me run. I'll call tonight. Love you."

I added wood to the fireplace and curled up on the couch where Christie joined me. It was time I admitted how tired I was of hearing Sandy this and Sandy that. "Christie, am I jealous? Of Dave's high school sweetheart?"

"What are you talking about?"

"I wasn't worried when Michelle warned me about her, and I managed to put her catty comments out of my mind. But I'm an ocean away now, and she's spending hours a day with Dave. If she's making a play for him, there's not much I can do about it."

"So what? He belongs to us."

I had to laugh at that. "To us, huh? He's certainly won you over."

"It's like Watson. He belongs to me."

"So, you're comparing Dave to a cat?"

"Why not? They both adore me, and Dave adores you, too. Why do you think I approved of him moving in?"

"You, little girl, are a trip. I didn't realize I needed your approval, but I'm glad to hear I got it."

I rubbed her head and thought about what she'd said. "I know Dave loves me, but he's only human. How would I react if an old sweetheart threw himself at me? That's a silly question. I'd be flattered, but that's it. Dave's the man for me."

Christie purred. "And you're the girl for him."

For someone who tried for months to steer me away from Dave, she'd certainly come around. Back then, I'd laughed about taking relationship advice from a cat. She'd been dead wrong, but now? She seemed awfully smart. She was right. I was letting my imagination run away with me.

I picked up my phone. "Hey Siri, play Billy Joel's "A Matter of Trust." As I listened to the words, I closed my eyes and smiled. *Sunday, he'll be home Sunday.*

CHAPTER FOURTEEN

DICKENS'S BARK WOKE ME up. "Leta, Wendy's here." Standing, I stretched and went to the door. A glance at my watch told me I'd only dozed off for fifteen minutes.

Wendy called to me as she climbed from her car. "Hi. I texted but when you didn't respond, I took a chance and came on by. Boy, do I have lots to report."

I yawned. "Come on in, I'll make tea."

"Did you speak with Lyle?"

"Oh yes, and Jonas too. I had soup at Toby's, but that seems ages ago. Shall I heat up some muffins?"

"What a coincidence. I had his soup of the day, but I always have room for a muffin." She started sharing her findings as we carried our snack to the sitting room. "My goodness, I found out lots. I spoke with Trixie, Jenny, and Jill, and I'm meeting with Barb later."

She held up my notebook. "I should have told you I took it with me. I typed our notes from last night and sent them to Mum and Ellie."

"It sounds like we've both had a productive day, and it's not over yet. Did you add your findings from today?"

"No. I thought you could do that as we talk it out." Wendy paced as she talked. "Let me start with Trixie, though it was Jill I interviewed first. I asked for her impression of Rick. I didn't want to lead the witness, so I didn't prompt her with anything specific.

"She remarked on his good looks, even though he was an older man. That made me cringe. You realize, don't you, that to people like Trixie, we're now considered old? Horrors."

"Given the unflattering grey hair comment from Dave's high school sweetheart, I'm all too aware."

Wendy wasn't about to let me dwell on that. "The good news for you is that your hair is a shiny silver. We blondes aren't that lucky when we go grey. That's why I shall forever remain a platinum blonde."

She summed up Trixie's take on Rick as fairly benign. He was nice. He told funny stories and listened to what others had to say. I laughed at her comment that he was friendly in the way most Americans are. That we tend to touch people when we talk and that he was a hugger like me. She didn't describe it as overly friendly or handsy as my co-worker Stephie had.

"Then, I kind of nonchalantly brought up Madge. I think I'm getting good at subterfuge. It was easy to mention Madge and how weird it was for her to get sick and for Rick to die—the same night, as though some evil spirit was afoot."

Laughing, I choked on my tea. "Evil spirit? You need to remember that idea when we get around to writing our books."

She grinned. "Pretty creative, huh? She didn't know about Madge being ill but told me she spent some time with her standing in line at the bar. Barb was moving as fast as she could, but it was a bit of a wait because the crowd was so large. I hope she raked it in that night. Anyway, Trixie and Madge chatted about the village, the bookshop, you name it. Just like the two of us talking to people in the line at Sainsbury's.

"You know how you have to lean over and squeeze in to give Barb your order when it's standing room only? Trixie and Madge found themselves behind Rick, and when he noticed them, he suggested they try the Cycling Cider and paid for their drinks."

"And?"

"You and I theorized he might have slipped something in Madge's drink, though I'm not sure why. But it was the perfect opportunity for him to do it. It would have been easy since he had his back to the two of them. When he pulled his wallet from his pocket, he could have grabbed a pill too. Not only that, it fits with the timing of Madge feeling ill."

I took a deep breath. "It's time I told you about Jilly. I still can't quite wrap my head around this spiked drink idea, even though we discussed it last night. It seemed far-fetched then, but Jilly did pretty much the same thing to Rick. You need to sit down. This is going to take a while."

"Okay. You've certainly piqued my interest."

"That's not the half of it. She was with Rick—next door—the night he died."

Wendy's jaw dropped. "And Gemma hasn't arrested her yet? Wait, does Gemma know?"

"No and no. And before you go there, I don't think Jilly did it. Don't ask me why. Hear me out, and then we can debate it."

My explanation of how Rick and Jilly wound up together at the cottage was quick. Jilly wanted to discuss the agenda. Rick put her off, but finally agreed.

"It's the rest of the night that sounds like something straight out of an old black and white movie. I can almost see Barbara Stanwyck and Gregory Peck as Jilly and Rick. Picture them drinking wine, Jilly on the couch, and Rick in the easy chair fiddling with the jigsaw puzzle. They're reflecting on people they knew ten years ago. It all sounds very convivial, doesn't it? Until it gets weird."

I described Jilly's reaction to the offer of whiskey and what she did to Rick's drink. "She almost nonchalantly commented that turnabout was fair play. Why? What does she know about him that we don't? And then, she suddenly gets the idea to crush sleeping pills in his glass?"

Wendy studied me, her chin in her hand. "Last night, we thought, 'gee, maybe Rick spiked Madge's drink.' I'm not sure how or why we got that idea, but I know I latched on to it. But now? What Jilly said, independent of us, makes me think there must be something to it."

"Yes, it's beyond strange. What would make her slip sleeping pills into his whiskey? I mean, who does that?"

"A woman who's had it done to her. That's all I can see. So, the lipstick and the belt buckle were all for show? Nothing happened between them because he passed out?"

"That's what she says. And she wrote the note to make him wonder."

We were both quiet for a moment, thinking our separate thoughts, until Wendy suddenly leaned forward. "You didn't mention the wine. The wine on his sweater. Did he spill it on himself?" She closed her eyes. "No, that doesn't make any sense. Did Jilly do it as part of her little scene?"

"She didn't mention it, and there's no reason she'd leave it out. If she didn't do it, or he didn't, then whoever killed him must have—but why?"

Wendy mimed throwing a glass of wine into someone's face. "There are only two reasons you throw a glass of water or wine or whatever into someone's face—to wake them up or because you're angry with them. Which was it?"

"If he was sound asleep, it must have been to wake him up—or maybe both. His killer was angry *and* wanted him awake. What a horrible thought."

"There could be a third reason. What if the killer did it to throw the police off his trail? Except I don't see how wine on Rick's face and sweater would do that."

Grabbing the notebook, I wrote as I talked. "Let's play it out. Rick gets dropped off at the cottage. Jilly arrives after that. They drink, she drugs him, and she does her thing with the lipstick and the note. She leaves, satisfied that she's taught Rick a lesson. The killer arrives and finds him unresponsive. Maybe he's come for a confrontation. He's angry and disappointed that he can't confront Rick, so he throws wine in his face to wake him up. Oh heck, it could go two different ways after that."

Wendy followed my train of thought. "One, Rick wakes up. The two men argue—it has to be a man—and in a fit of anger, the killer strangles Rick."

"Or two," I said, "the killer splashes wine in Rick's face, and when there's no response, he gets even angrier and strangles him." I shook my head. "Something's not working for me. Something I saw, but I can't quite grab on to."

"Would it help to—"

"Wait, I've got it. The wine. There were two bottles of wine when I arrived, both unopened. And Jilly specifically told me she washed her and Rick's glasses and corked the bottle of wine. If the killer threw wine in Rick's face, where's the other bottle? Hell's bells, I mentioned that to Gemma, but we didn't go anywhere with it. Two washed wine glasses, one dirty, two unopened bottles of wine, but no half-empty bottle. Where did it go? Gemma was sick and off her game, but what's my excuse?"

"Oh, let me see, Leta, maybe finding a dead body disconcerted you just a little? So, you missed an empty bottle. I bet the SOCOs found it. What's the big deal?"

"Probably nothing. It's just that Gemma and I thought—assumed is the better word—that three people drank whiskey and three people drank wine—the same three people, at least in my brain. Based on Jilly's story, she and Rick were two of the people who drank both whiskey and wine."

I blew out my lips. "Oh, for goodness' sake, I haven't told you what I learned from walking through the cottage with Lyle and Jonas. Lyle told us he drank whiskey with Rick when he picked him up to drive him to the pub, meaning he was the third whiskey drinker."

"I'm trying to follow you, Leta, but I don't see the problem."

"If the third person drank both wine and whiskey, and if there were only three people, then Lyle has to be the killer."

"Leta, I think there's a flaw in your logic. You and Gemma *assumed* there were three people, and they were the *same* three people. Maybe they weren't. For all we know, there was a party next door. Or Jilly and Lyle both lied to you. Why, I don't know."

If there's such a thing as confused silence, this is it. "Okay, setting aside the party idea, let me follow that thread. What you're saying is that maybe the same three people didn't do all the drinking. Lyle and Jilly both say they drank whiskey with Rick. That accounts for three whiskey tumblers. We know Rick and Jilly drank wine—that's two goblets. Lyle *may have* had a glass of wine *or* yet another person could have used the third wine goblet. So, it's possible four different people were at the cottage that night."

Wendy nodded slowly. "And that fourth person, not Lyle, could be the killer."

"Well, I certainly got us wrapped around the axle. Sorry."

"Don't be so hasty. All you did was ensure that we consider all the possibilities. It could still be only three people, which would put Lyle solidly in the frame. Do you think Jonas could help us sort this mess?"

Christie chose that moment to leap onto the couch. "If Wendy's not going to sit still, you need to make room in your lap."

"Not yet, princess, I'm busy taking notes."

Wendy grinned. "She's giving you the look, the same one Tigger gives us when he wants to curl up—usually in Mum's lap. Right now, I'm his only choice."

With a sassy meow, Christie replied to Wendy. "Too bad you're not as smart as Leta. You could understand Tigger if you were."

I whispered in Christie's ear. "Shush. That wasn't nice."

When Wendy patted her lap, Christie abandoned me. "Finally, an invitation." She landed in Wendy's lap with a thud.

"Oof! Guess she gave up on you." She stroked my happy-for-the-moment cat. "I say we let the cottage scenarios simmer, and we get back to the pub. Let me tell you what Jill had to say."

She paused when her phone rang. "What? FaceTime? Ellie does FaceTime?" The shocked look on her face was priceless.

"Ellie! I can't believe you're FaceTiming me. Is Mum with you?"

"Of course she is, luv."

Belle chimed in. "I'm right here. And I see you're at Leta's." She chuckled. "Oh! You've got Christie in your lap! Does she miss me?"

Looking her sweetest, Christie meowed, "Yes, Belle. When are you coming back?"

I heard Ellie and Belle oohing and aahing over Christie, and then Ellie got down to business. "Leta, we want to hear all about your trip with Dave, but first we want to turn in our assignment on RIBA."

"The short version is my trip was marvelous, ladies. I came home with a new dress for the holiday party, though I had to leave Dave behind. I'll tell you more later, so fire away. Cynthia told me a little about Lyle's design winning the RIBA award, but not much background on the organization."

When Wendy turned her phone to face me, I could see Ellie was beaming. "We've plenty of background, dear, but we'll try to give you only the highlights. Once I've typed up the notes, we'll send them along. The Royal Institute of British Architects didn't receive its royal charter until 1837, though it was founded in London in 1834. It's a terribly prestigious organization, and winning one of its awards is quite an honor. Holmes & White won the Regional Award for its reinvention of Ambleside Anglican Cathedral. The description reads, 'Now rescued, restored and sensitively modified for community use, Ambleside Anglican Cathedral retains its architectural integrity while providing modern facilities.' Surely, winning this award helped them land a spot in the Cotswolds Village Hall competition."

"Yes, Ellie. That's exactly what Cynthia said, but she didn't give me the history of RIBA."

Belle's face, framed by her soft white curls, appeared on the screen. "Oh, we've got more, Leta. RIBA also gives student awards, and we discovered that Lyle and his roommate jointly won the President's Medal for Students when they were at uni thirty years ago. It was also for a church. Only for the design, though, as student awards aren't for completed projects."

"Thanks, Mum. We ladies may have to take a road trip to see this Ambleside Anglican Cathedral. A grand excuse to travel, don't you think?"

A black paw tapped the phone. "Pfft. You only just got home, Leta. Can't you stay put for a while?"

I pictured Belle pointing at the phone as she spoke. "Oh, look at that, Ellie. Isn't Christie's paw adorable? Wendy, can you turn the phone so we can see her more clearly?"

Wendy aimed the screen at Christie, who sat in her Buddha pose with her paws together. "Mum, will I have to get you an iPhone next?"

"No, dear. My iPad is quite enough. I've been using it to keep up with our work with lost pets. Did you know that three dogs have been reunited with their owners while we've been in Tintagel?"

"Outstanding, Mum. Who knew you and Ellie would turn into such accomplished dog detectives? Much safer than investigating murders."

Ellie interjected. "Speaking of murder, we'd like an update. Leta, are you anxious about living next door to a murder scene? And why on earth isn't Dave there with you?"

Rolling my eyes, I gave her the short version of the Dave story. "Wendy's keeping me company, and we're making progress." I glanced at Wendy. "We'll send today's notes later."

Wendy nodded and promised to send them once they were typed. We knew that keeping the Cornwall arm of the LOLs in the loop was critical. The last thing we wanted was for them to cut their holiday short.

We finished with Wendy giving Dickens a belly rub for the benefit of Belle and Ellie and signed off. Dickens was happy, but Christie not so much, since she'd been dumped from Wendy's lap for the belly rub. Wendy and I debated shifting to wine before agreeing it was more prudent to have another cup of tea with half a muffin each.

"Leta, where were we when they called us?"

"We'd gone from saying it had to be Lyle to thinking there may have been a fourth person next door. Why don't you tell me what you got from Jenny and Jill."

"Right. Again, nothing definitive, just an observation from Jenny. One of the young designers offered Madge a seat at the other end of the bar after she got her cider. Who says chivalry is dead? He was standing there when Jenny walked up, and they talked as she waited for a drink. I used my line about Madge getting sick, yada, yada. It turns out they both noticed Madge looking a bit flushed, so much so that Jenny offered to take Madge to the loo, but Madge demurred."

"So, if someone spiked Madge's drink, it could have happened there at the end of the bar. And not when Rick handed her the cider." I shook my head. "I know Jilly mentioned roofies, but it still seems a bit of a stretch to me."

"The thing is when I wondered aloud what could have made Madge sick, Jenny had a sudden memory. She couldn't be positive, but she had the impression Madge took a pill. You know how some people toss their heads back to swallow? Jenny glimpsed that kind of motion."

"Are you saying that whatever made Madge sick could have been something she took herself?"

I thought about Trixie who couldn't take ibuprofen because it would trigger a severe asthma attack. *Could Madge have some similar issue? Some medicine she takes that interacts adversely with alcohol?*

When I said as much to Wendy, she pursed her lips. "I didn't get that far in my thinking, but you could be right. Didn't she tell you she wasn't a drinker? Maybe it never occurred to her not to mix alcohol with whatever pill she took."

I jotted more notes while Wendy pondered that idea. "Got it. Now what did Jill have to say?"

"Nothing about Madge. What she told me had to do with Lyle and Rick. She left earlier than Jenny and Trixie because she had to be at the inn at the crack of dawn. As she walked to her car, she heard voices and saw Lyle and Rick. She didn't know who they were, but when she described them, I knew right away. She said it sounded as though they were arguing—something about RIBA. Good thing Mum and Ellie came up with the background for us."

"Did Jill catch any specifics?"

With the customary scrunch of her lips, Wendy closed her eyes. I could almost see a sign above her head that read "Thinking in progress."

"Yes, the name Angus came up. Something about his work. And she heard one of them say, 'Don't pretend to understand architecture. You have no idea how concepts come to life.' That had to be Lyle, and he went on to say he had to call a client and couldn't talk about it right then. Seems like something you and I should pursue."

The unopened wine bottles next door sprang to mind. "RIBA! That reminds me, I found out that Holmes & White gave Madge a case of wine because of her work on the project that garnered the RIBA award—the redo of the church. And Bert got a humidor and cigars. The more I learn about the company, the more impressed I am."

"I have to agree with you. You don't often find that kind of camaraderie in the workplace. They all seem to genuinely get along. And before you correct me, I know that's a split infinitive."

"When your inner English teacher surfaces, it's a sure sign we need a break. My brain's on overload. How 'bout yours?"

"I'm with you. We can revisit all this when I come back to spend the night. Do you want to meet at the pub later? Let's say seven because I need to feed Tigger around six. Heaven forbid I mess with the routine Mum's got him on."

Dickens perked up at Wendy's comment. "Did someone mention food?"

Lifting her head, Christie meowed the answer. "You always think it's time for food, Dickens, but this time, you're right." She leaped from my lap and strolled into the kitchen.

"What just happened?" asked Wendy.

I joked about their reactions. "Oh, when Dickens hears food or pub, he goes on high alert. You said both, and he thinks going with me is a grand idea. We'll meet you there."

CHAPTER FIFTEEN

STUDYING MY FACE IN the mirror made me groan. My day was catching up with me. There was nothing for it but to start over, though I doubted the effort would suddenly make me look fresh and rested. I was applying concealer to the black circles beneath my eyes when my phone rang.

It was Stephie from the bank. "Good grief, Leta. I was already in shock over the news about Rick, and then your question about him spiking drinks threw me for a loop. I've never heard word one about him doing anything like that. Besides, if he's rekindled his relationship with Jilly, why would he need to spike anyone's drink?"

"Rekindled? You mean they were an item?"

"Of course they were. How did you miss that? And how awful for her now. They reconnect after all these years and then he dies. She must be devastated." She was, but maybe not for the reason Stephie thought.

I pondered Stephie's revelations as I applied blush and lipstick. Nothing short of an instant facelift was going to keep me from looking like death warmed over, but there wasn't any more I could do. *Jilly and Rick. Hadn't I told myself there was more to their relationship?*

Were they back together? Based on Jilly's story, I didn't think so. Did she want them to resume their romance? That seemed the more likely scenario. Was it her sense of being second choice that prompted her to drug him and leave the note?

And what was that remark about turnabout being fair play? Had he spiked her drink in the past? Or had she been someone else's victim?

And then it hit me. Was it the pot calling the kettle black? Maybe no one spiked Madge's drink, but if someone did, could it have been Jilly? Because Rick was paying too much attention to her? *Brilliant deduction, Leta. But where does it get you? What does it have to do with Rick's death?*

I put the kettle on and called Wendy to share my new ideas. "Thinking Jilly doctored Madge's drink felt like a bolt of lightning, but now it seems more like a small sparkler—not useful at all. What do you think?"

"It's food for thought. Rick and Jilly having a history gives me a new perspective and moves her higher up on the list of suspects. I know you don't think she belongs on the list, but think about it. If she wanted him back and thought he'd moved on, jealousy could have been the motive. What if she drugged him so she could strangle him?"

"But she had him back, at least for the night. If she wanted to rekindle the relationship, the opportunity was there. She could have spent the night. Something's off about her story, which begs the question of why she came to me at all?"

"Oh, that's easy, Leta. I mentioned the LOLs to her that first night at the pub. She came to you to find out what you knew and what the police thought. It could have been a calculated attempt to mislead you."

"Except, if she knew he was dead, why send me over there to find the body? Wait. I think I know. She didn't want to be the one to raise the alarm." I blew out my breath. "We could go on like this for hours."

"Look. Let's go with our original plan to enjoy dinner and see what surfaces. We'll touch base with Barb and leave it at that. Bring the notebook in case we have a sudden aha."

Armed with a cup of tea, I sat at my desk to work on the first column about the conference. This one would introduce the Village Hall Design Competition and some background on Holmes & White. Highlighting the RIBA award would be a nice touch.

I was adding notes about Lyle and Cynthia when something else hit me. *This is how it happens. Distract yourself and let ideas percolate in the background.* Who drove Rick back from the pub? It wasn't Jilly, and I now knew it wasn't Lyle. It might not be important, but it was a missing piece.

Jotting a note to ask around, I resumed typing my column. When my phone rang, I groaned. It was Jilly. *Not again.*

"Oh, thank goodness, Leta. I really, really need to talk to you. Can I come over now?"

"What's going on, Jilly? Can't you tell me over the phone?"

"No. I just spoke with Constable James."

"Just now? I thought he was meeting with you earlier."

"No. He was very kind about my wanting to do the bus tour with the group, so he met me at the village hall when the tour was over. Leta, speaking with him triggered a memory about the night Rick died."

"I guess that's good."

"No, it's not. Because it only hit me after he left, and I don't want to tell him until I get your take. Can I come over now?"

I looked at my watch. It was five, so I had plenty of time before I had to meet Wendy. "If you come now, yes."

Fifteen minutes later, Jilly knocked on the door. She accepted my offer of tea, and we made small talk while I poured tea and put a plate of cookies on the kitchen table. Dickens eyed the cookies but got the message when I shook my head.

Jilly cleared her throat and took a sip of tea. When she repeated the sequence without speaking, I assumed she was struggling to collect her thoughts.

"That night at the pub . . . I think I misunderstood something, and I think I made a horrible mistake. Did you see Madge playing darts?"

"Yes."

"Did you see her wince and grab her back the last time she threw? Bert spoke to her, and she waved him away and hobbled to the wall. She pressed her shoulders against the wall as though she were trying to stand up straight. Maybe she was trying to relieve the muscle spasm or whatever it was."

"No. I missed that." But Wendy saw it.

The sequence Jilly recalled was that Madge patted her pockets like she was searching for something but came up empty-handed. As she stood there grimacing, Rick approached her. "He had his back to me, but it looked like he handed her something, and she stuffed it in her pocket. She didn't exactly smile, but she looked, I don't know, relieved or something, and she pecked him on the cheek and put her lips to his ear."

Why didn't she tell me this earlier? Will I ever get the whole story of that night? "What did he hand her, Jilly?"

"I couldn't see, but I was convinced it had to be a pill. Not right then, but later when I helped Madge outside and she mumbled something about Rick and a pill. She wasn't really coherent, and I didn't realize until today that I'd leaped to the wrong conclusion."

"If it wasn't a pill, what was it?"

She rubbed her face. "It was a pill *case*, and it belonged to Madge."

Now I was completely lost. "It belonged to Madge? But Rick had it?"

"Oh hell. I know I'm not making sense. Let me try again. Yesterday, I saw her with a tiny blue enameled pill case. How was I to know she'd left her pain pills at Lyle's cottage when she had lunch with Rick? Even then, I didn't make the connection. How could I have been so wrong?"

"I'm not following you. How do you know she had lunch with Rick? Or that she takes pain pills and left them at Rick's? Did she tell you all that?"

"Yes, but not until today on the bus tour. We sat together, and she asked me to grab a bottle of water from George's cooler. When I did, she pulled out the little blue case and downed a pill. I had this awful feeling I'd been terribly wrong about what I saw that night, and I had to ask her. 'Is that what Rick gave you at the pub?'

"It took her a moment to reply, and then she told me about having lunch with Rick. That he'd thoughtfully opened a bottle of her favorite wine and given her some books. And how she took her midday pain pill and accidentally left her pill case on the table. Rick texted her when he found it and said he'd bring it to the pub. And that's what I saw. That's what he gave her."

"Jilly, help me understand. When you *assumed* Rick gave Madge a pill, what did you think was going on?"

Tears cascaded down her cheeks. "That he was giving her a pill for later. Like he gave me sometimes."

I would have been more shocked if Stephie hadn't told me that Jilly and Rick were a thing years ago. "Are you saying that you and Rick used drugs . . . when you dated? Like ecstasy or something?"

"Yes. I guess you could call it dating since he was separated. But mostly, we hooked up, and ecstasy was a special treat."

I am so naïve. Sometimes people take it unawares and sometimes on purpose. "So, you did ecstasy, and you thought that was what he was giving Madge? For later, meaning she was meeting him?"

"She smiled at him and pecked him on the cheek, so yes, that's what I thought. That they had a thing. I knew she'd done the design on his flat, and to hear him talk, they'd spent lots of time together. Just like we had back in the day."

"But, Jilly, Madge got sick. Does that happen?"

"To some people. You hear about bad reactions, but it never happened to me. It just made me happy, all aglow."

Processing what I'd just heard was like feeling my way through a forest filled with fog. "Jilly, I'm trying to take in what you've told me and connect it to what happened at the cottage." *Was it only this morning that she told me that story?*

"Based on that one interaction between Rick and Madge by the dartboard, you concluded that Rick planned to hook up with Madge later. Is that right?"

"Yes. No. It was more than that. He talked about her a lot, about how much talent she had, and they looked . . . they just looked like there was something going on between them. I could tell." *Good grief. Looked like?*

"Okay. I'm trying to understand, so go with me here. When Madge mumbled something about pills and Rick, you were convinced you were right, and you were furious with him. But when he invited you back to the cottage, you went. I thought it was because you wanted to ensure you were prepared for the meeting, but there was more to it, wasn't there? Were you hoping to rekindle your relationship?"

Jilly wouldn't look at me. Instead, she nodded as she stared into her cup of tea.

"Then why on earth did you drug him? Why didn't you spend the night?"

Her mug shattered on the stone floor as she spat the words. "Because I felt like second choice. Because I thought it was Madge he wanted to be with, not me. I *wanted* to spend the night. But something about the large drink and the words 'in the bed'— I felt like I'd fallen into the spider's web. It suddenly hit me that I didn't want what we had before. I wanted more. And I wasn't going to get it.

"That's why I drugged him. That's why I left the note. But I didn't mean for him to die!"

It was time to get to the bottom of this. "Jilly, you misread the scene between Madge and Rick, but I don't see it changing anything. Your thinking the worst of him didn't kill him."

"I feel like it did. Like if I hadn't put the sleeping pills in his drink, he wouldn't have died."

"Jilly, someone visited Lyle's cottage and strangled Rick. Nothing you did caused that." I saw no need to point out that Rick might have fought off his attacker if he hadn't been comatose. She felt bad enough already.

She sniffled. "Do you think I need to tell any of this to Constable James? I'd rather not, but I wasn't sure whether it would make a difference to his investigation or not. What do you think?"

Is this why she keeps unburdening herself to me? Am I her guide to how to handle the police?

Her next words answered my unspoken questions. "I'm sorry to keep coming to you, Leta, but I didn't know where else to turn. You've always been so approachable—so easy to talk to."

Both a blessing and a curse. "It's okay, Jilly. I honestly don't think it will change anything for Constable James, but you never know. It's possible that what you *thought* you saw between Madge and Rick could be a piece of the puzzle that will help him. I'll mention it to him. If he wants to hear it directly from you, I'll let you know."

CHAPTER SIXTEEN

POURING A GLASS OF wine was a priority after my Jilly conversation. I could only hope she wouldn't wake me in the morning with something else. It wasn't that I disliked Jilly. It was that I didn't relish my new role as her confidant.

I was more convinced than ever that she had nothing to do with Rick's death. Yes, she was angry with him, but drugging a man in order to strangle him was a cold, calculated murder. Jilly was way too scattered for that. I didn't think she had it in her.

It didn't take long to jot down this latest disclosure in my notebook. Certainly, I captured it all more clearly than she'd explained it. I sipped and mused, all the while rubbing Dickens's belly with my foot.

Had Jilly misread Rick's overtures to her, as well as his interaction with Madge? Maybe I was a sucker for happily-ever-after stories, but I wanted to think he liked what he saw in the more mature Jilly. Maybe he wanted to give the relationship a chance on a different footing. Rick may have been a player, but he wasn't stupid, nor did I think he would risk hurting her for a one-night stand.

Taking a photo of my bullet points, I texted it to Jonas first and then forwarded it to Wendy with a note saying I'd give her the color commentary at the Ploughman.

That idea bit the dust when Dickens and I walked into the pub. Wendy was already seated at a large round table with Madge, Cynthia, Lyle, and Bert. She motioned to a glass of white wine in front of the empty seat beside her. "They insisted we join them and wouldn't take no for an answer."

Dickens was thrilled and squirmed beneath the table, where he promptly got a handout from Bert. Madge was describing the day's tour. "George is an outstanding guide. He regaled us with local history and gave us ample time to explore the various village halls we visited. How he keeps all that information in his head, I'm not sure."

The pub was much less crowded tonight, and this was a more subdued conversation than the one on Monday night. I wondered aloud where the rest of the Holmes & White group was.

Bert took a sip of his beer. "They're off to dinner in Stow. Madge and I begged off, but we promised to join the brain trust at the village hall later for a spot of work." *Brain Trust. Interesting label.* I was more and more convinced Bert was one of the resistant old hands at Holmes & White.

Raising her glass, Madge complimented me on the morning's Myers-Briggs session. "We four already knew our personality types, but we all agreed you added new insights. Trust me, the fact everyone focused on you instead of their phones was a real accomplishment on your part. And they couldn't stop talking about the exercise with Dickens and Christie." She nudged Lyle. "May have to get an office cat and dog."

"If that's what it takes to keep those creative juices flowing, I'm all for it. How 'bout it, Leta? Can we adopt Dickens?"

Dickens stuck his head in my lap. "I'm not going anywhere, am I, Leta?"

"Not on your life. He's staying with me."

We ordered dinner and did a good job of avoiding the elephant in the room. Hearing about the many projects Holmes & White had done in London and other locales was enlightening. They ran the gamut from small residential designs to large commercial buildings, though nothing above four to five stories.

Wendy brought her napkin to her mouth. "Lyle, tell me more about the RIBA Award the company recently won."

"Bert, Madge, why don't you describe it. I may have come up with the original design, but you two modified it and brought it to life." He glanced at Wendy. "Like any project for an older structure, you start with a grand design, but you adjust as you encounter unknowns. As is often the case, the evolution in the design resulted in an outstanding final product."

I knew Wendy had introduced the topic to gather data, but it was fascinating to hear how the design of the church took shape. Bert and Madge were clearly enthused about the project. When I mentioned the article I'd seen at his cottage, Lyle told us that the idea dated back to his days at uni.

"Our professor chose random, sometimes abandoned, homes or churches for us to work on, and my roommate Angus drew a church in Ambleside as his assignment. Our challenge was to create designs that would make them usable while keeping the integrity of the original structure.

"Why Angus struggled so has always been a mystery to me. My assignment went quite smoothly, but I thought the Gothic Revival style of the church was much more intriguing, and I tried to help him every chance I got. I never could have imagined that all these years later, the church would want to remodel in almost exactly the way Angus and I envisioned. It was an assignment, nothing more.

"Truth be told, that's where my passion for Gothic Revival started. Sir Gilbert Scott, who designed the church in the 1800s, is well known for building the terraced block adjoining Westminster Abbey, and he was also an early recipient of RIBA's Royal Gold Medal."

Cynthia rolled her eyes. "If we could make enough money working only on mid-nineteenth century churches, that's all Lyle would take on. Thank goodness my passion is residential design. You never want to have all your eggs in one basket."

As the conversation shifted to the company's work for the Village Hall Competition, my role came up again. "Heaven help me," I said. "I'm waking up brain cells that have been in a deep sleep for years."

Lyle winked at me. "Rumor has it that you and Wendy have other talents you put to good use. Tell them about the Canine Caper."

Incredulous comments greeted Wendy's tale of what I always referred to as the modern-day version of *The Incredible Journey*. By the end, there were smiles all around.

She did a good job of brushing aside references to detective work. "Thankfully, Leta and I spend most of our time doing yoga, attending book club meetings, and shopping. We're quite talented at shopping."

It was Cynthia who gave the game away. "Oh, it's more than that. These two are the founding members of the Little Old Ladies' Detective Agency. Toby keeps me up to date about your work. First, it was figuring out who killed everyone's favorite housekeeper. I was still commuting to London when that happened. And I understand you later worked out who tampered with the Earl's car and caused the accident that killed him. Then there was the case in Tintagel. It's a long list."

Wendy was blushing, and I knew I was too. We tried to keep our detective work under wraps, and, instead, Cynthia had shone a spotlight on it.

When Lyle spoke up, I did my best to look unconcerned. "Ladies, are you looking into Rick's death? Or is that one a bit too close to home, so to speak?"

Once again, Wendy did her best to make light of our involvement. "Leta's understandably shaken by a murder next door, especially with Dave still away. That's why I stayed with her last night. I don't know which is worse—thinking someone Rick knew killed him or that a random killer is on the loose."

Tears formed in Madge's eyes. "I didn't know him very well, but I enjoyed working on his flat. He was open to suggestions and always appreciative of my ideas." *Boy, did Jilly misread that relationship.*

She glanced at Cynthia. "Did I tell you we had lunch Monday, and he gave me the most marvelous book about the Cotswolds as a thank-you gift? He even had my favorite wine on hand."

I caught a look of surprise on Bert's face and when Madge nudged him, I knew she'd seen it too. "What is it, Bert?"

"I'm just surprised about the book because he told me he had a bottle of wine for you. Very thoughtful of him to come up with a book, too."

An image of Rick at Toby's popped into my mind. "He had a gift-wrapped book from the Book Nook when I saw him Monday. I bet Beatrix helped him find it." And now I knew why Madge's favorite wine was at the cottage.

Lyle leaned toward Madge. "Thanks, Madge, for that reminder of Rick's thoughtfulness. All the police want to talk about is who disliked him, not what a good man he was. Being interviewed by them is unsettling, to say the least."

Pushing back his chair, Bert agreed. "Amen to that. I barely knew the man, but they kept asking about enemies and wanted every detail of our conversation on the drive from the train station to your cottage. I couldn't see how my explanation about Cotswolds golden stone and Rick's raving about the splendid job Madge did on his flat had any bearing on the case." He looked at Lyle. "How about a game of darts?"

When Wendy glanced at me, I knew exactly what was coming. "Mind if I join you? I enjoyed the game the other night." *Divide and conquer.*

Dickens wiggled his way out from beneath the table. "Look, Leta. It's Jenny." Turning around, I saw Jenny and Freddie coming in through the door. She waved as her date went to the bar.

Madge winked at Cynthia. "Told you Freddie took a liking to her. She's a nice change from his usual diva-type."

The two took their drinks to an intimate table in the corner, where Freddie pulled out a chair for Jenny. He spoke into her ear and walked over to us. "Hello ladies. Hi Dickens. I see I'm not the only one who blew off dinner in Stow."

Promising to be at the work session later, he said Jenny was helping with an idea for planters flanking bicycle racks outside the village hall. "She's absolutely amazing with flowers. You should see the photos of her work."

Madge rolled her eyes. "Flowers, is it?"

When he blushed, we all knew Madge was on the right track. To his credit, Freddie regained his composure soon enough. "Alright, we may have a few other things to discuss. You know I grew up in Cheltenham, right? We have loads in common."

It was nice to see two young people connect and get to know each other in person. If I were to believe what I read, it was all about dating apps these days. I thought about my chance encounter with Dave at the Olde Mill Inn and felt the smile spread across my face.

Cynthia watched me. "Smiling at young love, Leta?"

"More like slightly older love. Some might label it senior, but I think Dave and I have a few years before we fall into that category." That comment led to a conversation about the ups and downs of dating later in life, though I didn't have much to contribute. I'd had plenty of dating woes in my twenties before I married Henry and hadn't considered dating after he died. Dave and I just happened.

Madge listened intently as I described how I'd met Dave and wound up in a long-distance relationship. "Leta, you haven't stopped smiling the whole time. It's like a fairy tale."

That made me laugh. "Well, Prince Charming and Sleeping Beauty have their ups and downs, but yes, for the most part it's heavenly. And what about you, Madge? Is there a man in your life?"

"No, not exactly." *How do you* not exactly *have a man in your life?*

Bracing herself on the table, she winced as she pushed her chair back. When I gave her an inquiring look, she frowned. "It flared up again on the bus ride. My back. I see a visit to the doctor in my future."

As I watched Madge limp to the bathroom, Cynthia shook her head. "She's always had back issues, but since her mugging a year ago, it's gotten worse. She recovered from the broken wrist, but this has lingered."

"Guess I'm fortunate I only suffer with bad knees, and that comes and goes. When Bert helped me get Madge back to the inn the other night, he told me about the mugging. Was this in broad daylight or at night?"

"Early evening. Bert and Madge worked late, and he walked her to the tube, as he often did. When they stopped to get take-away, her phone rang, she stepped outside to take the call, and wham. A boy on a bicycle flew by and grabbed her purse.

"The way Madge tells the story, she was on the ground before she knew it, and Bert had the mugger up against the wall. It took ages for the ambulance to come, but Bert stayed with her the whole time. Took her home from A&E, got her settled, even brought her groceries the next day."

I thought of the many police procedurals I watched on TV. "It's like something you see on those shows set in London, with Bert in the role of hero."

That got a chuckle. "If you want to see him blush, tell him that. He hates to talk about it because we made such a big deal out of it at the office. We even hung a banner over his desk."

Rubbing my foot on Dickens's belly, I recalled the last time I got in a scrape. It was Dave who got me out, but Dickens had played the role of hero plenty of times.

Cynthia sipped her drink. "I've always thought of him as chivalrous, and since Madge's mugging, he's very protective of all the women in the office. It's so easy to think it will never happen to you, but he keeps reminding us to be careful. It's funny. He can be a tad overprotective, but he means well."

"How things change. Do you remember when men opened doors for women and gave up their seats on the bus or train? And then we went through a period when women resented that gesture and saw it as belittling. Perhaps I was never enlightened enough. I always appreciated men doing that. When it went to the other extreme, I was the one standing up for older women who clearly needed a seat when not a single man did. How do women see it these days?"

"Well, I for one, appreciate being looked out for. And the younger girls don't seem to take Bert's behavior amiss. They jokingly call him dad. I understand why he worries about us. It was bad enough that he witnessed Madge being mugged, but several years before that, his daughter was also the victim of an assault."

She explained his middle child was out with friends and woke up in bed with a man she hardly knew. She had no memory of how she got there, but her injuries told the story of a sexual assault. When she made it back home, her flat mates made her go to A&E, but they couldn't persuade her to press charges. "Isn't that what we women do, Leta? Convince ourselves that we're to blame, that we somehow give the wrong signal? Even with all the revelations from the Me-Too movement, we still have a long way to go."

"What a horrific experience for his daughter and for him. How does a parent deal with that? I guess being overprotective is a natural outcome."

When Madge rejoined us, we'd moved on to the more pleasant topic of an idea I had for Dave's he-shed. Given her look of pain, I wasn't surprised when she told us she was going to the inn. "I'm sorry to miss the group work, but I know they'll understand. They're always very solicitous of my spells. A pain pill, an ice bag, and a good night's rest will hopefully do the trick."

When she stood with her purse in her hand, Bert was Johnny-on-the-spot. "You don't think you're walking, do you?"

"Oh, the walk will help to stretch it out a bit. Get on with your game." They had a gentle back and forth before she finally agreed he could drive her to the inn.

It was like a set change in a play. Bert and Madge left. I headed to the restroom. Dickens stayed with Cynthia. Wendy and Lyle approached the table, and Wendy veered off to follow me. She was champing at the bit to tell me what had transpired during the dart game, but we didn't want to be overheard. "Listen," I whispered, "I want to get the CD covers from the car so I can show them to Cynthia. Meet me out there."

My idea for Dave's he-shed was to frame a collage of CD covers. We had a few favorite artists in common—Billy Joel, the Beatles, Van Morrison, and Gordon Lightfoot—so I'd pulled them from my collection and put them in a bag. I'd intended to show Cynthia the next day, but now was as good a time as any.

Lyle was nowhere to be seen when I stopped by the table to tell Cynthia I'd be right back and told Dickens to stay. Outside, I leaned against the car to wait for Wendy. After tonight's conversations, a few puzzle pieces had slotted into place, but large gaps still existed.

A car drove up, and two men got out. Another car door slammed. I thought I heard someone strike a match before a small glow appeared. A whiff of what I thought was pipe tobacco drifted my way.

Growing impatient, I opened the car door again and grabbed my notebook. Scrawling notes in the light from the dim lamp in the parking lot wasn't ideal, but I wanted to capture the gist of what I'd heard. RIBA, Rick's gift, the assault on Bert's daughter, overprotective, back pain. . .

"What are you doing, Leta?" called Wendy.

"I'm making notes. Where have you been?"

She lowered her voice to a stage whisper when she got to the car. "Sorry. I got waylaid by Jenny and Freddie. Such a cute couple. Shoot! It's cold out here. Let's save what I learned for when we get to your place. It's nothing earth-shaking. I picked up more info about Rick and Lyle at uni and what Jill overheard out here."

"And I just found out more about both Bert and Madge. I think we've had a productive evening. Let's call it a night once Cynthia looks at the CD covers, and then head home for hot cocoa in our jammies."

When I finished writing, I tossed the notebook in the back seat and grabbed the bag of CDs. "That will do for now. I think it's time we organized all this on those large flip-chart sticky notes." That was our go-to method for making sense of our discoveries.

Inside, Wendy tackled Barb while Cynthia and I discussed my CD idea. I watched in awe as Cynthia arranged and rearranged them on the table. "That's it," she said. "The simple way is the best. We'll lay them out one on top of the other and mat them in one frame. The perfect wall is the narrow one between the window and the door."

Looking past me, Cynthia gave a half smile. "I'm glad Bert's back. I'd forgotten how much he and Lyle like darts. They'll soon need reminding that we're due at the village hall."

She turned her attention back to the CD covers and snapped photos of them. "You can take them with you. I'll order copies and have this done in no time."

As she waved to Bert and Lyle and gave them a time out motion, I heard my Billy Joel ringtone. Dave's first words were, "Promise me we're never moving. I thought packing up my place was a bear, but Mom is making me crazy."

"Bad day, is it?" His tiny New York City apartment held mostly books, and that was bad enough. I couldn't imagine packing up sixty years of stuff. I'd downsized twice—once right after Henry died when I moved to a condo, and then again to move to Astonbury. It wasn't easy, but it had to be less stressful than what Dave and his mom were going through.

"Yes, but I *do have* some good news. I forgot to tell you I found your ring. It somehow wound up buried in my Dopp kit."

How it had ended up there was a mystery to me, but I was thankful he'd found it. "Listen, sweetheart, I'm at the Ploughman. Let me call you when I climb in bed, okay?"

Cynthia winked at me as Bert and Lyle joined us. "I take it that was Prince Charming."

"Goodness, if he ever hears you refer to him that way, I'll never hear the end of it." Bert and Lyle had amused expressions on their faces as Cynthia explained who Dave was.

"Is he still on schedule to be home by Sunday, Leta?"

"Yes. Fingers crossed that nothing comes up to delay him."

It was perfect timing when my phone chirped with a text from Wendy. "Ready?"

After pressing the thumbs-up icon, I pushed back my chair. "Time for me to head home. If I don't get some sleep, you may have to prop me up tomorrow."

CHAPTER SEVENTEEN

At home, Dickens wandered the garden while I tended to the fire in the sitting room. Christie let me know right away that my priorities were out of whack. "What are you doing? The fire can wait." I was striking a match when she dug her claws into my calf. "I'm hungry."

"What's it been, two hours since I fed you? And you have dry food in your feeder, too. Next time, I'm choosing a sweet cat."

As I fed the princess, I had an idea. Changing to a warmer jacket and adding a hat, I joined Dickens outside. "What do you think? Should we start a fire in the firepit?" It had been Dave's idea to add it in the spring.

For Dickens, it was no question. He thrived on cold weather, though this hardly qualified as cold in his book. I gathered kindling and several smaller logs and lit the fire. As usual, Dickens heard the car before I did, and he jogged to the driveway to greet Wendy.

I followed him to the side of the cottage. "Hey there, I thought we'd sit out back for a bit and enjoy our cocoa."

As we filled our mugs and grabbed several blankets, Christie twined herself around my legs. "Do you want to join us,

Christie? We have blankets." Her answer was to stand by the door.

Wendy went ahead of me with the blankets and mugs, while I retrieved the notebook from the front seat of my car. Soon, we were comfortably ensconced in our Adirondack chairs. Christie kneaded the blanket into a snug nest on my lap, and Dickens stretched out on the patio close to the fire. Wrapping her hands around her mug, Wendy suggested I start with the details of Jilly's latest revelations.

Notebook in hand, I gave her the highlights. "It was painful to hear how badly she'd misread the Madge situation. If not for that, she and Rick might have started anew. She would have stayed the night, and Rick might still be alive. Of course, depending on who killed him, if she stayed, she could have become collateral damage.

"I texted Jilly's latest tale to Jonas but haven't had any acknowledgement. I wonder if he's busy pursuing a new lead."

My scribbled notes from the pub were nearly indecipherable, but my memory of the discussion served me well. I described Bert's hero role in Madge's mugging and how he looked out for the women at Holmes & White. "It reminds me of a long-term assignment I had in San Francisco when I was in my forties. There were five of us who flew out there every week, and I was the only woman. The guys took turns looking out for me, and one of them always walked me back to the hotel after dinner before catching up with the others at whichever bar they had picked out."

Moving Christie from my lap, I put another log on the fire. "I wonder. Should we add Bert to our suspect list? Our nearly nonexistent suspect list? Maybe we need to investigate him a bit more."

"Probably not. Our biggest problem is that we can add suspects all day long, but we've yet to come up with a motive. Other than thwarted love for Jilly, which seems less and less plausible. Nothing for Lyle, much less for Bert."

Holding my hand out for her mug, I suggested a refill. Christie and Dickens followed me, no doubt expecting a treat. The sight of Watson lolling on the doormat made me smile. Only after I'd given all three of them treats could I refill our cocoa mugs.

For whatever reason, Dickens and Watson were sniffing around my garage. They must have given Christie a signal because she joined them as they rolled in the grass on the other side of the driveway. "Stay close," I called.

I never used to worry about Dickens taking off, but since he'd disappeared before Christmas last year, I was more cautious. Unlike Watson, Christie was a homebody, so I didn't worry about her.

I added wood to the firepit. "At the risk of being ridiculous, let's revisit Bert as a suspect. Cynthia said he was a tad overprotective. Is it possible that Bert observed the same interaction Jilly did—between Madge and Rick? Might he have gone to the cottage to confront Rick? Except being overprotective is a far cry from killing someone."

"True. And when you think about Bert's daughter, it's easy to see why he'd be overprotective. It's not necessarily a bad thing. We'll have to explore it more. Now, about Lyle. I bet you didn't know that conversations over darts can be more than small talk. Lyle was happy to tell me about uni and RIBA and how one thing led to another."

The discussion centered on the friendship among Lyle, Rick, and Angus. That long ago summer, the trio had been inseparable. Angus and Lyle saw it as their responsibility to ensure that Rick visited not only historic sights during his sojourn in

London, but also the best pubs. The lighter class load allowed more free time, and the trip to the Cotswolds cottage was a bonus.

As compared to the rest of the year, the summer semester seemed almost carefree to Lyle, and at first Angus felt the same way. As the summer progressed, though, Angus became more and more anxious, especially about the Ambleside project.

"I could hear the remorse in Lyle's voice, Leta. He felt he should have known Angus was approaching the breaking point. Instead, he attributed the moodiness and lack of focus to their late nights out carousing with Rick. What he didn't know was that Angus was bipolar, and he'd stopped taking his meds. Lyle's remedy was to spend more and more time helping Angus with his project. He didn't begrudge the time because he enjoyed immersing himself in the Gothic Revival style."

"Lyle told us Angus committed suicide. Was it that summer?"

"Yes, shortly after Rick went home. Do you remember Mum and Ellie telling us about the RIBA award Lyle and his room-mate won as students?"

"Yes. Was it the church project? Did they manage to finish it before Angus committed suicide?"

"No. Lyle completed it after Angus's death and turned it in to their professor. Sometime the following semester, his professor encouraged him to submit it for the RIBA student award as a joint project. And it won."

What an emotional roller coaster. "An idyllic summer that ended in tragedy. Followed by a prestigious award."

"Ah, but there's more. He gave the award to Angus's parents, and still stays in touch with them. Over thirty years later."

I couldn't see Wendy's face in the dark, but I knew she had to be smiling. I certainly was. "It could be time to strike his name from the suspect list. What do you think?"

"When you hear this next bit, you'll know why I'm leaning that way too. When I heard about Rick and Lyle arguing Monday night and that the word RIBA was part of the conversation, I was sure he should be on top of the list. Boy, was I ever wrong."

"How so?"

She moved to the fire and warmed her hands. "He volunteered that the last words he had with Rick were angry ones, and he'd have to live with that. The man takes an awful lot on his shoulders. He felt guilty about not detecting the signs of suicide in Angus. And now he feels bad that he and Rick argued and never had the chance to resolve their disagreement."

"What was there to resolve? What happened?"

Grabbing the poker, Wendy stoked the fire and then resumed warming her hands. "You told me about the newspaper article with the scribbled note—'roommate'. Seeing Ambleside in the article reminded Rick of Angus's project and what a wreck he'd been over it. He got it in his head that Lyle had taken credit for Angus's work. He brought it up over drinks at the cottage, but let it go. In the car park later, he flat-out accused Lyle of stealing Angus's idea. Some friend, right? It tells me something about Rick, but I'm not sure what."

"Oh, for goodness' sake. If Belle and Ellie could find the original student award, why couldn't Rick? Or did he even try to find out before accosting Lyle? He was a friend and a client, and Rick was staying in his cottage. If nothing else, the timing was awful. If he thought Lyle had done something dishonorable, why bring it up the night before an important meeting? Forget Lyle being a friend. You don't do that to a client."

The scenario brought Stephie's email to mind. "Remember the list of bullet points? I think it speaks to a pattern of erratic behavior. Rick was a no-show for an important meeting. Another time, his partner had to fill in for him at the last minute at an all-day session. Amidst all that, he was rumored to have a drinking problem. And now, months later, he accosts a client. What if the drinking problem was more than a rumor? What if he became accusatory because he had too much to drink?"

Wendy paced and nodded. "Maybe he went to rehab. Maybe he dried out and got his act together. At least enough to start fresh. But he couldn't escape his demons. He resumed drinking, and if Monday night was any indication, he drank a lot. It wouldn't be the first time someone's career tanked because of alcohol or drugs. That scenario is all too believable. And sad."

More and more data. Less and less clarity. "Aargh. Where does this take us? As awful as it to think Rick had a drinking problem, it doesn't get us any closer to identifying his killer."

"You're right, but let me play devil's advocate for a moment. That whole argument in the car park scenario? We only have Lyle's word for what happened. We can't ask Rick. What if Lyle's calm retelling of the argument was to throw us off the track? What if the accusation led Lyle to kill Rick?"

Why am I so reluctant to see Lyle as the killer? "Wow! That would be awfully calculated on Lyle's part."

If we followed Wendy's line of thinking, we could also say that we only had Lyle's word for how the joint RIBA submission and winning the student award came about. "Wendy, I hate to say it, but we could take it a step further. What if Lyle's rewritten history? What if Rick's accusation was true, and Lyle *did steal* Angus's work? Rick raising a stink about it now could ruin Lyle's career. People would say he stole the original design and used it years later for the Ambleside project. The latest award is fruit of the poisonous tree. I know I sound like a lawyer, don't I?"

With her hands on her hips, Wendy attempted to mimic Yul Brynner. "It's a puzzlement! That's what it is."

At least she'd made me chuckle. "Seriously. *The King and I*?"

Wendy burst into laughter when Dickens and Christie came running. "Look, I've attracted an audience. I see fame in my future."

On that note, we grabbed our mugs and blankets and headed inside. We'd done a good day's work but were no closer to solving the case and no closer to a motive. It was even possible we didn't yet have the killer on our list of suspects.

CHAPTER EIGHTEEN

My waking thought was to text Jonas. Grabbing my phone, I typed a message. *Did you see my text about Jilly's latest? I have more info on Bert and Lyle. Talk today? After lunch?*

As an afterthought, I typed, *How's Gemma?* What surprised me as I typed was that I'd heard nothing about DCI Burton sticking his nose into the investigation. Perhaps the death of a Yank didn't seem high profile enough to him. Okay, that was mean, but the man had never been anything but rude to me.

Jonas called immediately. "Leta, I'm on my way to see Gemma in Cheltenham. They admitted her to hospital last night."

"What? For the flu?"

"Yes. You wouldn't think so for someone as healthy as she is, but her mum says she was having trouble breathing and complained of pressure in her chest. Of course, you know Gemma went kicking and screaming, but it was a good thing. They're giving her fluids and some meds. That's all I know."

"And DCI Burton is about to take over the investigation, right?"

"No. I've dodged that bullet for now. Nearly everyone at the Coleford station is out with the flu, and he's got his hands full there. Awful for them, but a lucky break for me. I'm telling all my mates at the Stow police station to get the flu jab." It wasn't a funny topic, but I always smiled at the term jab instead of shot.

"Fingers crossed, you don't get it. Oh, something else before I forget. Did the SOCOs find an empty wine bottle anywhere? I had this sudden flash that there wasn't one on the counter next door."

"It was in the rubbish bin, Leta. Nothing earth-shattering there."

I could scratch that from the list of unknowns. "Thanks, it just seemed like a loose end. Now, did you see my text?"

"Yes, and I'm finding it hard to believe that her memories of Monday night keep surfacing in fragments. Thank goodness she's using you as her sounding board. Let me know when the next news flash comes in."

"Unless it's something that breaks the case wide open, I hope there's not one. The good and bad news is that I'm helping her with the meeting today, so if she has any late-breaking news, I'll be the first to know. What did you think of her latest memory?"

"That she got hold of the wrong end of the stick with this pill thing. Is she that dim?"

"Hard to say. Do you have time to hear what Wendy and I learned at dinner last night? Think of it as the type of detail we'll add for the characters in the Constable James mysteries, except this is about the players at Holmes & White."

He laughed. "I can see it now, another book in the series—*The Villain at the Village Hall*."

I got through the dinner table discussion about Madge's mugging, Bert's heroics, and the sad tale about his daughter. Jonas took the mugging in stride but expressed disgust at the roofie episode. "That kind of thing is all too prevalent these days. More in the big cities than in the Cotswolds, but I'm sure it happens here, too. Those pills are too easy to get hold of. It's bad enough that kids take them for kicks, but slipping them to a girl to take advantage of her—well, let's not go there."

Hearing him turn off the motor, I hurried to get in my question. "Jonas, before you go, does the idea that Bert's a bit overprotective give you any qualms about him? Is it something you should dig into?"

"I doubt it, Leta. Gemma interviewed him before she took to her bed, and there's nothing in her notes. I plan to get her thoughts on whether this load of tosh from Jilly changes anything, and I guess I can ask about Bert, too. I can't see that any of it matters to the case."

That meant we were back to square one, unless he was about to pull a rabbit from his hat. "Trust me, Jonas, I feel the same way about Jilly's revelations, but I thought it best to tell you."

"I know. You can never tell what will be valuable in something like this. You say you're helping her today. At the village hall?"

"There and in the woods and along the river. It's the day for team-building activities outdoors. Hope the rain holds off. I don't relish the idea of being soaking wet and cold. Can we meet afterward so I can tell you the rest of what I learned last night? Preferably in front of a fireplace? It may or may not be helpful, but as you say, you never know."

"You haven't led me astray yet, Leta, but mum's the word where Gemma's concerned, right?"

"Ha! Do you think I'm going to let on to her that I'm being a 'Nosey Parker'? Not on your life."

Leaving Christie curled up on the bed and Wendy dressing for yoga, Dickens and I walked to the village hall. There was a fine mist in the air. Hopefully, it wouldn't turn to a drizzle, but I'd tucked a small umbrella in my backpack just in case. Only once in my years of leadership training had I been forced to cut short the outdoor activities. On that day in North Carolina, we had snow and near-freezing temperatures. I wasn't willing to risk hypothermia for me or the participants, though a few of them wanted to keep going. There was no danger of it being that bad today.

The sun was just rising, and the design group wasn't due at the hall for another hour, but I knew Toby had already set up refreshments when I caught a welcome whiff of coffee.

Jilly looked relieved to see me. "Right on time. I've got everything set up. Do you want a cuppa to take along as we look it all over?"

"Yes. And let me put your mind at ease about talking to the police. Constable James feels no need to interview you again. Now, let's focus on today."

Armed with coffee, we walked to the woods bordering the village green. All the activities had a building component, and they would increase in difficulty as the morning progressed. First up was the egg drop. Jilly had suspended an egg high in a tree and provided an odd assortment of materials to use in lowering the egg to the ground without breaking it. It sounded simple, but of course, it wasn't. I'd seen many a smashed egg in my day.

Dickens was in heaven as we traipsed through the woods and along the riverbank to visit the locations Jilly had so carefully chosen. He snuffled in the fallen leaves and intermittently jogged ahead of us to bark at who knows what.

The task of dragging four by fours, cinder blocks, and other heavy materials through the woods had fallen to Jilly. All I had to do was observe and debrief the Holmes & White employees after each activity. The morning would culminate with the most challenging, that of building a bridge across the river.

"What do you think, Leta? Good spot for bridge building?"

"I think so. It's the narrowest spot and close enough to the stone bridge to allow them to send a scout to the other side to scope it out. I'm always amazed at the creativity of these groups. Given that we've got a bunch of architects today, I expect the structure to be a masterpiece."

Jilly laughed. "Unless they can't agree on the design and waste time bickering."

"True—the too many cooks in the kitchen syndrome. They'll have to decide quickly on a Head Chef, a Sous Chef, and more. I wonder whether we'll see the dynamic Cynthia described, where the veteran staff diss the input of the newer ones, and vice versa. Either way, I've forgotten how much fun this can be."

I thought about Bert and wondered how his overprotective tendencies would play out today. Based on what I'd observed so far, I expected Bert wouldn't be able to camouflage it in the heat of the moment. Time would tell.

When we returned to the village hall, Lucy was there munching on a muffin. "Hi, Leta. I'm here to take pictures to accompany your columns for the *Astonbury Aha!* It's a pretty dismal day, but I should be able to get a few decent shots." She held out her hand to Jilly. "I'm Lucy, and you must be Jilly. Cynthia mentioned you'd be in charge of this part."

The two chatted as I poured myself another cup of coffee and tried to resist the muffins. Bert, Freddie, and Madge arrived next.

I knew not to expect Lyle and Cynthia. The two planned to spend the day ensconced in the conservatory at the inn, catching up on work. They'd been in constant touch with their office assistant, and he'd scheduled several telephone meetings for them.

I was surprised to see Madge walking without a limp. "Madge, you look quite chipper today. Looks like the ice pack and a good night's rest did the trick."

"It sure did. I was afraid I'd have to stay on the sidelines today, but as long as I'm careful, I should be okay. By the way, Cynthia tells me you're a regular at the local book club meeting, and she plans to go tonight. Depending on how the day goes, I may join her."

Bert brought her a cup of coffee. "Better you than me."

Looking at me, Madge shrugged her shoulders. "He'll watch documentaries and mysteries on the telly, but read a book? No way."

I put my hand to my mouth and mimed whispering. "Each to his own, Madge, but I can tell you that Gavin, your innkeeper, never misses one. He's a big reader. And Beatrix chose the September selection to fit with this meeting."

Jilly called the group to order and shared a high-level view of the day—five outdoor activities, a debrief after each one, and finally back to the hall for lunch and a wrap up.

My job was to explain the point of spending half a day on all this. "While Jilly will give you the objectives for the activities, you'll need your brain cells for more than figuring out how to achieve them. Lyle and Cynthia didn't engage Jilly for fun and games. This is an opportunity for you to focus on working as a team. That's why we call it team *building*.

"Michael Jordan said, 'Talent wins games, but teamwork and intelligence win championships.' How does that apply to Holmes & White as a company today?"

Freddie mentioned Madge and Bert as talented individuals who brought home the RIBA award. "They had to be good at give and take."

"Exactly," said Madge. "We've all had wins on our smaller assignments, but large-scale projects require that several of us come together. We can't accomplish those alone."

"Now, think about what you learned from the puzzle activity and the Myers-Briggs assessment, and consider how you can use those takeaways today.

"I'll ask you three questions each time: What happened? So what? Now what? In other words, what did you *observe* as you attempted to reach the goal? What do those observations tell you? What will you do differently in the next activity? What will you do more of or less of? Our overarching goal for today and this week is to set you on the path to becoming a powerhouse team."

Bert cleared his throat. "How many of you have noticed the framed quote on Lyle's desk?" There were some nods and a few puzzled looks. "It's easy to see it every day without really seeing it. It's from Steve Jobs. He said, 'Great things in business are never done by one person; they're done by a team of people.' Lyle's a huge fan of Steve Jobs."

Nodding at me, Jilly stood. "That's perfect, Bert. Now, let's get this show on the road."

With Jilly and Dickens, I watched as the group tackled the egg drop. Their first challenge was to traverse a twenty-foot clearing to reach the tree. It was tricky because they had to do it without letting their feet touch the ground. Eventually, they figured out they could construct skis using the ropes and four by fours and use them to transport the team in small groups.

Lucy snapped pictures and listened to the back-and-forth. The first group to reach the egg took inventory of the materials at the base of tree and began brainstorming how to tackle the problem. The next group to arrive questioned all the original ideas. Valuable time was wasted bringing the latecomers up to speed.

With time running out, they went with Freddie's idea—the one he'd been repeating since the get-go. It was déjà vu for me when the egg hit the ground with a splat. I gave them a moment to indulge in some lighthearted recriminations—a few more serious than others—and then led the debrief.

Their takeaways were all I could have asked for. They recognized they adopted Freddie's idea because he was the loudest and most energized. Several folks admitted they were so busy thinking on their own, they didn't listen to the brainstorming. Still others said they should have invited input from their less vocal teammates.

They were more successful with the second activity, though they nearly didn't make it in time. Jilly called a fifteen-minute break after my debrief and pointed out the cooler of snacks and bottled water. What I wanted was more coffee, so I jogged back to the village hall. As I came through the door with a large cup, I saw Bert coming my way, unwrapping a cigar. He stuck the wrapper in his pocket and the cigar in his mouth.

He grimaced. "A bit nippy out here, isn't it?"

"There's plenty of coffee inside. Are you looking for a light?"

Pulling the cigar from his mouth, he shook his head. "No, I'm saving it for later, but it helps me think."

The faint aroma of the cigar brought back a childhood memory. I could see my favorite uncle, who liked to smoke a cigar after Sunday dinners. He used to let me open the box and choose one for him.

"Something on your mind, Bert? If it's about design, I'm of no use, but if it's about teamwork, I might be able to help."

He didn't answer right away. "How do you think we're doing?"

No one had ever asked me that before. "Not for me to say, Bert. What do you think?"

"I'd say a few of the lads could stand to listen to the ladies. They seem to pay attention to Madge, but not the younger women."

His observation was spot-on. "Are you going to point that out?"

"We'll see." He stuck the cigar back in his mouth and went inside.

The next two activities went more smoothly. Both times, the group selected a leader, and that helped to ensure all voices were heard. It wasn't until we got to the bridge building challenge that one of the women called Bert on the carpet when he said that the men should do the heavy lifting. "Oi. I go to the gym, you know! I can carry a cinder block as well as you can." He looked suitably abashed.

Some might see his comment as sexist, but I took it as an example of his overprotective tendency. Because Cynthia had mentioned that some senior members of the team were resistant to change, I'd been paying close attention to Bert. Perhaps that behavior was more obvious on the job, but I'd seen no sign of it today.

This was the last activity, and the goal was to build a bridge that would allow at least one person to traverse the river without getting wet. For this challenge, Jilly had provided a notepad and pencil in addition to the building materials. I was happy to see the group tap Madge as the leader. She immediately sent Freddie and one of the female designers across the stone bridge to determine a way to anchor the other end of the bridge.

Their design wasn't pretty, but it worked. It was a flimsy structure, with a rope suspended above it, attached to a tree on either side of the river. The girl who'd chastised Bert got the nod as the one to venture across, owing in no small part to how tiny she was. As she approached the middle of the bridge, the planks dipped dangerously low. She grabbed the rope and swung her legs just beyond the low part to avoid getting wet. Cheers went up when Freddie grabbed her and pulled her to the riverbank.

Lucy was having a ball. "Leta, I've got some great photos. Even got them all cheering, and a few of them leaping in the air."

Though it hadn't rained, the sky was growing darker. We sat on tarps provided by Jilly and did our final debrief. Luck was with us. The raindrops held off until Jilly dismissed us for lunch.

Toby had laid out a spread for us in the meeting room, and I gave the group time to eat before starting work on their takeaways to present to Cynthia and Lyle.

Looking around for Dickens, I spied him making the rounds of the lunch crowd. No surprise there.

Jilly toasted me with a cup of tea. "Great day, Leta. You haven't lost your touch. Now, I'm going to gather the equipment to put in my van before the rain gets any worse. I should be back by the time Lyle and Cynthia get here, but if not, give me a ring, please."

As she pulled up her hood, I saw Bert go after her with Freddie in tow. She'd be glad for the help. I texted Cynthia to let her know she and Lyle should plan to arrive by one. She responded that Lyle was out jogging, but she'd round him up.

Freddie was the first one back. He told me that the rain had stopped, and that he and Bert had quickly packed up the materials from the first three activities. Jilly insisted she could handle the others.

"Super. Grab some lunch. Is Bert right behind you?"

"Nope. When we finished, he went to find Jilly. Said it would go quicker with the two of them. Like we learned today, right? It's all about teamwork."

By now, I'd already given the team an extra ten minutes for lunch, so I kept an eye out for Bert. He was an integral part of the team, and I didn't want him to miss working on the presentation. "Dickens, I give up. Looks like we'll have to conduct a search and rescue operation."

I whispered in Madge's ear. "Would you mind leading them in pulling together the presentation? I'm going to track down Bert and Jilly."

Lucy offered to accompany me, and I suggested we head to where they'd built the bridge. "They're probably there by now, so let's head to the riverbank. Can't imagine what's taking so long."

The makeshift bridge was dismantled and the materials neatly stacked on the bank, but there was no sign of our two stragglers. I glanced up and down the river, to no avail, and called their names, thinking they might be on the other side. No response.

"Lucy, maybe we missed them, and they went to bring the van around. Let's split up. You walk toward the bridge over the High Street, and Dickens and I will go in the other direction."

"Sure thing, Leta. Do you have your phone? I'll ring you if I find them."

I walked all the way back to the previous site, but it was clean and tidy. "Dickens, they must be at the stone bridge." Retracing my footsteps, I looked back and forth between the riverbank and the woods bordering the path. Nothing.

"Dickens barked, "Leta, on the other side. It's a hand."

"Wait, Dickens," I called as he dove into the water. I didn't see a hand, but I recognized Jilly's red anorak. I jogged toward the bridge, trying simultaneously to keep Dickens in sight and holler for Lucy. The only way for me to get to the other side was the long way around on foot.

When the phone rang, I dug it out of my pocket. "Lucy, did you find Bert?"

"Yes, how did you know? I think . . . I think he was attacked. Did you find Jilly? I hope she's not hurt, too."

Telling her I was on my way, I dialed 999. "Need an ambulance. Two people injured on the riverbank near the High Street bridge. Yes, Astonbury."

I jogged to Lucy and Bert. She had his head in her lap, and his eyes were fluttering. "You stay with him. Jilly's on the other side, and I've got to get her out of the water."

The trees were thicker on the opposite side of the river, and I struggled to make my way to Jilly. I prayed that she and Dickens were both okay.

Jilly lay face down, her lower body in the water and her arms outstretched on the riverbank, one hand clutching a root. Dickens had positioned his body beneath Jilly's chin, and both their heads were barely above water. *How am I going to do this?*

Sitting on the riverbank, I put my arms beneath Jilly's shoulders and lifted and pulled for what seemed an eternity. Dickens squirmed from beneath her and clamped his mouth on a root. Finally, I maneuvered Jilly far enough onto the bank so she wouldn't slide backward.

Once I confirmed she had a pulse, I grasped Dickens's collar and pulled until he got purchase on the riverbank and could scramble up. "Dickens, are you okay? Are you hurt?"

He was panting and struggling to stand. I had my answer when he got to his feet and shook muddy water all over me. "Oh, thank goodness. That's my boy."

Licking my face, he barked, "I got her, Leta. Is she okay?"

"She's breathing, but just barely. And I hope she's not hypothermic."

As I stripped off my jacket and tucked it over Jilly, I heard sirens in the distance and prayed they'd be in time.

CHAPTER NINETEEN

From my position on the riverbank, I could see the flashing lights as the ambulance turned on to the bridge. "Jilly, stay with me." Her lips were blue and her breathing labored. I tucked my scarf around her neck and tried to work my gloves onto her stiff fingers.

When the EMTS arrived with a thermal blanket and a stretcher, they moved me out of the way. Only then did I turn to observe the bridge. A second ambulance pulled up, and I caught sight of Jonas and Lucy scrambling down to the other side of the river. Behind me, I heard the EMTs conferring. "Pulse good, blood pressure dropping. Ready? Lift."

I watched as they transported Jilly toward the bridge. It was Dickens who got me moving with a nudge to the back of my legs. I wasn't as nimble as the EMTs, who made it look easy to carry a stretcher through the brambles and brush.

As I approached the site where the makeshift bridge had been anchored, I noticed that the rope was still attached to the tree. It hung loosely, as it was no longer tied to a tree on the other side. Looking down, I saw a small shovel lying in the mud beside a cinder block dug into the riverbank. Another cinder block lay a few feet away, as though a giant had tossed it aside. Jilly must have been digging them up. There were plenty of footprints, which made sense given that two EMTS and I had been this way.

Did she go in the water here? "Dickens, I need to get my brain in gear. If Lucy hadn't found Bert injured, I might have thought Jilly lost her footing while trying to dig the cinder block out. But there's zero chance that she and Bert both accidentally fell."

Dickens was sniffing the mud around the shovel. "Look, Leta."

With his snout covered in mud, I couldn't make out the item in his mouth. *Is it a stick?* It wasn't until he dropped it at my feet that I realized what he'd found and where I'd seen it before. I took a picture of it and wondered how long it had been there. Was it dropped during the last activity of the day or later?

I made my way to the bridge and stood looking down. Bert was sitting up on the riverbank as the EMTs ministered to him. Though I couldn't hear him, his hand motions seemed argumentative, and Lucy throwing her hands in the air confirmed my assumption.

When she joined me, she was shaking her head. "Stupid git. He doesn't want to go to A&E. Says it's just a bump on the head. The EMTs cleaned and bandaged the back of his head and a scrape on his forehead, and they've told him he could have a concussion."

"Did he say what happened?"

"Not to me, but I caught some of his answer to Jonas. Says he was hit on the back of the head and must have fallen flat on his face. The mud smears and the scrape on his forehead jibe with that. He's lucky he didn't break his nose if he fell that hard. Who could have done this? Attack two people?"

Hearing my name, I turned toward the end of the bridge. It was Lyle running from the center of the village. "Leta, what's going on? Who's hurt?" He came to a halt and leaned over, panting with his hands on his thighs.

The ambulance carrying Jilly departed as I answered him. "It's Jilly and Bert. Jilly's in bad shape, but Bert seems to be faring a bit better." I studied Lyle. "Did you run here from the inn?"

"Yes, when Cynthia rang me, I thought it wouldn't hurt to get in a bit more of a run. She passed me in the car on her way." He pulled off his ball cap. "I thought the outdoor piece was over for the day. What happened?"

We told him the story as we watched Jonas, Bert, and the EMTs walk toward the second ambulance. Escorted by the EMTs, Bert was unsteady on his feet, but at least he was upright.

When Lyle jogged over to him, Bert groaned. "Tell 'em I'm fine, will you? Just a few scrapes. Don't need a hospital."

"Don't be ridiculous, Bert. If there's a chance you have a concussion, you need to have your injuries seen to."

Bert lost the argument. "Okay already, but tell Madge I'm alright. She doesn't need to worry."

Only Jonas's car remained on the bridge. "Lyle, can you instruct your team not to leave until I get to the hall? And Lucy, now that we've gotten Bert off to the hospital, let me ask you a few more questions about finding him, and then you'll be free to go." He glanced at me. "Leta, I'll get to you in a moment. I'll need you to show me where you found Jilly."

Gemma would have taken Lucy to the side, so I couldn't eavesdrop on the conversation, but not Jonas. "Now, Lucy, tell me what you saw in detail. How was Bert lying? Was he conscious? Everything."

Closing her eyes, Lucy took a moment to respond. I imagined her rewinding her camera to see the images. "He was lying on his back with his feet toward the river. If I had to guess, I'd say he'd fallen on his face and rolled himself over. That's because there was mud smeared on his nose and his chin. He was conscious because his eyes were open and he was mumbling, though I couldn't understand a word."

Her mouth dropped open. "Was I wrong to move him, to prop his head in my lap?"

He shook his head. "No, Lucy. You were only trying to make him comfortable. What else do you remember?"

"His shoes were caked in mud, and his hands were muddy. And, like I said, he had mud on his face. And he had a scrape on his forehead."

Jonas was jotting things in his notebook. "Did he speak to you at all, beyond mumbling?"

"Eventually. I asked him several times what had happened, and it must have finally penetrated. He said he didn't know—that he thought someone had hit him in the head because it hurt like the devil."

Beyond his being argumentative with the EMTs, she didn't have anything else to add. Now it was my turn.

"Leta, while we wait for the SOCOs to arrive, let's see where you found Jilly."

I felt like I was babbling as we made our way to the far bank, but Jonas listened patiently. I outlined the day's activities, ending with Bert and Freddie helping Jilly. He didn't object when I paused by the cinder blocks. "I can't be sure, Jonas, but I think she must have gone in the water here. There was no need for her to walk downstream where I found her. The path is clear from here to the High Street bridge, but beyond here, it's full of nettles." I held up my red hands. "Stinging nettles, apparently."

"Baking soda and water, Leta. That's what my mum always used on us to stop the stinging." He studied the area. "Not likely to pick up any useful footprints here. It's a muddy mess. What is all this?"

"Bridge building materials. Part of an exercise." I pointed out the cinder blocks, the rope, and finally, the object Dickens had retrieved.

Jonas pulled his ever-present notebook from his pocket. "Bert wasn't clear about where the attack took place. He's probably concussed. My immediate thought was that the attacker struck in two different places. Maybe Jilly first. Then he sees Bert across the river. Maybe Bert could even have yelled at him. So, whoever it was had to take out Bert too."

"The question is who was the primary target—Jilly or Bert? Was one of them in the wrong place at the wrong time? Or was the attacker after them both?"

"You're good, Leta. Whoever did this has to be the person who killed Rick Bradley."

"Because . . . they're eliminating possible witnesses—not to the murder but to—"

"Something that would point to the murderer!"

I concurred. "Exactly! Bert or Jilly or the two of them must know something that would point the finger at the real killer. And it could be a clue they don't even realize they have."

Blowing out my breath, I looked at Jonas. "Did that make any sense at all?"

"Unfortunately, it did. I've missed something critical, and I need to go back through all my notes. Bloody hell, Leta, could it be time to wallpaper your sitting room in notes?"

Thinking things through with Jonas was so much more rewarding than attempting to do it with Gemma. She only wanted my help up to a limit, and I never knew where that limit would be. One minute, I was a hugely observant and intuitive resource, and the next I was a Nosey Parker.

"Jonas, you know I have a notebook, too, right? We need to go through both. And we need to gather the LOLs and get to work before someone else gets hurt."

That settled, we made our way to where I'd found Jilly. That spot was also a muddy mess.

"You spotted her from the across the river, Leta?"

"Dickens did. Before I could stop him, he barked and dove into the water. I doubt I would have seen her if not for him."

He chuckled. "Once again, the hero dog saves the day. Tell me, will Constable James have a dog for a sidekick in the books you're writing? I'd like that."

Dickens preened and barked. "Say yes, Leta, please."

When Jonas's phone rang with a call from the SOCOs saying they were on the bridge, he gave them directions to where we thought the attack on Jilly had taken place. They were already at work when we joined them.

Watching them maneuver to take photos and bag items from the mud, I realized how narrow the path was. Whoever attacked Bert and Jilly had to have come down the path from the stone bridge. There was no way they could have come from the road above the river. The trees and brush were too thick.

Another idea floated through my head. "Jonas, do you think Bert and Jilly could have both been attacked on this side of the river? There are so many possible scenarios. It would really help if Bert could tell us what happened. Maybe Jilly went in the water, and Bert was knocked out cold right here. And when he came to, he made his way across the bridge to the other side. . ." *But why leave Bert alive?*

"So, instead of two separate attacks, it all happened here? Could be."

This time, the thought that popped into my head was an unwelcome one. When I closed my eyes and shook my head, Jonas cocked his head. "What?"

"Lyle's the last man standing."

He knew exactly what I meant. "You think Lyle—"

"He was on our list of suspects for Rick's murder. I didn't want him to be. It was Jilly and Lyle and even briefly, Bert. No plausible motive for any of them, but now I don't know."

"Well, maybe it will all come clear after I talk to Bert and, hopefully, Jilly. And I'll run things by Gemma, too. I'll let you know of any developments. Right now, I need to speak with the Holmes & White team."

Taking my time, I walked back to the bridge. Once again, I was a combination of hyped up and exhausted. When I was back on the bridge, I looked downstream as I called Wendy. I gave her the short version of what had just transpired, and the welcome news that Jonas wanted our help.

"Did I hear you right? He wants to use our Maisie Dobbs wallpaper method? Then you and I need to put our heads together before that."

"I doubt he knows about Maisie Dobbs, but yes. Too bad we don't have Belle and Ellie, too. This case is getting to be bigger than a breadbox."

"Speak of the devil—or devils. Mum and Ellie are back home. Mum's taking a nap now. She claims they came home early because they didn't want to miss the book club meeting tonight, but I'm not falling for that. They drove as far as Bristol and spent last night there to break up the journey."

"Whatever the reason, I'm happy to have their brainpower. I'll text you when I get home. Maybe the four of us can talk before we go to the Book Nook."

Dickens and I took the direct route across the bridge to the village hall but paused by the churchyard on the opposite side of the street. Not wanting to interrupt Jonas's questioning of the team, I waited until I saw him drive off.

I had to give Lyle and Cynthia credit. They'd put their team to work on the design proposal after Lyle arrived with the news about Jilly and Bert. That was already the plan for the afternoon, so the group set aside the teamwork presentation for later and shifted gears. The interior and exterior design teams had moved to two smaller rooms, leaving only Lyle, Cynthia, and Lucy in the large open area.

As the three approached me, Lucy called my name and motioned to the coffee. I gave her a thumbs-up and plopped into a seat. Both Dickens and I were a muddy mess, and which one of us was in more need of a bath was debatable.

Handing me a cup, Lucy hovered. "Do you want lunch? There are sandwiches left."

"I may go to Toby's for a mug of steaming hot soup, or I may go straight to Posh Pets to drop Dickens off. I don't think I can face giving him a bath."

Lyle and Cynthia must have sensed I needed to collect my thoughts, as they didn't do much more than greet me. As I sat with my hands wrapped around my coffee cup, Cynthia broke the ice. "Leta, have you gotten any word from the hospital?"

"No, nothing, but Constable James will keep me posted. How did the team take it?"

Lyle sat with his elbows on his knees, his hands grasped between them. "It was a blow, but they're taking it in stride. I didn't use the word attacked, just said that Bert and Jilly were injured and headed to the hospital. Made it sound like more of a precaution than anything life-threatening. And that's the truth, at least for Bert."

Cynthia shuddered. "Lyle told me as soon as he walked in, so we pulled Madge aside to tell her. As good of friends as she and Bert are, I thought she needed to know the circumstances. Lyle apprised everyone of the change of plans, and they got to work." She leaned toward me. "Did the EMTs give you any indication about Jilly? Do they . . . do they think she's going to make it?"

It was my turn to shudder. Pulling Jilly from the river brought back memories of my near drowning in the same river. The good news for Jilly was that it was September, not a freezing cold December like it was when I went in. "They didn't tell me, Cynthia. I can only hope for the best."

Lucy and I were the only ones free to go, and she offered to accompany me to the Tearoom. "I thought I could show you today's photos while you eat. Maybe take your mind off what happened after that." She gave me a sideways glance. "Knowing you, though, you don't want to be distracted because you're trying to figure it out."

"Yes, and no, Lucy. Yes, I'd like to see the photos. And no, the distraction won't bother me. Sometimes, distraction triggers breakthrough ideas."

When we arrived at the Tearoom, I looked in dismay at my jeans. "I'm almost embarrassed to go in looking like this. Guess Toby's seen mud before, though."

Today's soup special was tomato basil, one of my favorites. No one observing us as we quietly looked at photos would have guessed what kind of morning we'd had.

Toby brought us a plate of freshly baked snickerdoodles, and we invited him to join us. Dickens was especially happy at that turn of events, as he'd had nary a crumb from me.

When I nodded at Toby, he gave Dickens a pinch of cookie. "Thanks for letting me bring him in, Toby. I know he's a muddy mess."

"Unless he consorts with a skunk, he's always welcome. So, are you two done with the design team for the day?"

Holding up her camera, Lucy smiled. "Just looking over the photos I got today. Some great shots here, if I do say so myself. Care to see?"

"Sure." Toby listened attentively as Lucy scrolled and explained the activities. "I've not been to anything like this before, so I got a big kick out of it."

Toby interrupted the scrolling. "Hold on. Can you scroll back a few, Lucy? There."

He pointed to a shot of Madge and Bert conferring with their heads together. "I've seen them in the group at the village hall all week, but it just hit me who they are. I mean, I don't know their names, but they were in here together Saturday morning. Nice couple. This shot of just the two of them brought it back."

Saturday morning. Before the event kicked off Monday night. "Couple?"

"Oh yes, and they sat over there by the window. I asked if they were visiting for the weekend, and they said they were staying in Bourton. They liked their room and especially enjoyed the model village. I had no idea there were over thirty model villages in England. They've already visited one in the Lake District and another in Cornwall."

The look on my face must have worried him. "Leta, what is it? You look, I don't know, like you've seen a ghost."

"Not a ghost, but something I wish I'd seen sooner." *A missing piece to the puzzle.*

CHAPTER TWENTY

WHEN A CALL CAME in from Jonas, I stepped outside to take it. "Do you have good news?"

"Yes and no. Jilly's prognosis is good, but I was only able to speak with her briefly. She remembers Bert and Freddie offering to help her and vaguely recalls Bert starting to dismantle the bridge on the side of the river nearest the village hall. She's blank beyond that. Could come back to her later.

"Bert is a complete pain. Ever since they said he wasn't concussed, he hasn't stopped grousing about wanting to leave. As for what he remembers, no joy there. He's pretty sure he was where Jilly says she saw him last, but he's still foggy on that."

"Are they keeping Jilly? Can she have visitors?"

"She'll be here for a day or two at a minimum. On that point, Leta, I'd rather not publicize that she's doing well. Keep that under your hat for now."

"Jonas, what are you thinking?"

"It's not a fully formed idea, but we could give out that she's in serious condition and may not recover."

I was pretty sure where he was going. "Uh-huh. And if she does, her memory may not return, right? Are you planning to set a trap?"

"Like I said, Leta, I haven't worked it out yet. Just got to Gemma's room. More later. Bye."

His abrupt goodbye was no surprise. The less Gemma knew about my involvement in the investigation, the better. *Will he tell her about his latest idea?*

Attaching Dickens's leash, I started toward home. "Dickens, you'll have to ride in the luggage area for the trip to Posh Pets. No way you're getting in the back seat." My London taxi had a large open space that served as a trunk. He could comfortably sit there with his head resting on the seat back.

I knew what was coming when he put the brakes on. "Leta, I don't need a bath. I'm fine." We debated that point as we walked up the High Street toward Schoolhouse Lane. Anyone observing us would think I was a typical pet parent talking to her dog.

As we reached the corner, Freddie called to me from the village green. "Leta, Bert called Madge to say he's doing well but won't be rejoining us today. He's trying to check himself out. Do you have an update on Jilly?"

"Her prognosis isn't as positive as Bert's." In line with Jonas's request, I described her condition as touch and go and mentioned hypothermia. We stood quietly while he digested the information, and I absentmindedly tossed a stick for Dickens.

Freddie and I took turns throwing until Dickens lay at our feet panting. "When he won't give up the stick, Freddie, that's the sign he's tuckered out."

Seeing him with the stick protruding from both sides of his mouth reminded me of his discovery on the riverbank. "By the way, Freddie, I think Bert asked about his cigar. It could be it's one of the special ones Lyle and Cynthia gave him. Last time I saw him with it, it was right here on the green." I saw no harm in telling a tiny fib.

"Oh, right. He's a fiend for those things. He pulled it out of his pocket as soon as we started dismantling the team-building structures. Was chewing on it when he went in search of Jilly. Always makes me think of a character in an old black-and-white mystery movie. Funny, I don't think I've ever seen him actually smoke one."

Good old Freddie. He'd given me a critical bit of information. I still didn't know who the primary target was, but I knew Bert and Jilly had been together when the attack occurred.

I said goodbye to Freddie and motioned to Dickens, but before I could leave, Freddie blurted, "Leta, should we be worried? About our safety? One person's dead, and two have been attacked. Do the police have any idea what's going on?"

How much should I say? Is this an opportunity to put Jonas's plan into motion? "Freddie, based on what I've heard, the police suspect the attacks on Bert and Jilly have something to do with Rick Bradley's murder. Unless you were there that night, I doubt you have anything to worry about."

Freddie gasped and threw up his hands. "Well, I *was* there, but he was alive and well when I left him."

"Left him where, Freddie?"

"At the cottage. I drove him there from the pub. He didn't have a car."

Another question answered. Car number one was Freddie's. Car number two was Jilly's. Who arrived next? "Did you tell that to the police, Freddie?"

"Yes, to DI Taylor. She asked me how inebriated Rick was and what we discussed. I didn't think he'd had too much to drink. He wasn't slurring his words or anything."

"And your conversation?"

"There wasn't time for much. It was a short drive. He asked about my background and said Madge and Cynthia had been very complimentary about my work. And he was concerned about Madge taking ill, and hoped it wasn't serious. Said she'd done a bang-up job on his flat. I felt like he was looking forward to working with us. That's all."

Two texts arrived as I was unlocking my door. Wendy's alerted me she and the senior members of the LOLs would arrive at two, and Lucy's message was an offer to take Dickens for his bath. "I've already checked with Posh Pets, and they can take both Buttercup and Dickens." We agreed I'd put him in the garden so she could grab him and go.

I had barely enough time to take a quick shower and put the kettle on before the gang pulled up in the driveway. Belle and Ellie took turns regaling me with the highlights of their visit to Cornwall. Their return trip to Knight's Rest was like going home.

As we took our usual places in the sitting room, Christie leaped into Belle's lap and meowed, "Did you see Archie?" I thought of the hefty grey cat as Christie's long-distance boyfriend. They'd been inseparable at the yoga retreat we attended last year, and I'd teased her about two-timing Watson.

Belle chuckled as she stroked Christie. "Where's Dickens? We saw his friend Merlin romping in the lavender fields and Archie stretched out atop the reception desk. Of course, it wasn't the same without Dickens and Christie there, too." She tsk-tsked when I explained Lucy had taken Dickens for a bath.

Marker in hand, Wendy called us to order. "Enough, ladies. We'll never make it to the Book Nook tonight if we don't get to work. Leta, I've brought Mum and Ellie up to speed with the goings-on this week. Until this morning's attack, we'd batted around three pretty unlikely suspects—Jilly, Lyle, and, as a late addition, Bert. I move we strike Jilly and Bert from the list, which I know you won't like, Leta."

With a grimace, I agreed. "You're right. I don't, but I had to admit to Jonas that moving Lyle to the top of the list made sense—if only because we don't have a better option."

Wendy wrote *#1 Lyle* on the flip chart. "Since you've been closer to the action than any of us, have you learned anything that makes that assumption seem wrong?"

During my call immediately after finding Jilly and Bert, I'd shared only the headlines, not the details. I tried to organize my thoughts into bullet points. "If only I had conclusions rather than random details, but here goes. It's logical to say, 'tag, he's it.' He had the means and opportunity to kill Rick, though we've gone back and forth about whether Rick's accusation about the RIBA award could be a motive."

Though Jonas didn't know about the RIBA award, he'd easily seen Lyle as responsible for the attack on Jilly and Bert—if only because he was the only one left. "If we see him as the murderer, then it would follow that he attacked Jilly because she may have seen something. Heck, it's a wild idea, but he could have strangled Rick while Jilly was upstairs planting the note. But someone else could have done that, too. Like Bert."

With a flourish, Ellie pulled her laser pointer from her purse and circled the name Lyle with the red light. "I understand Lyle wasn't at the team-building event this morning. Why do you say he had opportunity?"

"Because he was out running and could easily have run to the river and waited for a moment when Jilly was alone. All it took was a strong shove to send her tumbling into the river. For that matter, I could have done it. If she was digging the cinder block from the riverbank, anyone could have snuck up on her."

Closing my eyes, I reflected on the additional details that had surfaced. "The puzzling piece is that I think Bert was helping Jilly when she went in the water. Even though Lucy found him on the opposite side of the river where it wasn't muddy, his shoes were coated in mud. That and the fact that Dickens found a cigar in the mud tells me Bert must have been there."

Three puzzled faces looked at me. *Right. Clear as mud, as the saying goes.* "Let me see if I can explain that more clearly. Bert wasn't on the far side of the river during the bridge building activity. The only time he could have dropped his cigar in that location was if he helped to dismantle the bridge. But he told Jonas he never went over there."

Belle turned toward the paper on the wall. "So, you're saying that Lyle attacked Bert and Jilly in the same location? I'm trying to envision the riverbank. Did he come through the trees and take them unawares?" She shook her head. "I wasn't there, but that doesn't seem likely."

"It's not, Belle. The trees are too thick there for anyone to make their way down from the road. Whether it was Lyle or someone else, it doesn't make sense to go after two people at one time. Not if you want to go undetected." I squinted. "What if someone planted the cigar to make us think it was Bert who attacked Jilly? Oh heck, I'm confusing myself."

Ellie fiddled with her laser pointer. "Was Lyle muddy? If he attacked Jilly, wouldn't his running shoes be caked in mud?"

Everyone's attention turned to Christie when she stood in Belle's lap, gave a little butt wiggle, and pounced on the red dot on the floor.

Moving the laser light around the chairs and to the rug in front of the fireplace, Ellie exclaimed at Christie's antics. "I've missed this. I haven't missed murder and mayhem, but this? We should play laser tag more often." She cleared her throat. "On a serious note, what puzzles me is why Lyle would attack Jilly and Bert but do such a poor job of it. If you're intent on eliminating witnesses, you do it. You don't mess about." *That's what Jonas said.*

Wendy scrunched her mouth to one side. "If not for Dickens, Jilly would have been a goner, but Bert? His injuries weren't life-threatening. Maybe the attacker was interrupted. Oh, for goodness' sake. Did Lyle see Lucy coming and leave the job unfinished? You said he ran onto the bridge, Leta. Maybe he came from somewhere close like the churchyard and not from the inn."

Going back and forth with that idea, we imagined a sequence of events. Lyle pushed Jilly in the river and planted a cigar to misdirect the police. He glimpsed Bert on the other side and panicked. It was possible that Bert didn't see Lyle or what he'd done. Lyle jogged to where Bert was, bashed him in the head, and was about to deliver the fatal blow when he spied Lucy. That was the problem. Our imaginings were possible, but none were conclusive.

Are we so focused on the scene of the second crime that we've lost sight of the first? What are we missing? "Wendy, write Bert on a flip-chart page, please. I think we need to capture what we know about him."

She frowned but wrote *#2 Bert* on a page. Beneath that she added senior architect, fatherly caretaker, and Ambleside church/RIBA award.

"There's something else. Toby thinks Bert and Madge are a couple."

Wendy's mouth formed an O and then a smile. "A couple? How sweet."

After explaining Toby had seen them Saturday and learned they were staying in Bourton, I posed a question. "Does this information make us look at anything differently?"

"It explains a few things," said Wendy. "We know he stopped Madge's mugger, and we saw that as the reason he was so protective of her. Knowing they're a couple also explains why he was Johnny-on-the-spot when she was sick Monday night and why he insisted on driving her to the inn last night. Gee, was it just last night?"

She rolled her eyes. "You know he would drive me crazy, right? I wouldn't be able to stand all that hovering. Reminds me of 'He-Who-Must-Not-Be-Named', he who was worried I couldn't climb to the top of Tintagel." She was referring to DCI Burton. Thank goodness she'd come to her senses about him early on.

Nodding at her daughter, Belle smiled. "I think we all much prefer Rhys, dear. And that reminds me, we had dinner with Jake on our trip. Such a nice young man."

We'd met DCI Jake Nancarrow in Tintagel during our yoga retreat, and he and Gemma were now an item. His easygoing nature smoothed her sharp edges, and I often wished he lived closer—for all our sakes.

I stretched my arms over my head. "We're getting nowhere fast. We've landed on Lyle because he's the last man standing—as I reluctantly said to Jonas. What if it's someone we haven't considered at all?"

Sipping her tea, Belle stared at the two pages taped to the wall. "The names I've heard from you girls are Bert, Lyle, Cynthia, Madge, Freddie, and Jilly. Unless it's a complete stranger or someone Rick Bradley met here in Astonbury, who could it be besides Lyle?"

How I wished I knew. "That's the problem, Belle. Let's stick with Rick Bradley's murder. Except for Madge, who was sick as a dog, they all had the opportunity and the means. That is—if you assume a woman could have done it as easily as a man. And motive? Jilly felt betrayed because Rick was flirting with Madge. Her jealousy led her to think Rick gave Madge—what? Ecstasy or something like that to put her in the mood? Goodness, I know so little about that kind of thing.

"Cynthia? Sorry, I can't go there. And Freddie is such a kind, likeable young man. If you had seen him blush about Jenny, you'd know it couldn't be him."

The corners of Wendy's mouth turned up. "What does it say about us that we refer to someone in their late twenties, possibly early thirties, as a young man?"

"That we know we're both old enough to be his mother."

Ellie aimed her laser pointer at the *#2 Bert* page. "Could jealousy be a motive not only for Jilly but also for Bert? Suppose he picked up on the same signals as Jilly did and misread them? Suppose he killed Rick in a fit of jealousy?"

Grabbing a marker, Wendy scribbled *jealousy* on the page. "I think it's a stretch, but we don't have much else. So, do we go to our book club meeting and noodle on this? Maybe regroup tomorrow after Jonas is able to interview Jilly again?"

I'd almost forgotten to tell them about Jonas's plan—such as it was. "On that note, Jonas has something up his sleeve—maybe setting a trap for the killer. My job is to be less than forthcoming about Jilly's prognosis so that people think she may not recover. We all need to be suitably concerned about her tonight."

Belle looked impressed. "That boy's come a long way, hasn't he? Perhaps he's been reading Agatha Christie and has a Hercule Poirot move in mind."

CHAPTER TWENTY-ONE

STILL SMILING AT THE thought of Jonas as Poirot, I tidied the sitting room and tried to do the same to my thoughts. Unfortunately, stoking the fire and staring at the paper on my walls didn't produce any lightbulb thoughts. There was so much we didn't know. I scribbled questions in my notebook and moved it to the office. Out of sight, out of mind. Perhaps pondering which outfit to wear tonight would clear my mind.

I laid a red merino wool turtleneck on the bed and decided on my pearl grey knitted scarf as the perfect accent. That combination would at least ward off the damp chill in the air.

Christie took up her sphinx pose in the middle of the bed as I spritzed and powdered in an attempt to look less haggard. "What do you think, princess? Good to go?"

Never one to mince her meows, she gave me her honest opinion. "Not your best, but it will do." That was nearly high praise coming from her.

When my call to Dave went to voicemail, I let him know I'd call again when I was tucked in bed. I pictured him surrounded by boxes, packing paper, and tape.

It's a good thing I walked. The Book Nook was the only shop open at this hour, so the cars lining the High Street and the full parking lot at the village hall meant Beatrix had a crowd for tonight's book club meeting.

Trixie had once again outdone herself with the window display. In each corner of the window, she'd erected a 3D wooden puzzle—one of Big Ben and another of Tower Bridge. Between these lay colorful coffee table books on architecture. The scarecrow outside the door had a pencil behind one ear and rolled-up blueprints in her arms.

As I admired the books on display, I texted Jonas again. I'd received only curt 'not now' responses to the several I'd already sent.

September's book club selection had been airplane reading for my trip to NYC several weeks ago, and I'd lost sight of the fact it was a mystery about murder at a corporate retreat in the Australian bushland. When we'd chosen Jane Harper's latest bestseller, it seemed the perfect choice to accompany the Holmes & White conference at the village hall. Now, *Force of Nature* was anything but. I wondered whether Beatrix would address life imitating art in her opening.

It was standing room only when I entered the shop. Beatrix was busy ringing up sales, and Trixie was pouring wine at a table in the corner. I saw Wendy, Belle, and Ellie seated together in the back row. Thankfully, Gavin waved and pointed to a seat next to him in the front row.

"Phew," I said as I sat. "I didn't relish the idea of standing up for an hour. Do you think this enormous crowd came out because of morbid curiosity?"

"No. I think it's that Beatrix coerced Lyle into doing a last-minute presentation on the restoration of the Ambleside church. She sent an email to her customers here and in Chipping

Camden at her other shop. Those coffee-table books are flying off the shelf, and I've seen several customers with the wooden puzzles too. I may have to get Big Ben for the conservatory at the inn."

The room grew quiet when Beatrix rang a small brass bell and stepped to the podium. Her opening was all about appreciation. She thanked the Astonbury businesses for supporting the conference, the town fathers for providing input to the design team, and Lyle for graciously agreeing to speak tonight. "The presentation on architecture will come first, and then we'll discuss *Force of Nature*. Let me address the elephant in the room. Given the recent tragic events, that conversation may be awkward for many of us. That's why I'll call a brief break before we go there. If discussing tonight's book isn't something you feel comfortable with, please feel free to leave at that point."

It wasn't until she invited Jonas to the podium that I realized he was there. "In that vein, Constable James has asked to say a word before we get started."

When Jonas strode to the podium, a hush fell over the room. "Thank you, Beatrix. First, we believe the murder of the American consultant and the attacks that occurred today to be the work of one individual. We are working round the clock, and an arrest is imminent.

"As for the victims of today's attack, one suffered only minor injuries and is resting comfortably. I am very sorry to say the second victim remains in critical condition." He gripped the podium. "Let me assure you that *you*, the residents of Astonbury, have no need to fear for your safety." With that, he thanked Beatrix and moved to the front door.

Is an arrest really imminent or is that statement part of Jonas's plan? Though Lyle was an engaging speaker, it was difficult for me to focus on his colorful slides of the before and after of the

Ambleside church. Listening to his smooth delivery made me even more convinced he couldn't be the killer. To me, that left only Bert or someone who'd never made our radar.

A text came in from Lucy as the crowd was applauding. "Buttercup and Dickens are having a ball. Can he stay for a doggie slumber party?"

I imagined the two four-legged friends in jammies. "Sure. I'll pick him up in the morning."

Turning toward Gavin, I stood. "I think I'm one of those who can't face a discussion of death at a corporate retreat. I'm going to make an early night of it."

I texted Wendy my plan and was nearly to the door when Madge called to me. "Leta, wait a sec, please. Bert wanted me to be sure to thank you for everything you did today. What a nightmare."

"It certainly was. How's he doing?"

She rolled her eyes. "Judging by his whinging, just fine. He's quite irritated at not being able to light a cigar in front of the fireplace at the inn. Cynthia and I didn't want to leave him, but he shooed us out, and I'm glad he did. Lyle did a marvelous job, as usual."

Jonas stood by the door with his arms crossed. "Leaving, Leta?"

"Yes. This topic's just too close to home."

He grimaced and gently took my arm. "Let's talk outside."

Crossing the street, we walked to the corner. "Leta, I'm tailing Lyle and I've posted a guard on the inn and the other cottage Holmes & White rented for the week. The closest I can get to a motive is something about that flipping RIBA award, and I'm convinced Lyle is our chief suspect. But I'm not leaving anything to chance."

"Is Jilly doing any better? Were your comments a ploy to flush the killer into the open?"

"Yes, on both counts. There's a guard outside Jilly's room, too. I predict Lyle will make another attempt on either Jilly or Bert. Gemma's money is on Bert because Jilly's too hard to get to and we're suggesting she may not make it. But I'm not sure. That's why I'm not leaving anything to chance."

"So, you think Lyle went after both him and Jilly?"

"I think Jilly was the primary target, and Bert was in the wrong place at the wrong time. Lyle attacked him because he was a potential witness to the assault on Jilly. The way that girl's been piecemealing information to us, I think she's withheld something vital, something she knows that would point the finger at Lyle. Why? I don't know unless she has a blackmail scheme in mind. I half wonder if the malarkey about the pill case was to distract us from Lyle. Whatever the reason, I think it's got Lyle worried."

He studied my face beneath the streetlight. "You and the LOLs haven't deduced something different, have you?"

"If only we were that good. Everyone but me thinks Lyle is suspect #1, but finding out Bert and Madge are a couple? Something doesn't fit. Maybe I'm grasping at straws because I don't want to think Lyle did it. Wouldn't he have been muddy if he'd been on the riverbank?"

Jonas chewed his lip. I much preferred that response to Gemma rolling her eyes. "I get it, Leta, but none of that changes the fact that Bert was a victim. How do you account for that?"

"I can't, but neither can I account for my sense that it wasn't Lyle. What if I'm right, and it's not Lyle but Bert?"

He patted me on the shoulder. "Then, if he tries to leave the inn, our officer will stop him. We're covered either way."

When he crossed the street to return to the bookshop, I walked on, deep in thought. Wendy would be at home with Belle tonight, and I was looking forward to a mug of cocoa in front of the fireplace and an early evening. Maybe talking everything over with Dave would provide some clarity. Once I was wrapped in my fleece robe, I'd call him.

Pulling my keys from my purse, I saw a basket of flowers by my door. *What on earth?* I carried them inside and read the note. *Surprise! See you tonight, sweetheart.*

Tonight? He's coming home tonight? When I dialed his number, the call went straight to voicemail, which I took as confirmation he was somewhere over the Atlantic. "You devil. I can't wait to see you. Call me when you get this."

Carrying the flowers to the sitting room, I turned in a circle, looking for the perfect spot, and nearly tripped over Christie and Watson, who lay curled together on the rug. "Watson? What are you doing here?"

"I'm here every night, Leta."

"Yes, but not inside. How did you get in?"

"Through the door."

"But the door wasn't open." *Unless Dave is already here? Is that part of the surprise?*

Christie gave a faint meow as she uncurled and stretched. "Is that you, Leta?"

Setting the flowers on the mantle, I knelt to rub her soft black belly. "Of course, it's me, silly girl. Now, tell me, is Dave home?"

She wobbled to her feet and stretched again. "How would I know?"

"I think you two are in cahoots with Dave. He's upstairs, isn't he?" I tiptoed up the stairs, expecting to find my boyfriend napping as was his custom after a trans-Atlantic flight.

Dave wasn't there. The bedroom was too neat—no suitcase, no jacket, nothing.

Christie trailed behind me and jumped on the bed. A dreadful thought crossed my mind. "Christie, is someone else here? Who let Watson in?"

She yawned as only a cat can. "The man who fed me. The food tasted much better than ours."

My eyes grew wide. "What man? Is he still here?"

After stretching into a downward dog position, my little cat yogi sat up and tilted her head. "I'm not sure. I took a nap."

She took a nap, and a man was here . . . or maybe still here. Who is it? What does he want?

My next panicked thought was to text Jonas, except my phone was on the kitchen table. At the top of the stairs, I listened for footsteps or some sound that would tell me whether the intruder was still in my cottage. Without conscious thought, I reached beneath the bed for the cricket bat.

My clueless cat studied me. "What's with the bat?"

I hissed at her. "Christie, whoever was here, he doesn't belong in our house."

And now what? If he's still here, can I even swing this thing hard enough to hurt him? Do I race for the door? Do I wait to be cornered up here? A horrifying image of being bound and gagged on my bed spurred me to action.

Tiptoeing down the stairs, I sprinted toward the front door. The deadbolt. The doorknob. So close. I sensed his presence seconds before he tackled me and threw me to the floor. The cricket bat flew from my hand.

With his knees pinned to either side of my torso, my attacker grabbed my scarf. As he pulled, he grunted, "You're *not* supposed to be here."

No, no, no! I bucked. I twisted. I clawed at his hands. A loud buzzing erupted in my ears.

As my vision dimmed, I glimpsed a blurred brown shape hurtle past my head. The pressure on my neck eased—but not enough. My last conscious thought was of Dave.

"Leta, can you hear me?" When I blinked, the voice resumed. "That's my girl. Can you open your eyes?"

The pinpricks of light were my first clue that all was not well. I blinked again, but my vision didn't clear. Raising my hand to my throat, I tried to speak, but only a croak came out. Something was terribly wrong.

The last thing I remembered was walking home and finding flowers on my doorstep. What did the note say? *Dave. Is Dave here?*

The kiss on my forehead told me everything I needed to know. "Leta, I'm here. Jonas has things under control, and the ambulance is on its way."

That made me open my eyes despite the stars. "No," I croaked.

"Yes. We need to get you checked out."

"What? Why?"

"You don't remember? Maybe that's for the best."

A sandpaper tongue licked my chin. "We got him, Leta. Me and Watson."

"Who?"

Christie and Dave spoke over each other. "Don't know," meowed Christie. "Bert," said Dave. "And here's Jonas. He'll fill you in."

"You were right, Leta. It wasn't Lyle."

Wincing, I turned my head toward him. "Bert? Why?"

"The paramedics just got here, so I'll give you the headlines while they tend to Bert's injuries. After that, you'll be on your way. The best part is that one of the cats bit a chunk from his ear."

This time, Christie licked my nose. "That was me."

Every word took effort. "I don't understand."

Jonas spoke in a low voice. "Bert broke into your cottage. He came in through the boot room. When he attacked you, he was felled by two wildcats."

"Why me?"

"He's not saying, but he had your notebook tucked in his coat. I suspect he was worried about what you knew."

When I tried to sit up, the room spun, and I fell back on the couch. "The river?"

Jonas correctly interpreted what I was asking. "His injuries must have been self-inflicted, Leta. It was a crafty bit of misdirection. Scalp wounds bleed like the devil, but they're not serious."

I felt like a broken record. "Why?"

"I don't know why. But it must go back to Rick Bradley's murder. I think Bert killed him, and he attacked Jilly because he thought she knew something. Once I book him for your attempted murder and breaking and entering, questioning Jilly again will be the next thing on my list. Regardless of whether she knows it, she has the answers."

If I had any doubt that I'd almost died, hearing the words attempted murder brought it home. Conversation swirled above me as I lay on the couch and faded in and out.

When I next opened my eyes, I saw the interior of an ambulance. A paramedic applied an ice pack to my neck and then examined my eyes. She murmured soothing words. "You're doing fine. Your bulky turtleneck and wide scarf kept your assailant from applying consistent pressure. Put simply, they got in the way, and the attack cats took care of the rest."

She smoothed my brow and chuckled softly. "This is one for the books. A woman saved by her cats. And, of course, the timely arrival of her boyfriend with his cricket bat."

My cricket bat. Closing my eyes, I pictured Bert bruised and battered and sincerely hoped he was in much worse shape than I was. *Is there really such a thing as cat scratch fever?*

After a CTA scan revealed no soft tissue or carotid damage, the doctors impressed upon me how very lucky I was to be alive—and relatively unscathed. Another few seconds with no oxygen to my brain would have been fatal.

It was nearly dawn when we got home, and the only thing I wanted more than my bed was a shower. Dave worried I would fall if left to my own devices, but I finally persuaded him to go downstairs to make coffee and try his hand at grits.

The sight of my neck in the mirror was a stark reminder of my attack, as were the bruises on my arms and legs. I rummaged in my pajama drawer for a high-necked flannel gown and topped it with my fleece robe.

In the kitchen, Dave was stirring a pot of grits large enough to feed an army. "Leta, sweetheart, I would have helped you down the stairs. Let's get you to the couch. Tell me what you need."

The trip from my bed to the kitchen had exhausted me, so I didn't have to be asked twice. I let him shepherd me to the sitting room and tuck a blanket around my legs. When he returned with two mugs of coffee, he joined me on the couch.

"Do you want to talk about it?"

I leaned my head on his shoulder. "Not yet." Normally, I would have been burning with curiosity about what had transpired last night, but I felt strangely detached, as though it had happened to someone else. I wasn't sure what that was a sign of. Maybe a near-death experience?

I'd been in more than a few precarious situations, but this one seemed different. It wasn't that I'd seen my life flash before my eyes. It was more that I'd felt my life ebbing away.

The doctors couldn't predict when the memory of the attack would surface—if it did at all—but already, I'd glimpsed a few fragments. There was only one I was determined to hold on to.

Setting my mug on the table, I turned to Dave. "Do you remember the day you offered to leave New York to be with me? We were sitting here, just as we are today, when you said, 'I love you, Leta Parker, and I don't want to lose you.' In those last terrifying seconds last night, that's what I heard."

I took his face in my hands. "I love you, Dave Prentiss, and you're not going to lose me."

His encouraging words as I tried a spoonful of grits made me think of a father coaxing his toddler to eat. "Can't you eat a bit more, sweetheart? If not grits, how 'bout some hot chocolate?"

"I promise I'll try again later. Right now, I think bed is the best thing for me."

He was happy to oblige, and we spent the rest of the morning in bed with Christie tucked between us. Dickens took up his usual position on the floor by my nightstand. It wasn't until midmorning that I woke from a fitful sleep and heard the soothing sound of the shower. I lay on my side and watched as Dave emerged from the bathroom, a towel wrapped around his waist.

An anxious expression crossed his face. "Did I wake you?"

"No. I've been awake off and on. Are you coming back to bed?"

"In a moment. There's a chill in the air, so I thought I'd bring in some firewood first. Are you comfy? Do you need anything?"

It was nice to be fussed over. "Not a thing."

CHAPTER TWENTY-TWO

I OPENED MY EYES again when he climbed into bed and tucked the covers over me. "Tell me about your mom and the packing. Did you get it all done?"

"Yes, finally. The library, Goodwill, and the local thrift shop loved us, and Mom seemed in better spirits when I left. It can't be easy to move after all these years, but she's beginning to look at it as an adventure. She has two friends who live in the retirement community, and they're already making plans."

"She'll be closer to your sister, too, right?"

"Yes, and she'll still have her car. She's closer to Michelle and to the local bookshop. Mom's like me. A convenient bookshop is a necessity." He hopped off the bed. "That reminds me. I brought you something. I hope you're proud of me. It's the only one I kept."

Digging in his suitcase, he stuck something in his pocket before grabbing a larger item. "A Nancy Drew book for my very own Nancy Drew." He sat on the bed and handed me a worn copy of *The Spider Sapphire Mystery.* "And here's your garnet ring. I almost forgot."

Both items warmed my heart—the ring I thought I'd lost, and a book to add to my collection from my childhood. I didn't have my Golden Books, but I had *Nancy Drew*, the *Bobbsey Twins*, *Heidi*, *Black Beauty*, and a host of others.

I slid the ring on my finger and held up my hand. "I'm so glad you found it, and it looks like you cleaned it, too."

He explained he'd asked the jeweler to clean it when he took his mom's jewelry in. "It was Sandy's idea to clean it up."

"And how is Sandy? I bet she was sorry to see you go."

His lips quirked up. "You figured that out, huh? It took Michelle stating the obvious for me to see it. I was on my way to realizing it without Michelle, especially after Sandy made a few disparaging comments about you finding a dead body. As if you somehow manufacture trouble."

"And you say I'm oblivious to admiring glances. This sounds well beyond that. So, Sandy was a huge help, but her intentions weren't entirely altruistic."

"Pretty much. Michelle said Sandy hadn't gotten her hands dirty in years, so her being at Mom's day in and day out was a sure sign something was up."

I kissed his cheek. "Well, your personal trouble magnet is glad you're home."

After spending several more hours in bed, I felt marginally better—still sore and listless, but better. Even my throat was much improved, thanks in large part to the tea and cocoa Dave plied me with. Well, that and taking my phone, so I wasn't tempted to talk to anyone. Somewhere, he'd come up with a small brass bell so I could summon him as needed.

When I rang for him around one, he entered with a bow. "At your service, madam."

With my best husky Marlene Dietrich voice, I requested a hot buttered rum. "Don't ask me why that entered my mind. What

I really want is to take you up on your earlier offer of scrambled eggs. I'll even come downstairs to eat."

"Are you sure? Room service is part of the package, you know."

I promised to be down in fifteen minutes. Splashing my face with water, I noticed the red dots sprinkled around my eyes. *Petechiae.* Those and the marks on my neck weren't something I ever thought I'd experience.

I pulled out leggings, a black turtleneck to hide the awful marks on my neck, and my favorite oversized Georgia Tech sweatshirt. I considered these my comfort clothes.

Christie greeted me at the foot of the stairs. "You're alive!"

"Thanks to you, princess. I hear you came to my rescue."

She led the way into the kitchen. "Me and Watson. It was a team effort." *Modesty? Would wonders never cease?*

Wrapping me in his arms, Dave kissed the top of my head. "I've been wanting to do this since I got home. Now, are you ready for brunch—or whatever meal this is?"

"More than ready." I smiled when he fixed two plates of scrambled eggs, toast, and grits. "Don't be stingy with the grits. I think we'll be eating them for the next week."

"They seem to multiply as you cook them. It's a good thing we like 'em."

We ate in companionable silence, me more slowly than Dave, as swallowing was uncomfortable. Dickens, who hadn't left my side since my early morning return, was the recipient of several bites of toast.

My little hero dog had been beside himself about not being here to protect me. "I would have chased him, Leta. As soon as he opened the door, he would have been a goner." There were several pointed references to Christie and Watson being poor substitutes for a dog.

Pushing my plate to the side, I put my elbows on the table. "Dave, disjointed memories of last night are coming back—like a movie trailer. I remember taking the flowers to the sitting room and thinking, maybe you were already here. Probably because I sensed a presence in the house. It was only after I climbed to our bedroom that I realized you weren't."

I closed my eyes and replayed the scenes in the sitting room and the bedroom. "Wait. I remember now. It was seeing Watson inside that made me think you were upstairs, waiting to surprise me. Let me think. There was something else, too."

Sharing this next part was tricky. I couldn't very well tell him what Christie said about someone feeding her. "Christie was acting odd, but I didn't pick up on it right away. She was down-right wobbly in the sitting room, and she didn't dart up the stairs in front of me like she usually does. It was like she was tipsy.

"Then I hear you asking me to open my eyes, but nothing between the bedroom and then. I don't even know when you got here, but the paramedic mentioned something about 'my boyfriend and his cricket bat.' Can you tell me what happened?"

Dave lifted Christie to his lap. "What do you say, princess, should we tell her you had too much tea?"

"What?"

"Jonas noticed a half-eaten saucer of cat food on the kitchen table and knew you would never feed Christie on the table. That led to the SOCOs taking the saucer and the contents of the trash can with them for analysis. Bert dosed our girl with chamomile tea—not a cup of tea, but the leaves. Jonas's theory is that he took the tea bags and canned cat food from the inn and mixed it all together planning to use it on Dickens. An empty can and the torn tea bags were in the kitchen trash."

I scratched her sleek head. "So, that's what was wrong with you, and here I thought you were drunk." Tweaking her ears, I sat back. "But why drug Christie?" I put my head in my hands. "There must be an explanation, but I'm in no shape to figure it out.

The corners of Dave's mouth quirked up. "You know you don't have to, right? That's Jonas's job. For now, it's enough that fragments are coming back to you. For what it's worth, I bet Christie was driving him crazy crying for treats, and he gave her the food to shut her up."

Christie meowed, "He said something about me being a pest, but he gave me food, so that was okay."

"Now, let me tell you the rest of the story. I planned to surprise you when you came home from the Book Nook, so I parked down the road until I saw you go inside. Thank goodness I had my keys in my hand because when I stepped up to the door . . . all hell was breaking loose inside."

He closed his eyes. "I heard screeching and through the window, I saw you struggling on the floor, a man sitting on your legs with the ends of your scarf in his hands. It all happened so fast. I opened the door. Christie leaped to his chest. Watson was on his back. I grabbed the cricket bat and walloped his back and his head, and it was over in an instant."

"Did I pass out? Is that why I don't remember much?"

"According to the paramedics, if you did, it couldn't have been for more than a few seconds. Once he got a good grip on your scarf, that's all it would have taken to . . . to cut off the oxygen flow."

I took a deep breath. "In other words, you arrived just in the nick of time."

Christie leaped into my lap. "We wouldn't have let him hurt you, Leta."

"How did he get in?" I was still struggling to refer to my attacker as Bert, and I supposed it was because I didn't remember seeing him. To me, Bert was the jovial dart player, the caring, overprotective man who worked for Lyle. Yet, I *had* suspected him.

"The same way as your intruder two years ago. He broke the glass in the door to the boot room. Jonas taped cardboard over it, and I've already called the glass shop. We're going to have to do something about the door. Heck, we may need an alarm system. This makes three times someone's broken in."

I didn't like to think of needing something like that in my fairy-tale cottage. But maybe he was right. "I wonder whether Jonas has charged Bert with Rick's murder and the attack on Jilly?"

"Jonas called me to see how you were and promised an updater later. Given that your phone's been ringing off the hook all day, maybe you have a voicemail with some answers."

Handing me my phone, he shooed me to the sitting room. "See what you can find out. I'll be there once I've cleaned up the kitchen."

My phone showed dozens of messages—a handful from Wendy and Ellie, one from Cynthia, one from Madge, and three from Jilly. The rest were from other friends in the village. I listened to Jilly's first.

In her first two messages, she expressed her concern about what I'd been through and how I was recovering and asked that I call her back. The third was a short, tearful plea to call her.

With a sigh, I leaned my head against the sofa. I knew I'd have to speak with her eventually, but I dreaded the drama. My assumption was that she'd be tearfully apologetic, and I wasn't up to comforting her—not yet.

Instead, I listened to the remaining messages and began scrolling through my texts. It was times like this that reminded me of how fortunate I was to have so many caring friends.

My scrolling was interrupted by barking followed by voices in the kitchen. The murmurs from whoever had arrived were too soft to make out, but I could hear Dave's testy responses quite clearly. "Not right now. She's resting. No, it's not."

The approaching footsteps told me that whoever it was had ignored him. To my dismay, the gatecrasher was Jilly. So much for not being ready to deal with her.

As the words tumbled from her mouth, she held out a bouquet of flowers. "Please, Leta, I won't take long. Constable James said I needed to come clean with you, and once I do that, I promise not to bother you again."

Dave walked in behind her, a scowl on his face. When I nodded and pointed at the easy chair, he interpreted my gestures. Snatching the flowers from her, he strode from the room, muttering something about audacity.

I was glad that she seemed to have recovered from her near drowning. Both of us had been through awful experiences, and the sooner we got this conversation over with, the better. "Jilly, I suggest you make it quick. It's not often I see Dave angry."

"I will, Leta, I promise." She ducked her head as tears filled her eyes. "I am so sorry. If I hadn't been such an idiot, Rick wouldn't be dead. And if I'd told you the whole story from the start . . . maybe Bert wouldn't have attacked you. I don't know. All I know is I owe you the truth—all of it. Constable James made that very clear. He threatened me with obstruction of justice, and I probably deserve it."

She waited a beat, as though hoping I'd respond. *Not yet*, I thought.

"Here's what I left out. I went to the pub after I left Rick. I didn't want to be alone. Bert was there quizzing his co-workers about what Madge had to drink. He thanked me for taking care of her and said he was trying to figure out what made her so sick.

I . . . I heard myself telling him that Rick had given Madge a pill, something to take the edge off, and it may have made her sick instead.

"I can hear him now slowly asking, 'Why would he want to do that . . . take the edge off?' And I told him. Told him that was Rick's thing when he was into someone. Leta, the words were out of my mouth before I could pull them back. I was angry with Rick, and I was jealous of Madge. It was a stupid, mean thing to do. And I just know that's why Bert killed Rick."

I knew she was expecting me to tell her she wasn't responsible for Rick's death, but I was too bruised and battered to find the right words.

"But, Leta, he didn't seem angry then. It was almost as though he was thinking aloud. He told me Madge took strong medicine for her back and he couldn't imagine her mixing anything with it. He mentioned maybe calling her doctor in the morning if she wasn't better. Then he clapped me on the back and thanked me for telling him. And that was it.

"I didn't even think about that conversation until I saw Madge with her pill box. And even then, I didn't want to throw Bert under the bus! I didn't think he'd murdered Rick. I just worried the police would *think* he had. Like on the telly. Leta, I'm so, so sorry. Everything is my fault."

What would I have done in her shoes? Stupid question, Leta. You'd have gone straight to the police. Sure, it was standard police thinking to see everyone as a suspect, but would they have seen Bert as a person who would kill a man he barely knew because he gave Madge a pill? Would they have dug deep enough to find out Bert and Madge were a couple—a fact that would lend credence to the idea he'd killed Rick?

"Jilly, I agree that your words probably prompted Bert to confront Rick. But what Bert did when he got there was his choice. You are not responsible for his decision to kill Rick."

What I said to her was true, but there was a piece of me that saw her as partly to blame. She had made so many bad decisions. Slipping sleeping pills into Rick's drink. Assuming he'd given Madge a pill, and, worse, telling that to Bert. And the topper? Failing to come clean from the get-go. Would Bert have attacked the two of us if she'd told Constable James everything in the beginning? I didn't think so.

"Leta, thank you. I know I did some stupid things, but I never meant to hurt anyone. I'm sorry for dragging you into this. I feel awful about what happened to you. And I nearly forgot to say thank you for pulling me from the river. Constable James says I owe you my life."

Those words were the kick in the pants I needed. I knew she'd be haunted by Rick's death for a long time to come. That was enough to deal with. What she didn't need was the added burden of feeling responsible for what happened.

Describing Dickens's actions was a good place to start. "It was Dickens who spotted you, and he helped to keep your head above water. I'm just glad we got there in time."

I leaned forward so that she would hear my next words clearly. "Think about everything Bert did. He killed Rick. He tried to drown you. He nearly killed me. Neither you nor I are to blame for his actions. You have to remember that, Jilly."

Her nod told me I'd gotten through. As she left, she pecked me on the cheek and whispered. "Thank you, Leta, I will."

Dave must have been waiting patiently for her departure because it wasn't long before he came in with two cups of tea. "I heard most of that. Do you want to talk about it?"

"Thank goodness, you heard it. I don't have the strength to repeat it all, but I'd love to hear what you think."

"My first thought was 'who does something like that?' It was bad enough she drugged Rick, but spreading that story? It's like a toned-down version of *Fatal Attraction*." He must have seen the appalled expression on my face. "Okay, not as bad, but still."

"There's no doubt she made some bad decisions, and her reckless words may have prompted Bert to confront Rick. But I find it hard to imagine the type of sustained fury that would lead Bert to snap and strangle Rick. He takes Jilly's pill story at face value. He's enraged and drives over there and *kills* him. And he doesn't think twice? I wonder if there was something else that happened between him and Rick."

"Leta, I know it sounds far-fetched, but keep in mind what you said to Jilly, he pushed her into the river and tried to kill you, too. It almost makes you wonder whether he has a history of aggravated assault. Don't the experts say this kind of behavior builds?"

My head was starting to ache. "I think I'll leave that for Jonas to figure out. I *do* want to know what made him attack me and Jilly, but I need to rest before I can handle much more."

"You may be in luck then. We've had an offer from Belle and Wendy—Belle's homemade chicken soup. I had to all but bar the door to keep Ellie, Belle, and Wendy away. They have all kinds of news and want to see you."

"A nap, chicken soup, and an update—in that order—sound like a great idea, as long as no one expects me to be the life of the party."

That got a chuckle. "When has anyone ever accused you of being the life of the party? Oh, wait. You mean before nine, right?"

I almost threw a pillow at him, but it would have taken too much energy.

CHAPTER TWENTY-THREE

FOOTSTEPS ON THE STAIRS woke me up, and I rolled over to see Wendy standing in the doorway. "Dave gave me permission to tell you we're ready to eat. How are you feeling?"

"Like I've been drugged, but it will pass once I splash some water on my face."

Sitting on the side of the bed, she studied me. "You know, Leta, maybe it really is time for us to write about murders instead of investigating them." She shifted her gaze to the window above my bed. "I can't believe I said that, but it bears thinking about."

All I could do was nod. I had neither the inclination nor the energy to disagree with her. Maybe, after we put this case to bed, we'd get serious about the Constable James series and find it easy to shift gears. After all, we'd stumbled into second careers as modern-day Miss Marples. Perhaps we could stumble back out.

Downstairs, Belle was stirring the soup while Dave set the kitchen table. Ellie was slicing a loaf of homemade bread. "Compliments of Caroline," she said. "My loaves never look this pretty." Caroline was the part-time cook at the manor house, and anything from her kitchen was a treat.

In unspoken agreement, we ate without broaching the topic that was uppermost in our minds. Dave entertained us with the saga of helping his mom pack up her house and had us all laughing as we enjoyed our meal. When Ellie suggested he might have a new career ahead of him, he feigned horror. "No way. I'd be still there packing if not for a high school friend who owns a business doing just that."

Wendy insisted on washing the dishes while Dave carried in more firewood. When we were all settled in the sitting room with our beverages of choice, Wendy pulled out a colorful spiral notebook. "Jonas has ours, Leta, so I found a new one today. I've captured most of what we've learned since your attack, and I also invited our favorite constable to join us later. If he can get away, he will."

She flipped pages and grimaced. "I cobbled together the pieces from Jonas and Jilly with bits from Cynthia and Lyle. Do I start with the murder or the attack on Jilly?"

As Christie leaped into her lap, Belle suggested Jilly's attack as the best place to begin. "Let's cover what provoked Bert to go after Jilly and then Leta. We can come back to Rick's murder."

"Right, Mum. Leta, Dave shared your conversation with Jilly about what she said to Bert at the pub after she left Rick that night. Jonas supplied the missing pieces—the sequence of events that caused Bert to worry about that conversation several days later."

I was puzzled. "Wendy, how does Jonas know the sequence of events? Did Bert spill everything?"

"Only as regards you and Jilly. He hasn't revealed anything about Rick Bradley's murder. Jonas had enough physical evidence to link him to the attack on Jilly, and he was caught in the act here, so he was more forthcoming about those incidents."
Incidents. As though they were no big deal.

She held up her hands and ticked her fingers as though checking items on a list. "Honestly, I have to wonder if he would have suspected anything if not for Cynthia's comments. Everything came to a head for Bert that night. First, he heard her description of our detective activities, and that raised an alarm bell. Next, he saw you writing in your notebook in the pub parking lot that night, and he overheard bits of our conversation before we went inside.

"Do you remember he drove Madge to the inn that evening? When he returned, he was perfectly positioned to observe and overhear us. After you finished with the notebook, you tossed it into your car—"

That shook loose a memory. "Yes! I tossed it in the *back* seat, but when I went to get it for our chat by the firepit later, it was in the *front* seat. So he looked at it? Out there in the dark?"

"Got it in one. He couldn't read it all, but enough to worry about how much we might know, and he eavesdropped on us when we were drinking our cocoa. Can you believe it?"

"He what? Where was he?" I rewound the video in my brain. Building the fire, grabbing blankets, getting mugs . . . Dickens and the cats on the far side of my garage. "He was next door! That explains why Dickens and Watson were checking out the driveway. Did he tell Jonas he was there?"

Christie meowed, "Hey, I was there too. We found one of those smelly brown things."

I pinched the bridge of my nose. "Did he drop his cigar?"

Wendy's mouth popped open. "Yes! When the SOCOs were here, Jonas had them search your property and Lyle's for any sign that Bert had lain in wait. They found a cigar, but it wasn't fresh, so to speak. How on earth did you know about it?"

Shrugging my shoulders proved an easy dodge. "So, what I'm hearing is that not only did he read the notebook, he also heard

our suppositions." I winked. "And your Yul Brynner imper-
sonation." After I explained the reference, I asked the obvious
question. "Why would he tell all that to Jonas?"

Dave ran his hands through his hair. "I'm not sure about
that, but I can see why he attacked you and Jilly. Think about
it. The notebook, your brainstorming session—both including
everything Jilly told you. Taken together, it would have made
him worry that all three of you knew too much. That could be
why he pushed Jilly in the river and then came after you."

Wendy shook her head. "Not exactly, Dave. Jonas thinks Bert
was worried about what *wasn't* in the notebook. If Jilly was sharing information with Leta, it appeared she hadn't yet revealed
the most damning piece of evidence—something that could be
seen as motive."

Placing my hand on Dave's knee, I frowned. "I think I see.
Bert realized Jilly was confiding in me, but there was one piece
missing in what he overheard and managed to read in the dark.
There was no mention of Jilly returning to the pub and talking
to him *after* Rick passed out.

"It wasn't in my notes because I didn't know. I only found out
about it today when Jilly came over. Given the pattern was that
she first told me something and then shared it with the police, he
had a problem."

Dave covered my hand with his. "He needed to ascertain what
you knew, Leta. If Jilly had already told you, all bets were off. But
if she'd kept quiet about that conversation, he had a quick way
out. Not to be overly dramatic, but the solution would be for
her to take her secret to the grave."

Ellie pursed her lips. "That sounds like a line from a B movie,
Dave. So matter-of-fact. Do you think it gets easier to kill someone after the first time?"

A disturbing image surfaced for me. "We see it in mystery novels, and we witnessed it in real life in Torquay, didn't we? Thank goodness we didn't have a repeat in this case."

When Wendy closed her eyes and shook her head, I could tell she was struggling to push the unwelcome memory away. She held up the notebook. "Not for lack of trying on Bert's part. Following your logic, Dave, the first step was to determine how much Jilly had shared with Leta. Bert arrived at the village hall early yesterday morning on the pretext of looking over the progress on the design. What he really wanted was an opportunity to talk to Jilly.

"If you can believe it, she broached the subject herself by apologizing to him for her misread of the pill situation. She told him the same thing she told you, Leta—how she saw the pillbox on the bus ride and figured out how wrong she was. Did she tell you that today? That she apologized for causing him undue concern?"

"No. And that was unbelievably stupid on her part."

Belle tickled Christie's chin. "If she watched any mysteries on the telly, she'd have known better."

"She clearly hasn't read any Miss Marple or Agatha Raisin," said Ellie.

"Oh, it gets better, ladies. She told him how Leta convinced her to tell Constable James and how much better she felt after doing that. So, he knew she shared that part with the police, but she didn't mention telling Leta anything else. That sealed the deal. Or at least, that's what Jonas is supposing. He knows from Jilly what was said. What he doesn't know is Bert's thought process. Or at least he didn't the last time we spoke."

The thought process of a killer. "The only thing left to determine was how and when to get rid of Jilly. And, of course, time was of the essence."

Dickens barked moments before I heard the car pull into the driveway. When Dave went to the door, he returned with a haggard Jonas James. He didn't get to say much more than hello before Wendy hopped up and offered him a bowl of soup.

Everyone but Dickens, Belle, and I returned to the kitchen. Though fragments of conversation floated our way, I was sure nothing of importance would be discussed until we were all in the same room.

Belle nodded towards Dickens. "He's become quite a Velcro dog, hasn't he? It's not often he misses an opportunity for a handout."

Leaning against my leg, Dickens barked, "I thought I was a hero dog, Leta. What's Velcro?"

"You're still my hero dog, Dickens." I smiled at Belle. "It's true. He hasn't left my side since we got home, but I'm sure he'll get to back to normal soon."

Looking uncomfortable, Jonas returned to the sitting room by himself. "Leta, could I speak with you on your own, please?" He glanced at Belle and back at me, and I could tell he didn't want to ask Belle to leave.

"Sure, Jonas. Let's go to my office." Dickens, of course, followed us.

In the soft light from the desk lamp, Jonas looked sheepish. "The thing is, Leta, I owe you an apology. If I hadn't dismissed your idea out of hand, if I'd considered for one moment that Bert might be the killer . . . I would have done things differently. You almost died, and it's my fault!"

"Jonas, you're not responsible for Bert's attack on me. I admit my brain is fuzzy, so let's play this out together. If you thought my suspicion was worth pursuing, what would you have done differently? Follow Bert instead of Lyle? But you already had a guard at the inn and the other cottage. The only other thing you could have done was to post a guard here, and neither of us had any reason to think that was necessary."

"Aargh, you're right. I would have asked more questions, but I didn't have anything concrete to go on. It's just that I was trying to lay a trap for whoever killed Rick Bradley. And it followed that the killer also attacked Jilly and Bert . . . and I made a hash of it."

"But your actions didn't cause Bert to target me. That's on him. We didn't know he'd eavesdropped on me in my garden. We didn't know he'd grabbed my notebook and read enough to worry him. Only a crystal ball would have told us what was coming."

His shoulders relaxed, and he gave an audible sigh of relief. "Thank you, Leta. I still owe you, though."

I smiled. "I'll be sure to keep that in mind."

When we joined the others in the sitting room, Jonas took center stage. "Wendy told me how far you've gotten, so let me cut to the chase. We've been interviewing Bert off and on all day. Even Gemma came in. She looks like hell, but she's all but nailed him to the wall with her questions.

"Bert's confessed to pushing Jilly in the river, and he couldn't deny attacking you, Leta, since he was caught in the act. He went to great lengths to convince us he didn't plan to hurt you—that you surprised him.

"Doesn't much matter. Surprise or not, he reacted by trying to kill you. As for Jilly, he chewed on what she said yesterday morning and decided he had no choice. It was the proximity to the river that gave him the idea of pushing her in. He just needed the right opportunity with no one around. That's why he offered to help her clean up, though Freddie following him almost thwarted his plan."

I pictured him chewing on his cigar. "I bet that's what he was pondering when he looked so serious during the break. And no matter what he did to Jilly, he had to come up with a way to eliminate himself as a suspect. Pure evil."

Jonas agreed. "You're right, Leta. He had to think it through. The idea to bash yourself in the head with a rock doesn't just pop up on the spur of the moment."

Ellie shuddered. "And then, Leta ruined his plan by spotting Jilly clinging to the riverbank. Is that why he came after her? He was angry?"

"No, Ellie. We gave out that Jilly likely wouldn't make it, so that was one loose end handled. But he couldn't be sure what else Leta and Wendy knew. Maybe they weren't privy to the full story about Rick and Madge and the pills, but sitting in the hospital, he began to fear he'd overlooked something. At least that's how he tells it.

"He'd only read their notebook in the dark car park, and he convinced himself he needed to see what else was in it. I feel pretty sure he would have killed Leta and Wendy both if he thought it was necessary. He was spinning out of control. But when he broke in here, he only wanted information. Leta was supposed to be at the Book Nook. He knew that from Madge."

I leaned forward. "Jonas, you told me you had an officer watching the inn. How did Bert leave unnoticed?"

His face turned red. "He went out through the patio door, unseen by my officer. Gemma hasn't yet decided how to discipline her. Even if she missed him exiting the inn, how she missed a car leaving the inn is a mystery to me."

And I came home early. "Is there a reason you didn't start with Rick Bradley's murder? Have you charged him with that, too?"

"Not yet, Leta, but we will soon. The fingerprint evidence should be back tomorrow, and we've found a shirt in Bert's room with a wine stain on the cuff. Gemma's sure his fingerprints will be on the dirty wine glass from Lyle's cottage, which must have been used to throw wine in the victim's face. And probably on the bottle in the rubbish bin."

Dave frowned. "So, it was only a matter of time before you identified him as the killer? Pushing Jilly in the river, attacking Leta, that was all for naught?"

"For him, yes. For us, much as I hate to say it, it helps cement the case against him. A good solicitor could have argued the fingerprints came from earlier in the day because Bert drove Rick to the cottage from the train station. Even the stain on his shirt could have happened then."

My head was throbbing. "Jonas, I'm afraid I need to rest, but first, please tell me what his motive was for killing Rick? Was it as unbelievable as what Wendy and I theorized? Did he drive over there already planning to kill Rick? Did he kill him for giving a pill to Madge? There must be more to it."

"We don't know, Leta, but we have a possible scenario. To-day, we re-interviewed Madge, Lyle, and Cynthia. This time, we asked questions about Bert, looking for indicators of motive in his words or actions. Of course, none of them wanted to implicate him, but they had to answer us.

"Leta, Wendy, your notebook was a tremendous help. We used the attack on Bert's daughter as a lever and learned from both Cynthia and Lyle that Bert had taken a 90-day leave of ab-sence after it happened. It was then that he began displaying his overprotective tendencies—nothing disturbing, just different. Madge admitted she was alarmed by how badly he injured her mugger, especially when the police questioned her about what she saw. In the end, they didn't charge him, so she convinced herself she'd overreacted.

"Again, using your notes, we asked Madge about getting sick at the pub. She was reluctant to tell us what happened, but finally, she did. It turns out she took an extra pill that day, at lunch, because her back was already acting up. She didn't eat more than a bite or two before taking her evening pain pill. That, coupled with wine at lunch and the beers at the pub, made her sick, though she didn't figure it out until a day or so later."

Belle interrupted him. "In the dark ages, when I worked in A&E, we saw a few instances of that. I understand it's much more prevalent now, with so many drugs readily available. If, as Leta and Wendy say, Madge isn't a drinker, it would have been a simple mistake for her to make."

I could hear Bert telling me that Madge didn't drink much, and Madge telling me the same thing the next morning. "How did she figure it out, Jonas?"

"Well, this is where it gets interesting. It seems Bert harangued her—my word, not hers—about what she'd done. He actually asked her if she'd taken anything besides her regular pills. She kept telling him no, that she didn't know what made her sick, but he wouldn't let it go. That's when it occurred to her she might have messed up. She counted her pills and saw she was one short. He apologized for harping on it, but she thought he seemed a tad taken aback."

Was he trying to rationalize what he'd done? "Because, if that's why he killed Rick, he'd made a dreadful mistake. What do you think, Jonas? Is that why he did it?"

"As ridiculous as it sounds, it's the only motive we have, and only because the LOLs supplied it."

Springing to his feet, Dave pointed to Jonas. "I have an idea. Are you game to try something different? I've written so many articles about this genre, I can picture how the murder may have played out. Let's do this like a scene in a play, one from a murder mystery."

Jonas threw up his hands. "Why not? If nothing else, maybe we'll have a few laughs."

"Okay. I'll play Rick Bradley, and you be Bert. We know the victim was comatose, and that Bert threw wine in his face. So, you come in, see me slumped in the chair, and play the part. I picture you growing angry. You want to confront me, but it's no use if I don't respond. So go along with it. I've heard enough from Leta about Rick Bradley to play his role. I may be way off base, but let's give it a go. No wine in my face, though!"

"There's one more thing you need to make the scene complete." I planted a kiss on Dave's cheek. "Our victim had a lipstick mark on his face."

Dave grinned and slumped on the couch. Jonas stood in front of him with his hands on his hips. "Rick, look at me. I want to talk to you. Come on you git, wake up. Bloody hell, how much did you drink?" Jonas grumbled a bit more and grabbed Dave's collar to shake him, before picking up an empty cup and miming tossing wine in his face.

Dave leaned his head back and slurred. "What? What d'ya want?"

I stood and whispered into Jonas's ear, and he followed my prompts. "What did you give Madge? I know you gave her something."

His head lolling, Dave played along. "Huh? Nothing. Didn't give her a thing."

Now, Jonas was getting in the spirit of it. "You drugged her, didn't you? To get her to sleep with you?"

"Are you crazy? Why would I do that? I don't have to drug women." Dave blinked and wiped his mouth. "Can have any woman I want . . . what would I need with Madge?"

It almost looked real when Jonas sprung at Dave and wrapped his hand around his throat. Dave made elaborate choking sounds before succumbing.

When he stopped moving, Jonas stepped back and looked at me. "Blimey, it could have happened that way. I couldn't wrap my head around Bert going over there and choking the life out of the man. What if he only wanted to confront him, not kill him? And Rick provoked him. He said something to set him off. It could have been about Bert or Madge. If Bert was already angry, an insult would have been like putting a match to a fire."

Straightening his collar, Dave looked at me. "What do you think, Leta? Would our victim have said anything like what I came up with?"

"I think so. Caught off guard like that, he wouldn't have watched his words, and I can imagine him responding in a macho way. Like, 'Who me? Need help with women?' If he uttered the slightest slur against Madge, Bert could have snapped."

"Unbelievable, and yet not," Jonas said. "If nothing else, it gives me a scenario to prod Bert with when the time comes."

Wendy frowned. "You know, Bert bloodying his head was a master stroke on his part. His mistake was breaking in here. Especially if, as you say, the fingerprints and wine stain are easily explained away."

My mind was traveling a different path, and I only half heard her. "I wish I'd made the cigar connection earlier."

"What do you mean, sweetheart?"

"That first morning in the cottage, I picked up on a strange aroma, but I couldn't place it. All the clues were there. The smell at the cottage. Lyle telling me and Jonas that Bert smoked cigars. The same smell at the village hall when Bert unwrapped his cigar. The cigar on the riverbank. Heck, that had to be what drew Dickens toward Lyle's cottage when we were sitting by the firepit.

"And Jonas, the SOCOs found a cigar near here. They say smell is the strongest memory trigger. Unfortunately, for me, it only made me think of my favorite uncle. Not Bert."

Jonas shook his head. "It's an interesting connection, Leta, but like the fingerprints, a good solicitor would probably explain it away."

My yawn alerted my friends that it was time to wrap things up. Wendy stood. "Jonas, where does that leave us?"

"Once the fingerprint analysis comes in, it'll be all over but the shouting. We'll confront him with that, and charge him with Rick Bradley's murder—with or without a confession. Gemma will interview him again early tomorrow morning. After another night in jail, he may be more willing to talk."

CHAPTER TWENTY-FOUR

DAVE AND I SPENT a quiet Saturday on our own. After another big breakfast of scrambled eggs and heaping servings of leftover grits, we visited Martha and Dylan and then spent the rest of the day reading, relaxing by the fire, and puttering around.

It was midafternoon when Cynthia texted a question about Dave's he-shed. "I'm glad to hear you're doing better, and I'm wondering if you're up for a brief visit. Remember, I told you I had a surprise on the way? It was delivered next door to Lyle's, and we'd love to come set it up for you. Maybe around five?"

My response was an enthusiastic *yes*. I'd asked Dave not to peek inside his shed without me, because I wanted to see his reaction when he did. This would be the perfect opportunity for the unveiling.

The idea for the shed had started as a way to give Dave a spot where he could spread out and write—a spot other than the kitchen table. In his small New York City apartment, he'd scattered papers, books, and scribbled notes everywhere. I could stand the mess short-term when he visited, but once he moved in, the constant clutter drove me crazy. A he-shed was the perfect so-lution. As we worked together on the design and his excitement grew, I realized it was much more than that. It was an affirmation that Schoolhouse Cottage was *our* home.

When I was honest with myself, I knew I was the one who needed the affirmation, not Dave. I had never expected our long-distance romance to last. How could it? He was the first and only man I dated after Henry died. And there was an ocean between us. *Enjoy it while you can*, I'd whispered to myself, *because happily-ever-after endings are the stuff of Hallmark movies.*

How was it I'd been the picture of self-confidence in my career, but not in my love life? Did it start with the college boyfriend who dumped me? Or was it all the failed romances before I married Henry? Had I unconsciously embraced Ben Franklin's philosophy that being a pessimist was a safeguard against disappointment—at least as far as romance was concerned?

And now? The thoughtful, caring man I'd fallen in love with had left his life in New York City to join me in England. *I've been lucky in love twice.*

By five, I'd made myself presentable, chilled a bottle of champagne, and prepared a plate of cheese and crackers. "Dave," I called, "can you get the champagne flutes from the top shelf, please?"

He wandered into the kitchen with a bemused expression on his face. "Champagne?"

"Yes, for the official unveiling of your he-shed. We'll wait for Cynthia and Lyle to arrive before we pop the cork."

When a text came in from Cynthia advising us to watch from the sitting room, Dave and I glanced up in time to see Lyle trundling a dolly through the garden to the shed. It was loaded with a large flat box. Dave strode to the window. "That thing's huge. What on earth is it?"

"I have no idea. Cynthia picked it out as the crowning touch for your shed."

We watched the two of them wrestle the thing through the door. Twenty minutes passed before Lyle carried the empty box out and Cynthia brought up the rear with the dolly. They were all grins as they leaned the box and the dolly against the garage.

"This must be Prince Charming," Cynthia exclaimed. That brought a blush to my cheeks as I introduced Dave.

We carried the champagne and hors d'oeuvres to the sitting room, where Dave did the honors. "Here's to the design team—Cynthia, Lyle, and Leta. I've enjoyed watching the shed go up, and I can't wait to see the interior. If it's anything like what you did with this place, I'm gonna love it."

The four of us, followed by Dickens and Christie, trooped to the shed, where Cynthia flung open the door. "Enter."

When a three-paneled wooden screen caught my eye, I gasped. "The screen! Oh, my goodness, it's perfect. Just think, Dave, you can easily tuck all kinds of paraphernalia behind it."

Dave winked. "What you really mean is I can hide my mess in the blink of an eye. You don't fool me for a minute, Leta Parker."

Walking from side to side, he came to a standstill in front of the framed book and magazine covers. "Leta, this . . . is . . . amazing. I knew it would be special, but I never imagined all this. The portrait of Dickens and Christie, the magazine covers—you made it mine." He lifted me off my feet into a bear hug.

Cynthia beckoned us behind the wooden screen. "Let me point out one more thing. I had this fitted with something special for the two of you."

A squeal escaped my mouth. "A whiteboard! How did you come up with that idea?"

"Exactly the reaction I was hoping for, Leta. What do you think, Dave? I see you using it to capture ideas as you write, but barring that, a little birdie told me it might come in handy for a certain detective agency."

"The clueless old codger at your service, madam. Yes, I can see it now. We may be able to avoid wallpapering the sitting room with flip chart paper. With the wood-burning stove in here, it's an all-weather room, so we're set."

Darting behind the screen, Christie meowed, "Dickens, look at this. It's like a cave. Perfect place for a nap."

After checking it out, Dickens gave his approval. "All it needs is a dog bed."

Lyle picked up a rectangular package from the desk and handed it to Dave. "One last thing."

"More?" As he tore off the brown paper, a grin spread across his face. "Tuppence, did you pick this out? It's perfect."

I could tell Cynthia was pleased with his reaction. "I chose *Partners in Crime*, Leta, because I thought it was more fitting."

She grabbed Dave's arm and tugged him outside to admire the stonework and window boxes. For a moment, Lyle held back. "Leta, thank you."

"For what, Lyle?"

"Constable James told me that despite the deck being stacked against me, you were the one person who couldn't be persuaded that I'd killed Rick. You hardly knew me, but somehow, you had faith in me. Talk about knowing someone. I've worked with Bert for years and still can't believe it was him. I wonder if we'll ever know why he did it."

"A good lawyer will urge him to stay mum on that, Lyle. We can guess, but we may never know for sure. Madge may have a better idea than we do. Speaking of which, how is she? I can't imagine how it must feel to learn your boyfriend is a murderer. Has she said anything?"

"Barely a thing. Only that the police asked lots of questions about the pain medicine she takes and her relationship with

Bert—the relationship neither I nor Cynthia knew anything about.

"And, of course, I owe you for pitching in to keep us going. Without you, this week would have been an unqualified disaster. I mean, it *was* a disaster in so many ways, but at least not for the rest of the team. If anything, the tragedy drew them closer together, and their final design was a masterpiece. The drawings and the scale model are on display at the village hall. I hope you'll stop by soon to see what they came up with."

I assured him I would, and we chatted about the plans for his gran's cottage. He wasn't sure he had the heart to keep it, but he didn't need to make that decision any time soon. He could rent it out as he'd planned and decide later whether he could ever again be comfortable in it.

After Cynthia and Lyle left, Dave insisted on moving his files and laptop into the shed. "You relax while I get things set up. Then we can decide what to do about dinner. I'm thinking takeaway from the Ploughman."

I must have dozed off because the next thing I knew, I smelled hamburgers. "Dave, is that you?" After Thursday night, I didn't want to assume. I'd have to get over that.

He stuck his head in the room. "Yes. Ran into Peter and Lucy and got us the same thing they had. A hamburger and a salad. They asked about you, and I told you'd be your old self soon. And before I forget, Jonas popped in while I was waiting."

"Well, don't make me beg. What did he say?"

"The fingerprint evidence gave them what they needed to charge Bert with Rick Bradley's murder. And get this. Gemma couldn't get over his approach to interviewing Bert. He used the scenario we acted out and asked Bert what Rick said to set him off. Suggested it was something about Madge.

"It worked just like it does in the movies. Bert lunged across the table and yelled to leave Madge out of it. Jonas touched a nerve, and Gemma thinks he's brilliant."

I beamed like a proud parent. "There could be a promotion in his future, and that would make a great ending for the Constable James series. I intend to get serious about that now that we're back home. The only thing on my plate for the next several months is helping with the Fall Fête, so I should have plenty of time."

Dave poured the wine. "Do we have plans for next Friday night?"

Closing my eyes, I pictured our calendar. "No. Is there something you want to do?"

"Have dinner in Northleach, like we would have last night if someone hadn't been under the weather."

He may be the most romantic man I've ever known. "Our anniversary! I put it out of my mind because you weren't due back until tomorrow, and then life got in the way. I'm sorry I forgot."

This September marked the two-year anniversary of our first date. Dave had arranged his travel schedule last year to ensure we could celebrate year one at the same restaurant. He'd even given me a box of chocolates, as he had the first time we went out. *Two marvelous years.*

Dave lay on the bed, watching me as I dug through the closet on Friday. "Will you wear your red dress tonight? The one you wore the first time I met you?"

I'd pulled out a black skirt and was searching for just the right top. "I can, though my bruises aren't quite gone. Wrapping a scarf around my neck instead of wearing a necklace would just about camouflage them." The night we met at the inn, I'd worn my favorite red dress, my black boots and a necklace of jet and crystal beads.

"What time are our reservations?"

"We need to leave here by 5:30."

That was earlier than usual. "They must be busy tonight."

"Let's just say that getting our table by the fireplace at the right time was a challenge." He winked. "But when I told them the occasion, they worked us in."

It was a special night, so I treated myself to a leisurely bath with my Shalimar bath oil. I was applying my makeup when I heard Dave bound up the stairs, followed by Dickens. "How was your run?"

"Great. Dickens was fired up the whole way. I missed running with him while I was at Mom's."

He disappeared while I was blow-drying my hair, and when I emerged from the bathroom, there was a surprise waiting for me. Atop my dresser was a bouquet of red roses and a notecard that read, "Roses for the lady in red." *Lucky in love indeed.*

I greeted him with a hug when he jogged back up the stairs. "You sure know how to make a girl feel special."

"That was my aim."

With a bit of fiddling, I eventually wrapped the scarf so that it hid the yellowing bruises on my neck. The long sleeves of my dress covered those on my arms, and my tights and knee-high boots took care of the rest.

Reaching for my bottle of Shalimar, I was about to add the finishing touch when Dave stuck his head out of the bathroom. "Wait, Tuppence, this is the part I like to see. The spritz."

That's how he referred to my habit of spraying perfume in the air above my head. When he said he'd never seen a woman do that before, I told him he must have led a sheltered life. With a grin, I curtsied before spritzing. "Happy, Tommy?"

"Always."

In typical Cotswolds fashion, the weather had briefly turned dry and warm—not hot by any means, but a balmy 60° F. I decided my black pashmina would do for the evening and headed downstairs.

Dave hollered, "By the way, I've already fed them both, and Dickens has been out. Be down in a flash."

When he turned left out of the driveway, I was confused. "I thought we were going to Northleach."

"We are, but first, we're taking a slight detour."

We passed the donkeys and turned into the Olde Mill Inn. Instead of walking in through the front door, he led me around to the patio, where a cheery fire glowed in the outdoor fireplace. "Oh, are Libby and Gavin having one of their parties?" The two often invited their local friends to join the inn guests on Friday evenings for cocktails. In fact, that's where I'd met Dave.

I realized there were no other guests and that a single table for two sat in front of the fireplace. On it were two red roses in a vase, two glasses, and a bottle of wine. Looping his arm in mine, Dave escorted me to the table. Someone, I assumed Gavin, had uncorked the bottle, and Dave filled our glasses. "Happy anniversary."

Laughing, I looked around. "I take it Libby and Gavin are in on this. Will they be popping by at any moment?"

A familiar voice came from behind me. "Funny you should ask. My job is to memorialize the occasion and vanish."

It was Gavin. He asked us to lean together and clink our glasses. The photo with the fire in the background captured the moment perfectly—Dave with a sly grin and me with a wondering look on my face.

As Gavin departed, Dave sat back and eyed me. "Leta, to mis-quote Roberta Flack, the first time ever I saw your face, I knew there was something special about you."

"And to my astonishment, you asked me out. You know, I tried to tell myself it wasn't a date, that you were planning a travel article and wanted to pick my brain."

"Oh, it was a date alright. Typical of you not to realize that."

We reminisced about his meeting my friends that night. Wendy and Peter had been there, along with Toby, Rhiannon, and Beatrix. Even Gemma had put in an appearance.

"Do you remember that Dickens took to you right away, but not Christie?"

He chuckled. "Dickens pretty much takes to everybody, so that's not exactly high praise. Thank goodness Christie's changed her tune. At least, I think she has."

"Trust me, she's decided you're okay. She wouldn't sleep on your stomach unless you met with her approval."

Taking a final sip of his wine, he stood. "Okay, Tuppence, we need to get a move on if we're going to make it to dinner."

Twenty minutes later, we pulled up to the Wheatsheaf. The host escorted us to what we considered *our* table in front of the fireplace. On it was a vase holding two red roses. I looked from the flowers to Dave. "Two roses for two years?"

"You're catching on."

It was here, on our first date, that we'd had a lengthy conver-sation about everything under the sun. But it wasn't only small talk. I told him about Henry's death and my decision to live in the Cotswolds. I heard about the ten-year relationship he'd had with a girlfriend. We discovered we had writing in com-mon, though he earned a living at it, while I considered myself a dabbler. He wrote about books and authors, and I was an avid reader.

Still, he was visiting from New York City, and I lived here. It was a heavenly evening, but I never once thought anything would come of it.

The waiter poured our wine, and Dave raised his glass. "Here's to two happy years."

I blinked back tears. The doctor had told me I'd be emotional after my attack, but I knew it was more than that. I hadn't married Henry until I was in my thirties, and I didn't expect to find love again after he died. And here I was. "In so many ways, it's been a whirlwind, hasn't it?"

Dave nodded. "All the goodbyes, the reunions, the phone calls—we made it work. And look at us now."

Another delightful dinner and we were on our way home. Unlocking the door to the cottage, Dave let Dickens out and ushered me to the kitchen.

My mouth dropped open. On the kitchen table, I saw a vase holding two roses, two lit candles, and a bottle of champagne with two flutes. *Two candles for two years.*

As Dave came up behind me, I leaned against him and turned my face up for a kiss. "You are the most amazing man. Thank you for the flowers."

He wrapped his arm around my waist. "The site of the first hug."

"When you forgave me for thinking you were, how did you put it, 'the devil incarnate.' I still can't believe how well you took that."

"What can I say? I'm not that easily scared off."

Christie leaped to the table. "Now that you're home, can we play with them?"

Where they'd come from was a mystery, and what was even more amazing was that she hadn't yet touched them. I tapped her nose with my finger. "Don't even think about it, little girl. They're not for you."

Handing me a glass of champagne, Dave steered me to the sitting room. I stopped in my tracks when I saw the mantel lined with flickering candles. In the center stood two red roses in a tall crystal vase.

"More flowers and candlelight!" I took a sip of champagne and wondered aloud. "Who lit the candles and chilled the champagne?"

"Your neighbors. I had the flowers delivered to Deborah's, and we put Timmy in charge of guarding them. I bet he didn't let Spot anywhere near them." Spot was the name Timmy had given his calico cat.

He led me to the couch and sat beside me. "After you apologized again for misjudging me, do you recall what happened here the next day? I'll give you a hint: It was another first."

Closing my eyes, I remembered our lunch in Broadway. I pictured him bringing me home and putting an icepack on my knee, and . . . "Our first kiss!"

He leaned in and kissed me. "Something like that?"

"Hmm . . . Close, but not quite. Maybe you should try again."

"All in good time. Tell me, have you enjoyed the trip down memory lane?"

"You know I have. You're quite the tour guide."

"I love making memories with you, sweetheart." He caressed my cheek. "In fact, I love everything about you."

His dark eyes twinkled, and before I knew it, he was on one knee. "I want to make memories with you for the rest of our lives."

I gasped as he pulled a tiny velvet box from his pocket. When he opened the lid, a diamond ring twinkled in the candlelight.

"Will you marry me, Leta?"

The words flew from my mouth in a half-laugh, half-cry. "Yes, yes, I will!"

Dave's chest rose and fell gently as he lay beside me. With my arm draped across him, I tilted my hand back and forth and admired my ring. It fit perfectly because the jeweler had matched the sizing to my garnet ring—the one I thought I'd misplaced.

A smile stretched across my face. An enchanting evening, a proposal fit for a Hallmark movie, and a bedtime story about how he'd planned it all. He'd long pictured his mother's engagement ring on my finger, with our September anniversary as the timing for his proposal.

He set the plan in motion by asking his mother for the ring. "She was overjoyed," he said. "I think she'd given up hope I'd ever find the right woman, and she was convinced you were the one."

The plan was to get it while we were in Connecticut, bring it back to England, and have the delicate filigree setting restored and repaired in time for our anniversary dinner. Had that worked out, he would have borrowed my garnet ring for a day, and I never would have missed it.

I chided myself for my misgivings as he described Sandy's role. "She may have started with ulterior motives, but when I showed her the ring, she jumped right in to help. Not only did she know a jeweler experienced in working with filigree, she also persuaded him to complete the repair in time for my departure."

Orchestrating a fairytale proposal was so like Dave. In our two years together, I'd even sometimes wondered whether his thoughtfulness was too good to be true.

Every detail was planned—the visit to the inn, the reservations at the Wheatsheaf, and Deborah handling flower and candle duty. After my trip to A&E spoiled things, he'd rescheduled it all. And it had come off without a hitch, right down to my ecstatic answer.

When I rolled over, Dave followed me and pulled me tight. "Happy, sweetheart?"

I breathed a sigh of contentment. "Happier than you'll ever know."

The End

Book XI
She thought she'd turned the page on murder. But after an author takes a lethal leap, is she back at Chapter One?
Read ***Manuscripts, Meows & Murder*** to find out.

Want to learn more about Leta's life before she retired to the Cotswolds? Curious about how Dickens & Christie became part of the family? Find out in ***Paws, Claws & Mischief***, the prequel to the Dickens & Christie mystery series. Join my newsletter today for exclusive access to the subscriber-only area of my website, where you'll find your complimentary copy of the prequel, plus much more! Enjoy behind-the-scenes content, recipes from

my books, and an ever-growing list of books mentioned in my
stories. New content is available every month—don't miss out!

Would you like to help others discover the world of Dickens
& Christie? If so, please leave an honest review on Amazon,
Goodreads, and/or BookBub. Readers depend on reviews to
help them decide what to read next. It doesn't have to be a book
report! A short *I love it* is all it takes.